WREATH, IN SUMMER

A Wreath Willis Novel

Judy Christie

©2015 by Judy Christie

ISBN: 0996155023
ISBN 9780996155021

For more information about author Judy Christie, please see her website at www.judychristie.com.

Published by Brosette & Barnhill Publishing, LLC
P.O. Box 6103, Shreveport LA 71136

For Annette
who devoted her life to helping children

1

Wreath climbed up into the store window and ripped the last graduation banner down. A moment of sweet memory fluttered down with it.

She descended from the window and draped the sign over a sofa. Maybe she'd hang it in her bedroom for the summer. *Was that cheesy?* She'd never had a room of her own before, so she wasn't sure.

She dragged an old stepladder from the workroom to the front, climbed back onto the platform and hoisted the ladder. Who needed a gym with a workout like this?

On tiptoes, she concentrated on the spray bottle of vinegar and razor-blade scraper, and tackled stray scraps of tape. The late-afternoon sun blazed through the plate-glass window, and she wiped a trickle of sweat out of her eyes with the back of her hand. The display space, a permanent stage for Wreath's design experiments, felt like the inside of a terrarium.

The banners had been a surprise, and Faye insisted they leave them up. But a week into June was past time to rearrange the showroom. With her haul from a thrift shop last weekend, she should have the fresh display finished before Law picked her up.

That brought a grin.

Wreath Wisteria Willis was ready for a nice, normal summer with Law. Tonight's movie with Mitch and Destiny was a start.

No weird secrets.

No more headaches for Faye and J.D.

Most of all, no creepy stalkers. *Bye, bye, Big Fun.*

Spraying cleanser on the window, she scraped extra hard and wiped the rivulets with a rag from her pocket. She tilted her head to inspect her work and squinted in the bright light.

Getting rid of smudges was not as easy as it looked. She raised the scraper blade. Her hair was in her eyes, and sweat trickled down her blouse.

When the bell on the door jangled, she bit back a groan. Turning, she worked on her disheveled hair and called out. "Over here. I'll be with you in a minute."

No one answered, and she frowned. Maybe it was the mailman? Or Faye had forgotten something?

She craned her neck. A stranger with wild red hair in a ponytail of sorts strolled toward the back of the store. His head moved from side-to-side as he looked around.

"May I help you?" she said.

The guy whirled, and his eyes widened.

Self-consciously she patted her hair again.

Without speaking, he walked toward her, his long legs gobbling up the distance between them. As he moved closer, a beam of sunshine turned the scruffy stubble on his unshaven face almost a golden red.

Nothing else about him was golden.

He wore a paint-splattered long-sleeved shirt—odd for June in Louisiana—and cargo pants frayed around the hem. A tattoo peeked from underneath his collar but Wreath couldn't tell what it was.

His mouth was set in a tight line and his eyes were serious. While he couldn't be much older than she was, the combination of clothes and his expression made him look ferocious. His gaze roamed around the store, then back to her, but he didn't speak.

Wreath gripped the razor handle tightly and hopped down from the window.

"May I help you?" She took a step behind a wingback chair as she repeated the question. She glanced at the sidewalk in front of the store. *Empty.*

J.D. had closed early and gone to Lafayette with Faye for shopping and dinner, their first real outing since Wreath had run away to Lucky. If anything unusual happened today, they'd probably handcuff themselves to her.

She had to get rid of this guy. He kept looking around, his gaze lingering on each section of the store, including the desk.

You're out of luck, buddy. After Big Fun snatched their cash, they didn't keep more than a few dollars in the store.

Wreath looked through the window at the hardware store bench again and waved at the vacant spot. "The owner's next door," she said. "She'll be back in a second."

The guy grunted what might have been an assent. Or annoyance. Hard to tell.

"Were you looking for something in particular?" *A hairbrush?*

3

He shook his head, that ponytail-knot-thing flopping. He was tall, his shoulders broad.

"If you want a job, we're not hiring." Wreath grabbed words she hoped would move him along. It would take some doing to get this guy ready for a job interview.

"I'm not looking for work," he said. His voice sounded like he'd come from a South Louisiana bayou, and something about it made Wreath shiver.

"Of course you're not," she said under her breath.

Methodically popping his knuckles, he shuffled his feet, clad in a pair of athletic shoes without laces. He smelled like he had been mowing lawns. Not stinky exactly but earthy.

The big old clock over the back door ticked in time with Wreath's thudding heart as they stared at each other.

"I'm looking for a girl," he said, his accent definitely intriguing. "Her name's . . ." He fished a scrap of paper out of his pocket and squinted at it. "Willis." He looked up at her, a slight frown on his face, then back at the paper. "Wreath Willis."

Wreath clutched the back of the chair, the razor blade catching on the fabric and ripping it like a zipper being unzipped. When she jerked the blade back, she widened the rip and nicked her palm.

"Ouch!" She winced when blood dripped on the chair. They had just bought that from a flea market down in Grand Coteau. Bloodstains were not good for business.

But the sight might scare Mr. Wildebeest away.

She held up her hand and squeezed it to make it bleed more. Her mind was grinding like Faye's homemade ice cream freezer right before it overheated. "If you'll excuse me . . ."

He didn't move, clearly not affected by the blood. "Somebody said she works here," he said. The bayou accent had lost any appeal.

Wreath shook her head and dabbed at the cut with the rag she'd used on the front window. The leftover vinegar stung. "Who told you that?"

"A guy I know." His hazel eyes, almost the color of the whiskey Big Fun used to drink, were clear and intense. "Do you know her?"

In Wreath's experience, guys like this didn't arrive bearing good news. "I might could give her a message for you," she said. Her nonbleeding hand fidgeted with a button on her vintage blouse.

"So you *do* know her?"

"Why are you looking for her?" Wreath had no intention of telling him anything.

"It's personal."

What *personal* business could she have with this—this person?

His sigh conveyed aggravation with the force of a yell. "I heard she knows Fred Procell," he said.

Wreath's hope for normalcy slid away faster than the seconds ticked on the old clock. She backed a step toward the front door. "Who are you?"

He tapped his foot. "Just tell me where I can find this Willis girl."

Before she could stall further, a door slammed out front. An unfamiliar pickup had pulled into the first parking spot. A tall guy climbed out.

The vise on Wreath's heart loosened.

Law was early.

The miracle of his arrival, though, brought a knot the size of an ostrich egg to her stomach. She hated to drag him into anything else to do with Big Fun—or Fred Procell or whatever he was calling himself this week. Wasn't jail supposed to keep him out of her life for good?

"Who's that?" The stranger retreated a couple of steps as he spoke.

Her legs felt wobbly, like the time she'd had the flu. "A friend."

"Does he know Wreath Willis?"

"I'll ask him."

The guy didn't respond, and Wreath walked toward the door. As she pulled it open, she glanced over her shoulder. The stranger loped toward the rear and didn't look back. His hand was on the back door when Wreath burst out front where Law stood.

Why was he looking for her?

Law practically jumped up and down when she stepped outside. He looked as excited as he had when Wreath returned on graduation day. "Surprise!" he yelled.

She glanced back into the showroom, then threw her arms around his neck. She gulped in the familiar soapy smell. He felt solid and comforting and clean—and normal. Law's eyes—kind eyes, not hard and glinty—widened.

"Wreath?" He pulled back, his enthusiasm toned down a notch. "Don't you want to know what my surprise is?"

The white pickup was parked in the front space, right behind her bike. "A truck?" she said.

The grin burst back onto Law's face. "Yes! My grandparents gave me a truck for graduation!"

She willed herself not to look back at the store.

"You should see your face." Law put his hands on her shoulders. "You're more stunned than I was."

This was the kind of guy she wanted looking for her.

In his green state park polo and khaki shorts, Law could make you take up camping. Although it was barely June, he was tan from his expanded job assignments. His dark hair was neat, though in need of a trim—waiting until closer to college, probably.

"You're early," she managed to say.

"I wanted you to be the first to see it. Don't you love it?"

"It's great. Wow," she repeated. *Focus, Wreath.* Here was Law, euphoric with excitement, and her thoughts pinged around like the video game in the corner of the last café where Frankie worked.

"Want a ride?"

"Definitely!" Then she grimaced. "But I can't leave yet. I'm the only one here."

Law frowned and looked past her. "I thought I saw Faye when I drove up."

"That was some guy who stopped in." Wreath fought the urge to nibble on her fingernails. "He was looking for—"

"A job?" Law jumped in. "Hardly anyone's hiring this summer." But he had moved back to his truck, and his hand rested on the front fender. If he'd been a cat, he'd have been purring.

She would not spoil Law's moment with more drama, and she amped up her excitement. "Lawson Rogers! A new truck! How? When? Give me all the details."

He strolled over to open the driver's door. "Hop in."

Sliding onto the seat, the blue upholstery soft on her legs, Wreath grabbed the steering wheel.

"Try the radio. Crank it up."

She fiddled with the controls. Clarice was out of town, but surely someone would let her know if Big Fun got out of jail.

"You can drive if you want."

Wreath gave a strangled laugh. "I'd better get a license first."

Law helped her as she climbed out of the cab.

"I'm stunned," she said.

"I know, right? My granddad sweet-talked Mama." He shrugged. "She said it's my life and if I want to be tied to them . . ." Law hesitated. "Do you think I should have waited until I can afford one on my own?"

"Don't be ridiculous." Although she knew how he felt. "They love you, and you graduated with honors."

"Not as many honors as you." He put his arm around her and squeezed. "It's hard to compete with the fantastic Wreath Willis."

She blushed. "Stop being goofy." She grabbed his hand and pulled him toward the store.

"I'm serious." He pushed the store door open. "This Wreath Willis girl is awesome. Smart. Funny. Brave. And did I mention sweet?"

"I don't believe you did."

"Pretty too."

She gave him a playful shove. "You make me sound almost as good as your pickup."

"Give me a few days and I'll let you know." His grin was powerful. Wreath wanted this moment to last forever.

But her gaze darted around the room. The only sign of the other guy was a slight musky scent. Would he come back?

More to the point, *when* would he come back?

Law pulled her down onto a mid-century sofa. It was green vinyl and not nearly as comfortable as the seat in Law's truck. "When can you close up shop?"

"An hour or so? Most of the stores close earlier these days."

"Summer." He clasped her hand.

"Oww." She grabbed at the cut.

Law pulled her hand closer for inspection. "What'd you do?"

"I was trying to get that tape off the window." She pointed to where the banner had hung. Now would be a good time to tell him about the guy.

But he gave her palm a soft kiss. "Better?"

"Much." Everything was better with Law here. She wasn't a scared girl on the run. Law was the best friend she'd ever had. On graduation day he'd kissed her right here in this room.

He draped his arm around her shoulders. "I'm happy about your truck." Wreath hesitated. "Now you can come home on weekends."

He frowned. "Everyone says classes are super hard your first quarter. And I'll have to work nights and weekends."

Her stomach ached. "It's going to be lonely without you in Landry."

"Not if you go to Tech too," he said. "Me, you, Destiny."

"Do we have to talk about this again?" She clutched a handmade pillow against her chest like a shield.

"Come on, Wreath. A community college with no four-year degrees? You were valedictorian."

"I'm lucky that even RPCC accepted me after I ran off."

He took her chin in his hand. "That's behind you."

But it wasn't.

Wreath was one big heaping pile of her past, and she did not intend to dart from place to place. "I need to stay put," she said.

"You're staying put for the summer." A rare note of exasperation entered Law's voice. "And Landry will always be home."

"Exactly." She gestured around the store. "I like it here."

He sighed. "This was supposed to be a high-school job."

Wreath fidgeted, her ear tuned to the back. All was quiet, except for the clock and the occasional hum of the A/C.

Law tilted his head. "You saved the store from closing. Don't you think Mrs. Durham can take it from here?"

She propped her new blue Converse All-Stars, a gift from her grandfather, on the coffee table. *She had a grandfather.* Another reason not to go away to school. "I want things to stay the way they are." Her voice was almost a whisper. "I wish you didn't have to go."

His mouth was a grim line. "If I stay here, I'll wind up like my parents and every other loser who can barely pay the bills."

"Thanks a lot." Wreath looked down. "Then I guess you're going, and I'm staying."

A moment of pained silence slipped by, then Law gave her ponytail a playful tug. "We're both here for two more months, right?"

She gave a tiny nod.

"Let's make a pact to have the best summer of our lives."

What if her new life was like one of Frankie's schemes, bright and shiny one month and dry as Faye's St. Augustine grass the next?

"Starting right now!" Law pulled her to her feet, and they stumbled against a coffee table. As they regained their balance, he danced her, laughing, toward the back of the store. They skirted two wingback chairs and ran into a rack of vintage dresses.

Wreath glanced in the workroom and in every corner. She wanted to get close enough to lock the back door.

"Two months to goof off, watch movies, eat pizza," Law said. "Mitch got so many gift cards for graduation he'll probably buy for the first month."

He twirled her around again. She looked everywhere. The stranger had vanished.

"No worries about what's ahead," Law said.

Wreath had fretted about the future for as long as she could remember. But now she had a roof over her head, plenty to eat and a little money in her pocket. She pushed the backdoor stranger out of her mind. "I can try," she said.

Law gave her a tight hug. "You're not alone anymore." He danced her around the entire showroom one more time and wound up at the front door.

"I'm going to teach you to have fun," he said. "Nothing— no homework or grades or junkyard or anything—will get in our way." He bowed. "Just a summer of fun."

"Summer of fun," she repeated with a salute. "I'm in."

2

Faye and Wreath walked out of the house on a hot Thursday morning the next week, Wreath convinced she'd made a big deal out of nothing.

The guy must have drifted on, a harmless unknown remnant of her past. Reminders like that might show up from time to time, but they wouldn't derail her plans.

She shook the thought off with a toss of her head, her ponytail flopping. "I'll race you," she said, walking over to her bike, next to Faye's new small car under the carport.

"Couldn't you ride with me once in a while?" Faye asked. "We're going to the same place."

"What if I need to run an errand or something?"

Faye opened the car door and paused. "It's time for you to learn to drive," she said.

Wreath rolled her eyes. "You and J.D. are ganging up on me, aren't you?"

"We're trying to badger you into letting us buy you a car. Horrible, aren't we?"

Wreath hopped on the bike, putting her pack in the basket.

"Law's grandparents got him a truck," Faye continued.

"But Law knows how to drive." She was uneasy about being too dependent on Faye and J.D. She adjusted the short 1960s skirt, studying the rickrack Faye had added to the hem.

"That looks cute with your long legs," Faye said. "I knew it would."

"We should have left it at the store."

Faye put her hands to her face. "What am I going to do with you?"

"Summer is slow. We need to sell more."

"One skirt won't make the difference. I brought it home because I wanted you to have it."

"You give me too much."

"So you've mentioned." Faye said. "But you're a good advertisement."

"We need to come up with new ideas."

"Wreath." Faye sighed. "Humor me. Relax and enjoy yourself for a few weeks. Business will pick up in the fall."

"But I'll be working less in the fall." Wreath squeezed the handlebars. "I should take fewer classes."

Faye looked into her eyes. "That's a good idea," she said. "Or you shouldn't go to college at all. Hang around the store; dust; scour garage sales."

Wreath tilted her head. "You're being sarcastic, aren't you?"

"You think?" Faye smoothed her hair, freshly cut into a bob and colored with a hint of red.

"But—"

Faye held up her hand. "You're going to college full time. End of debate. We'll find a student or retired person to help. You can train her. Or him."

Wreath groaned. "I can work more than you think I can," she said. "My school schedule will be way easier than high school." She gestured toward the house. "Especially since you're letting me live with you."

"My motives are selfish."

"Right."

"Seriously. Who'll take care of J.D. and me when we're in the nursing home? You need to be able to earn a good living."

Wreath turned the bike toward the street with a smile. "I'm leaving now."

"Most seventeen-year-olds are dying to drive," Faye called.

"I'm special," Wreath said and flew down the driveway on her bike, waving. "See you at the store!"

With the day already heating up, she liked the feel of the wind on her face. Several of Faye's neighbors were watering their thick grass, and an occasional mist blew across her bare legs. The birds were happy and hopped around in search of worms. The sky had the unique blue of Louisiana summer.

Why would anyone choose a car over a bike on a day like today? Frankie never owned a car. They'd walked or ridden the bus or bummed rides. Which was how Wreath planned to get to RPCC in the fall, with several of her Landry High classmates.

Not everyone needed to move away. Some people understood that roots were important.

A horn sounded as Faye's car shot around her, then the car slowed and the passenger window lowered. "I'm winning," Faye said and zoomed off.

Wreath shook her head. Love—in a variety of forms—had certainly lightened Faye's heart.

One of those loves, J.D., was sitting with Faye on the bench in front of the hardware store when Wreath rolled up.

"About time," Faye said. "You're getting slower."

"You drive too fast," Wreath said. "Doesn't she, J.D.?"

"You think I'm getting in the middle of an argument between my granddaughter and the woman I'm going to marry?" He shook his head. "I'm smarter than that."

Wreath's mouth dropped open. Faye went still.

"You're getting married?" Wreath said. "When?" Then she looked at Faye. "You didn't tell me."

With her eyes wide, Faye looked from Wreath to J.D. "I didn't know."

None of the three spoke for a moment, the sound of Thursday morning traffic covering the silence.

"I guess I'm not as smart as I thought I was," J.D. said. "I did not mean to say that."

"Oh, my," Faye said.

"I intended to ask you when we went to dinner in Lafayette last week, but I chickened out."

"She is pretty scary," Wreath said.

"I try," Faye said.

They all laughed, a nervous, excited mixture.

"But this is a much better time, here with my two best girls." J.D. lowered himself to one knee. "I don't have a ring yet," he said. "I was hoping Wreath could help me pick one out."

"I'd love to," she said.

"Are you trying to impress me with how long you can stay on your knees like that?" Faye asked.

J.D. smiled and took her hands in his. "I'm in pretty good shape for an old guy."

Wreath figured she should leave them alone, but her feet felt riveted to the cement. Delight and something that surely couldn't be jealousy coursed through her veins.

"We haven't been seeing each other very long," Faye said, her eyes bright with what might have been tears on someone else.

"But we've known each other for years."

"And time goes fast," Wreath said, taking a step closer. "Get on with it."

Faye's face was serious. "You're okay with this, Wreath?"

"Okay with my grandfather squatting on the sidewalk for half the day? Sure." She looked at him, a lump in her throat. "You guys are a wonderful couple. I'm more than okay with it."

Wreath reached past J.D. and picked up a small container of yellow snapdragons from his display of bedding plants. "Here," she whispered, putting the small cardboard pot in his hands.

J.D. winked at her and turned back toward the bench, flowers extended. "Faye Durham, I've fallen in love with you." He hesitated, and sweat popped out on his forehead. "Might you do me the honor of becoming my wife?"

Faye took the flowers and swiped at her eyes. Even the traffic noise seemed to stop. "I never planned to remarry after Billy died." She sniffed the flowers, her gaze still on his. "Then Wreath burst into my life and next thing I know . . ." She made a shaky sound. "The world is full of surprises."

J.D. got to his feet and sat on the bench next to her.

"That better be a 'yes,'" Wreath said.

"I would be thrilled to be your wife, J.D." Faye put her arms around him, dirt spilling out of the little pot as they kissed. And kissed.

Wreath cleared her throat. "You two lovebirds can stay out here making out," she said, "but I need to open the store."

They pulled apart, and J.D. reached for Faye's hand.

"Not even a romantic moment keeps Wreath from her work," Faye said. "What are we going to do to loosen this girl up?"

"This summer's a blast already." Wreath knelt and hugged them. "Do you want to get married in the store? It could help business."

Faye and J.D. laughed, giddy like kids.

"Let's not get ahead of ourselves," Faye said. "We want to get you settled first."

"I am settled."

J.D. reached out and touched her shoulder. "You've been through a lot, Wreath." The joy left his face, replaced with an emotion Wreath knew too well. Regret.

"So have you," she said. Her hands felt sweaty. "I'm super happy for you."

Faye let out what sounded suspiciously like a giggle, and J.D. grinned. Was that what Wreath's father had looked like when he fell in love with Frankie?

Walking toward the store, she stopped and whirled around. "Does this mean Faye will be my grandmother?"

J.D. smiled. "I suspect it's the main reason she said 'yes.'"

3

Wreath should head toward the brick home, the one with a lawn man and air-conditioning. Faye would have supper cooked before Wreath went out with her friends, and there would probably be a present waiting at her place at the table.

Never had she been given so many gifts.

But she had time for a quick bike ride—and that would allow Faye and J.D. a few minutes alone. After all, they had only gotten engaged last week. And she needed to clear her head.

She locked the front door; a lone lamp gave the store's interior a homey glow. She made sure the back door was locked at all times. All was secure. And no sign of that guy for two weeks. Probably gone for good.

"Want a ride?"

She dropped the key and squealed.

J.D. approached from the hardware store. His smile vanished. "I didn't mean to startle you," he said and bent to pick up her key ring.

Wreath's hand trembled when she reached for it. "I was thinking about a quick bike ride," she said. "Guess I got lost in thought."

"Everything okay?"

"All good. I'm riding out to the park to talk to Law about our plans." She paused. "I won't be long."

"Faye says we're having chicken and dumplings for supper," he said. "We'll save you some."

"Thanks!" She headed toward her bike, chained to a post in front of the store.

"Wreath?" J.D.'s voice stopped her, and she turned. "Are you upset about us getting married?"

"No!" Her hands fell to her sides. She wasn't in the habit of hugging, and it seemed too soon. *A grandfather. Unreal.*

"I shouldn't have proposed like I did." He looked like an embarrassed teenager. "Got caught off guard."

"It was sweet," she said. "Spontaneous—and romantic." Although she was fairly sure most kids didn't talk to their grandparents about romance.

He cleared his throat. "I didn't mean to intrude," he said. "I don't know much about this grandfather business."

She squirmed. She wouldn't mention the stranger unless he showed up again. But her list of concerns was long enough to give J.D. something. "The store's slow. I need to get things in order to start RPCC in August." She hesitated. "All my friends are going off to school."

"Faye and I are a little old to hang around with but . . ." He hesitated. "But we love spending time with you." Her grandfather simply looked at her, his face a mask of concern. Her mother had stared at her like that. It was a tender look, as though Wreath were the most wonderful thing in the world.

She took a deep breath. "Do you ever worry about the future?"

He moved a half step toward her, then stopped. She wondered if he was nervous too. "I worry about your future. I want you to be happy. Other than that? I try to take things as they come."

"Did you learn that after . . ." She couldn't force the words out.

"After your father was killed? Yes." He pulled a bandanna out of his blue-jean work pants and wiped his forehead. "John David was a special boy, and his mother and I had worked hard to have a child." He flushed. "You probably didn't need to know that."

"I want to know everything about my dad." Wreath's words were almost a whisper.

"When that train hit him, I lost my bearings." J.D. wiped his face again and sank onto the bench. "Everyone loved him. He was a real people person, like you. Made good grades. Ran track. I struggled to be thankful that we had him as long as we did."

Wreath couldn't bear the weight of his words. "What if we talk later? I'd better go if I'm going to get back before dark."

J.D. and Faye always fretted when she was out on her bike at night, and he stood quickly. "I shouldn't have held you up."

"I want to hear more," she said. "Just maybe not now." She walked toward her bike with an off-key chuckle. "Don't eat all the dumplings."

"Wreath?"

Her bike wobbled when she paused.

"I'm grateful you showed up."

"So am I."

The road to the park—and on to the junkyard—was familiar and comforting. With the summer sun approaching the tree line, the sky glowed blue. The drifting clouds reminded her of the way she felt. Unmoored. Floating. Not quite sure where she was headed.

She pulled over into the shade and took her journal out of her backpack. After drawing the clouds with her pen, she made a list:

1. *Don't be afraid of change.*
2. *Stick to your plan.*
3. *Forget about that guy with the wild hair.*

She would call Clarice's office to learn the status of the case. She'd been warned that she would need to testify, but she'd ignore that for now.

A wave of unexpected homesickness for the junkyard hit Wreath, and she pedaled past the state park. Were the rabbits and squirrels happy to have their sanctuary back? Were green lizards sunning on warm rusty hoods, showing off their red pouches?

She snorted and did a U-turn into the park.

Her life was in town now.

She rode toward the office and inhaled the humid summer air. The trees were dense and so green they looked like they could smother you. She could almost feel redbugs crawling onto her skin, and sweat trickled down her face.

She stopped to buy a pass, then veered to the left. Law's truck, its wax gleaming, was parked outside the big tin shed, alongside a golf cart with a Louisiana decal on the back of the seat. Law enjoyed checking on campsites in his "rolling office" and puttering around the park on errands. Between the job and his Louisiana Tech plans, he was happier than she had ever seen him.

He rounded the corner of the building and thrust his hands behind his back. "Perfect timing," he said. "I just went on break."

She cocked her head at the sound of a whimper. "Are you holding a dog?"

"No, Ms. Willis." He pulled his hands around. "Two dogs."

"Oooh! They're adorable!" Wreath's voice came out like a squeal from a Landry High cheerleader. The smaller puppy whined, and she reached for it. "What kind are they?"

"Part-lab and part-who-knows-what," Law said. "We found them abandoned by the gate this morning."

"Why do people do that? Couldn't they at least take them to a shelter?"

"These two are lucky." He scratched the puppy between the ears, rewarded with an exuberant lick. "My boss says some are killed, others picked up for dog fighting."

She shuddered. "Big Fun's friends were into that," she said. "He'd take Mama's tip money to bet—or buy booze. That's so evil I can't bear it."

A moment passed, then Law reached over to pat her shoulder. "He's behind bars," he said quietly. "Big Fun can't hurt you, Wreath."

She drew in a breath. Looked into the eyes of the dog she held. And tried to sound casual. "Do you think anyone in town knows Big Fun? I mean, he lived around here sometimes."

"Like his family?" he shrugged. "Who knows?"

"I was thinking more about friends, acquaintances." Big Fun wasn't a family man. He was a drifter, moving from one crime to another.

Law frowned. "You're doing it again."

"Doing what?" Although Wreath knew.

"He's. In. Jail. End of story."

Then he seemed to soften. "I wish I could block out all those memories," he said. "The scary ones."

"They'll fade in time . . . or at least that's what everyone says." She swallowed. All the puppies in the known universe wouldn't make this easy. "Your dad's at the parish prison where Big Fun is, right?" She rushed on. "Does he ever get in touch with anyone? From jail, I mean."

"My father?" Law looked away. "He talks to my mother every now and then. But I don't hear from him." Then he met her eyes. "Has Big Fun tried to contact you?"

"I'm not sure." She had to trust the people who cared for her. But it was hard.

"Because if he did, you need to tell Clarice. There are ways to keep that from happening. Restraining orders and police, for instance."

"I can't tell Clarice. She and Sam are on a mission trip in Haiti for six weeks. They left Sunday."

He took a step closer. "What happened, Wreath?"

She could see her fun summer collapsing with her next words, like a big row of dominoes. *Click, click, click.* Just like that everyone would freak out.

But she had promised to quit keeping secrets, and she'd already dodged the topic with Faye and J.D. "A young guy came by the store looking for me."

"And?"

Her toe drew an *X* in the dirt, and she stared at the foot as though it were attached to someone else's body. "I didn't admit that I was me."

She made another *X*.

"Where's this going, Wreath? Because I swear I'll kill Fred Procell if he tries to hurt you again."

The puppies whimpered as Law spoke.

"Shhh," she whispered. "It's okay."

"What'd he want?" Law's voice was harsh.

Her toe scratched a third *X*.

"It was the day you got your truck." She winced as his eyes flew open wide. "When you showed up, he left . . . but not before he mentioned Fred Procell."

"Why didn't you tell me? We could've called the cops."

She drew a line through the *Xs,* staring at the ground. "I'm tired of being the girl who brings trouble."

"So he hasn't come back?"

She shook her head. "I want to have a normal summer. I don't want everyone watching me like hawks on telephone poles."

"I get that," he said after a second. "But you have to let me know if you're in trouble."

"Will Big Fun ever go away, Law?"

"One of these days." He brought the puppy up under his chin. "At least he wasn't your dad."

Wreath touched his sleeve.

"The preacher says we're not supposed to hate anyone," Law said. He gave a laugh that didn't sound like him. "But he probably never went with his grandfather to bail his father out."

"That's why you work so hard," she said after a moment. "And why you're ready to get out of Landry."

"Let's say that I understand why you don't want to reopen the Fred Procell discussion." Law took the puppies and sat them on the ground. They nipped at each other and rolled in the dirt. "It feels like everyone's waiting for me to screw up like my parents did."

"Your grandparents aren't," Wreath said.

"If it weren't for them, I'd probably be homeless like you were."

She pulled the more adventurous pup back toward them, fighting her raw feelings and hating the bleak look she saw in Law's eyes.

"Can we change the subject?" he asked. "This isn't fun at all."

But Wreath ignored him. "I wish I had known my father. I wonder if he was anything like my mother."

Law reached down and picked up the dogs, who squirmed and whined. "Puppies, Wreath. Fun."

She twisted her mouth into a wry smile. "Still on for the movie tonight?" she asked.

"Sure." He smiled, his eyes crinkling at the corners.

Wreath leaned in to give him and the dogs a hug.

"You tell me if that guy shows up again," he said into her hair.

She nodded, bumping into his chin. "We can sic a puppy on him."

He chuckled, and she pulled back, picking up her pack. "I'd better go. Faye and J.D. wait supper for me, even though I tell them not to," she said. "The puppies were fun."

He held them up to her face. The black one gave a quick bark and licked her chin. "They're free. Want one?"

"I'd better not," she said.

Although she'd need something to stop the loneliness when Law and Destiny left for school.

4

Wreath propped her bike by a chain-link fence, watching the Saturday crowd gather at the flea market. A couple of older men in fluorescent orange vests directed traffic, collecting five dollars for parking. Not even eight o'clock, and the parking area overflowed.

Five bucks to park in a field. A definite reason to ride a bicycle.

Last summer she avoided the Junque Mart. It had been hard enough to get to work without adding miles to her day.

But Faye told her this place was big competition, and Wreath insisted on reconnaissance. Living with Faye was so easy, she craved an assignment. "A junk spy," she'd said and twirled an imaginary mustache.

Perched in the middle of a field on the outskirts of Landry, the flea market was busier than downtown had been last Christmas. A line had formed to pay two dollars to enter. Charging customers to shop? What a concept.

A quartet of portable toilets was visible on the outer edge of the lot. Wreath wrinkled her nose. After a year in the junk-yard, she preferred indoor plumbing.

As she stepped past the ticket booth, the market was alive with noise and smells. A middle-aged woman hawked beignets and coffee. A boy from high school sweated over the bubbling vats of hot grease.

Wreath dug money out of her pack and bought a café au lait and a trio of beignets, powdered sugar drifting down the front of her T-shirt that commemorated a Guns N' Roses concert, her mother's favorite eighties band.

Jostled by the crowd, she stepped back toward the entrance and surveyed the area.

The market was laid out with a central hub. A makeshift stage was set up in the middle with a big man sitting on a raised platform, talking through a portable PA system.

Younger than Faye but not as young as Frankie, the guy wore aviator sunglasses and black motorcycle boots, the kind with a ring on the ankle. He had on a camouflage shirt with a name tag that Wreath couldn't read.

But she thought she knew who he was.

"The owner's a real showman," J.D. had said over their lunch yesterday. "He's that Theriot guy who has that motel on the edge of town."

"I never cared for him," Faye said. "Heard he'd steal your watch and then ask you what time it was."

"He's a con man?" Wreath asked. She'd been studying J.D.'s face. *Should she tell him he had a spot of mustard on his chin?*

"That's his reputation," Faye said and reached over to wipe off the spot. The gesture was so personal that Wreath almost felt like she was watching them kiss again.

She was happy to set out on her own today, even though she'd asked Law to come. But most weekends he had to work. That hadn't stopped them from staying up too late on their movie night with Mitch and Destiny, though. They'd even managed a midnight pizza.

Law would warn her to stay away from Mr. Theriot with his toothpick and static-y mic. Probably with good cause. When he glanced down at Wreath without a hint of a smile, he called to mind Big Fun.

She scurried on.

A country craftsman was selling wind chimes and iron bottle trees next to a woman with bird feeders made out of old china plates. A portable fan made the chimes tinkle, a happy sound her mother loved.

The memory caused Wreath to look around, almost expecting to see Frankie in the crowded area. Her mother would have adored this place.

But of course she wasn't there.

Wreath gave one chime a gentle push. When she inhaled, the smell of roasted peanuts drifted across the aisle.

Just beyond, a booth promised pedigrees on German shepherd puppies. Wreath knelt at one of the portable pens and touched the soft fur. It reminded her of the ones she'd seen at the park.

"Purebred," a man in white shorts and a tank top said. "I'll make you a good deal."

"Oh, thanks, but I don't have a place for a dog."

"Everyone has a place for a dog," he said and turned to an approaching couple. "Purebred," he said. "I'll make you a good deal."

The first booth of used merchandise looked more like the Dollar Barn gone bad, packages of plastic toys and cheap knickknacks. They didn't call this the Junque Mart without cause. But there was good stuff mixed in.

In only a few months of picking antiques and vintage merchandise with Faye, Wreath had learned to spot the good at a glance. Stamped tablecloths—probably 1950s— were inexpensive at one booth, and pink Depression glass sparkled at another. Definitely worth bringing Faye for a look.

Wreath circled back around and bought a small crystal vase to resell and two fried pies for Faye and J.D. Then she did a quick assessment of the exits and glanced over to make sure her bike was still by the side entrance.

She had hidden for so long that it was hard not to think of ways to escape. But no one was paying her any attention, and she felt foolish. *Normal girls don't scan for trouble.*

With shoulders thrown back, she followed the packed red-dirt path to a picnic table, next to a booth peddling turkey legs.

The market felt foreign to Wreath, as separate from downtown as the junkyard was from life in town. The carnival atmosphere was rowdy and oddly appealing.

Why did Law think she needed to move away? Life was right here in Landry.

Tons of ideas for window displays surrounded her. She could even sketch the bright summer produce in her diary. She pulled it from her pack and fished for colored pencils.

A small smile emerged when she flipped through the entries, lingering on the most recent one. *SUMMER OF FUN,* written in all capital letters. Underneath she doodled a heart and one of the puppies Law had found. Too bad they weren't out here to be adopted. Maybe the parish's one animal shelter could set up a booth.

She tapped her pen on the picnic table and wrote the date. Her heart dipped. More than a year had passed since she'd made her first entry on the run.

But that was the past, as Law reminded her. She had the summer ahead and loved the list of activities she had compiled:

1. Spend time with Law. Dates?! 2. Go out with Law, Mitch and Destiny. Movies? Pizza? 3. Get to know my grandfather. Weird. 4. Come up with a summer party at the store. Surprise for Faye? 5. Check on advance reading for college.

That last one almost made her laugh out loud. Destiny had complained for days about the books she had to tackle before she left for Louisiana Tech. Wreath had already read several on the list and wanted more. She was a booklover, while Destiny and Law preferred television and video games.

6. Decorate my room. Faye chuckled when Wreath asked to tack the graduation banner to the wall. Apparently she could do anything she wanted, even paint. And J.D. volunteered to provide the paint.

She and Frankie lived in rent houses and never spent money on improvements. The most her mom had invested in was a furry hot-pink pillow for her bed from a local discount store. "You deserve something pretty," Frankie said when Wreath protested that they didn't have enough money.

7. Help the puppies. Those cuties at the state park haunted her. But she was working and about to start college. She couldn't take care of a puppy. Besides Faye's house was spotless. Maybe an answer would pop up.

Wreath jumped to the next page. *STORE IDEAS,* she wrote. She drew a few lines, sketching the glassware. Louisiana sizzled in summer, all bold and bright. She added the red of a rocker in the booth across from her. That would be perfect for the front window.

While Wreath drew, the aisle filled with a wave of moseying people, a clump of whom stopped near the edge of the far booth. Wreath contorted her body to see what had drawn their interest.

She froze.

It was him. The red-haired guy.

Even though his hair was down today, nearly to his shoulders, he wasn't hard to identify. Not only had he haunted her thoughts—no matter how much she pretended otherwise—he was wearing the same clothes he'd had on in the store.

Long sleeves again, despite the heat.

He stroked a German shepherd puppy like those near the entrance, his head low. *If only she could get a better look at his face.*

A group of older people in purple T-shirts blocked her view, though, as they stopped for a sample of bread-and-butter pickles. After what seemed like forever, they meandered on and formed a choir on risers at the end of the arena. Someone shook a tambourine, and the noise level rose.

Scrunching down, Wreath peered around the bodies.

A little boy sat on the ground at the feet of the stranger. Probably no older than five, he was blowing on a plastic kazoo. His T-shirt, jeans, and oversized blue-and-white cap—like a train engineer would wear—were beyond dingy, and his face was pale, as though he'd not been outside for months.

But his smile, which occasionally beamed through a break in the stream of people, radiated a freshness that Wreath had seen only in the very young.

From time to time he would look up at the guy and say something. The redhead would glance down, his face softening almost imperceptibly. While the child looked carefree, the guy wore somber like a cloak, but he didn't look as scary as she remembered.

Unlike the humans, the dog was shiny and clean, a red ribbon around its neck.

As more customers strolled by, the boy looked up, blowing harder on the instrument. A young woman dug in her purse and pulled out a bill. Wreath watched it drift into a yellow plastic pail. Straining her neck, she saw a pile of money and watched a man add a few coins.

The kid was a pint-size panhandler!

Wreath sat back down. What kind of person used a child like that? Even in the leanest days, her mama had never begged for money. Although they could have used it.

This had to be illegal, ill-treatment of a child or something. But Wreath had seen through the years what happened when strangers interfered where they weren't wanted. Trouble.

If she did nothing, though, the boy might get hurt. He looked scrawny. What if he was being starved? Or had been kidnapped?

Surely the guy wouldn't be out in public if he'd taken the child. Although they were stationed at the very end of the flea market, near an exit. And every few moments he would scan the crowd, his gaze roaming from side to side. Had he seen her?

She put the journal back in her pack and rose. She needed to walk away from whatever was going on. Someone else could handle it.

But what about that child? He was far more defenseless than the abandoned puppies.

She inspected the crowd a segment at a time. Was the kid's mother in on it?

She walked closer. Why didn't someone intervene?

When she was a few steps away, the boy tugged on the guy's shorts. "Mommy," he said and pointed.

The guy scanned the crowd, and his eyes narrowed when he noticed Wreath.

"Mama!" The boy's voice rose. The word exploded with distress.

The guy squatted, still holding the dog. "Where, Jack?"

The boy's lower lip trembled as he looked around. He shook his little head. "She's lost again," he said with a sniff. "We're never gonna find her."

With his mouth twisted, the stranger patted the boy on the head, the way he had the dog. "It was probably someone who looked like her, sugar." His voice was soft, that same Cajun accent discernible even over the choir.

Then he straightened, his eyes now fully upon Wreath. "What do you want?"

Wreath clenched her fists. "You've frightened that child."

"That's on you," he said.

The little boy picked up the hem of his shirt and wiped his nose, which was streaming snot. Wreath couldn't tell if he'd been crying or had a cold.

She fumbled with her pack and pulled out a Kleenex and a five-dollar bill. She handed the child the tissue and dropped the money into the pail. "You came into my store two weeks ago looking for . . ."

The guy wasn't listening to her. The kid, eyes wide, tugged on his sleeve and pointed toward the aisle. Whatever he said was swallowed by the exuberant music.

The redhead turned to stare, first toward the choir, then at a group of people buying Louisiana peaches. He swore under his breath, the curses loud as the music went soft.

A few customers jammed nearby stepped back, and the aisle opened up. The announcement man steamed their way. His dark glasses were now hooked over the neck of his shirt. His jaw was set.

The redhead's eyes moved from side to side. Like someone trapped.

Wreath knew that look.

He was about to run.

He grabbed the kid's arm with one hand and thrust the dog at Wreath. "Here."

She took a step back.

The guy let go, and Wreath caught the dog, pawing wildly, in mid-air.

"He won't bite," the child said solemnly.

The annoyed man was nearly to the booth, chewing on a toothpick.

"Damn!" the guy said.

"You said we aren't supposed to say that word." The boy jutted out a hip and pointed a finger covered in chalk.

"We're not." He scooped the kid up in one arm. Then he grabbed the money out of the plastic pail, crammed it in the pocket of the cargo shorts, dropped the bucket and tightened his grip on the child.

"What's going on?" The toothpick wiggled at the question. The man's name tag said *Theriot. Proprietor.* Underneath it read, *Put up or shut up.*

Nice marketing.

Wreath watched the grungy guy sprint behind shelves of perfume and around the side of the building, the child's arms around his neck.

"Hey! Put that boy down!" She started to chase him, but the dog squirmed nearly out of her arms. She stumbled as she fought to catch it. "Stop!" she yelled, and the dog barked.

By then the guy and the little boy were out of sight, hidden by a line of incoming cars. She prayed they weren't run over.

Theriot had stepped so close that she could smell onions on his breath. She turned. "That guy took that child."

He shrugged.

"But he's . . ." She stopped. What could she say? *Dirty? Shady? Looking for me?* With the little boy, he didn't seem as scary.

And then she saw the pair weaving through the parking lot.

"That's my bike!" she screeched.

The puppy yelped and fought again to get down.

But Wreath clutched him tight while she watched the guy pedal across the grass parking lot. He steered with one hand, the other holding the child close to his chest. As he approached the road, he slowed and shook his head.

Theriot pulled out a whistle and blew three short blasts. It fit right in with the rousing patriotic song the oldsters were singing.

The bicycle thief rode on, disappearing into traffic.

The beignets and coffee rose in Wreath's throat. Her bike was her independence. And what was she supposed to do with the dog? What about that poor little boy? And why was that guy looking for her?

"Was he panhandling again?" Theriot said.

She nodded. "He stole my bike."

"Traded it for a dog, eh?" The question came with a smirk.

She looked down at the puppy.

"There she is!" A loud voice cried out a few yards away, and the dog barked, a series of sharp yelps. A woman about Faye's age barreled toward Wreath. She was tall and blond and looked like a pro wrestler—with a scowl to match. "What are you doing with our baby?" She grabbed for the dog.

Wreath sidestepped her and held the puppy close.

The dog-seller in the tank top plowed through the crowd, choir still singing. "Move aside," he demanded. People took a step or two out of his way and stared as he strode right toward Wreath.

"Aha! The girl who doesn't have a place for a dog." His mouth was pressed into a straight line. "Why are you holding the pick of the litter?"

"I have no idea," Wreath said. She looked at the beautiful dog with its wolf-colored coat and dark ears.

"This girl should be arrested," the woman said. "Her accomplice too." She looked around. "Wherever he went."

"He got away?" The dog-seller frowned.

The woman scowled. "Like you care! I told you not to loan him Gretel, percentage or not."

At the commotion, part of the audience from the choir performance migrated toward them. A claustrophobic wall formed around Wreath, and the dog gave a baby-sized growl.

"Ooh, poor Gret-Gret." The woman shoved people aside. "She senses the tension." *Gret-Gret* bared her teeth.

"Whoa," Theriot said. "We got a little fighter on our hands." He lowered his voice. "What you asking for that one?"

The woman glared. "This girl stole our dog,"

"No, I didn't!"

"Give me the dog," Theriot said.

Wreath inched back, bumping into a man eating a corndog.

"Get your hands off her," the blond woman bellowed. Wreath wasn't sure who she was talking to.

The crowd had begun to murmur. Some people scurried away, others moved closer. A young guy held up a cell phone, videoing the disturbance.

Theriot swatted at the phone. "Put that thing away."

"Free country," the guy said.

"Private property." Theriot nodded at a man in a *Security* T-shirt, then looked around. "My apologies," he said with a toothy smile. The shift in his expression was so extreme it was like watching a slide show. A chill ran down Wreath's spine.

Gretel strained toward Theriot, then seemed to think better of it and drew back. The woman reached for the puppy again. Gretel whined, and Wreath reluctantly let her go.

She didn't know what was going on, but the dog did not belong to her.

The woman kissed the puppy on the nose. Gretel replied with a series of vigorous licks, paws flying. The dog-seller looked at Theriot. "You seriously interested?"

"Could be."

"She'd fit right in." He jerked his head toward the back of the flea market.

Theriot shook his head. "Not now."

"She's a good 'un. Think about it."

"Move on along, folks." Theriot turned toward the entrance.

"Wait!" Wreath said. "We need to call the police. I need to tell them about that child—and my bike."

Theriot was shaking his head before she finished speaking. "Private property," he said again and pointed to a sign posted on a utility pole. "We're not responsible for lost items."

"It's not *lost*."

"If you call the cops, I'll have you charged with dog theft," he said. "Those folks will back me up." He nodded toward the retreating couple. "The sheriff don't care for thieves."

"But . . ." She drew in a breath and reached for her backpack. She was going to get her bike back.

5

Wreath stood near the entrance of the flea market and pondered how to get back to town. Law was still at the park. Faye or J.D. would flip out. Destiny was working.

"Need a lift?" A woman with a smile and a pile of hair had walked right up beside her.

"Oh, um, I . . ." Wreath tried to place the woman as she stammered.

"Joyce!" the woman said. "As in *Pies by Auntie Joyce.* I didn't make near enough pies today, and I've run plumb out. Heading home to make more. Want a ride?"

She walked as she talked, her long skirt almost dragging the ground. Wreath followed in her wake.

"I watched that whole hullabaloo," Joyce said as they neared a beat-up minivan with giant fried pies and a phone number painted on the side. "That's a shame about your bike."

"So you saw that child?" Wreath climbed in, the cluttered interior scented with apples and cinnamon.

The woman cocked her head. "Didn't see a child," she said. "But I watched that dog trying to get at Mr. Theriot. Dogs sense things like that, they say."

"That poor puppy," Wreath said. "She wanted attention."

"She don't want the kind of attention that man gives dogs." The woman shivered, and she glanced at Wreath.

"What do you mean?"

"Mostly rumors." Joyce looked around. "I'd better not say. That man's got a long reach."

"But his flea market is crazy busy . . ."

"Just because he's got a mean streak doesn't keep people from looking for a bargain," Joyce said. "Summer's s-l-o-w around here, in case you haven't noticed."

"We're steady downtown, not much more, though."

Joyce shook her head. "Can't draw a consistent crowd downtown," she said. "So we put up with Theriot."

Frankie probably would have minded her own business. "What kind of mean streak?" Wreath asked.

"I've said more than I should." Joyce adjusted the radio to a gospel channel as they pulled up to the store.

Wreath opened her door. "Would you like a soft drink or coffee? I can show you what we have, introduce you to the owner."

"Aren't you a sweetie? But I've got to make twenty dozen pies by in the morning. With the weather so pretty, Sunday will be a big day."

"Well, thanks for the ride."

Joyce leaned out her window as Wreath walked toward the store. "You be careful around Theriot, you hear?"

"I don't even know him."

"Don't matter. He noticed you today, and he won't forget."

Before the van was barely rolling, Faye and J.D. rushed from the furniture store.

"Where's your bicycle?" Faye asked.

"Is that blood on your backpack?" J.D. said.

Wreath looked at the pack, hanging from her arm. Sure enough, a blob of red oozed out.

She touched it with her index finger. Then she stuck the finger in her mouth. "That's cherry fried pies," she said. "I must have sat on my pack getting into that van."

"Did you have a flat tire?" J.D.'s voice was calm but his eyes were sharp.

Prepare for worry. "Some guy stole my bike."

"At the flea market?" Faye's tone was outraged.

"Let's go inside, and I'll tell you all about it. You can have a smushed fried pie and a cup of tea."

2

Faye and J.D. tightened their lips at her decision not to call the police. Then Faye argued, and J.D. studied Wreath with that unnerving serious expression.

Would they override her? Maybe even go behind her back?

She knew why she didn't want to place the call. This was the kind of fracas Frankie got in. Wreath wanted no part of it. She didn't want to connect in any way with Theriot. She especially didn't want to get tangled up with the red-haired guy.

"Please sit down," she said and pulled the pies out. "It wasn't that big a deal."

"Would you mind telling us exactly what happened?" J.D. said. He settled into his regular recliner next to Faye's big roll-top desk.

"We worry about you." Faye bypassed her recliner for the wooden desk chair. That meant she had no intention of relaxing.

Wreath patted her shoulder and smiled. "I've got this."

"Okay, okay," Faye said. "We know. You're independent. But this is—"

J.D. looked at Faye and gave a sight shake of his head.

Wreath bit back a smile. Apparently he knew more about being a grandfather than he let on.

"So," she said on a loud breath. "I went out to the flea market."

"Cut to the chase," Faye said.

"And you say I'm stubborn."

"If you two don't mind," J.D. said. "The bike?"

Wreath outlined nearly every detail to Faye and J.D., the day imprinted on her mind. But she didn't mention that she'd seen the guy once before. Judging from their reaction to the bike theft, their anxiety would explode with mention of the stranger in the store.

She spent more time on the little boy and bypassed her encounter with Theriot. The last thing they needed was for her to bring another bad guy into their lives.

"We should at least tell Shane," J.D. said. "He can check with the sheriff's office."

Frowning, Wreath leaned forward.

"We insist," Faye said. "I saw him and Julia in the backyard not five minutes ago. They just got back from one of their runs." As usual, her tone implied she had no idea why Julia chose to run long distances.

"I'll fetch them." J.D. sprang up.

"It's *not* a big deal," Wreath said, but J.D. was already slipping out the back door.

Faye put her hands on her hips and studied her. "You love that bike. Why aren't you more upset?"

"I'll get it back. He couldn't have ridden far carrying a child."

Shane caught the words as he and Julia walked in. "Now, Wreath," he said, "don't try to play detective. Someone who will steal a bike will steal anything. And this dude might be dangerous." Wearing shorts and a running shirt, he looked more like an Olympic athlete than a law-enforcement agent.

Julia, also in running clothes, rushed over to Wreath. She and Shane were training for a marathon in New Orleans and trying to coax Wreath into running it with them. *No way.* She'd run too long out of necessity to take it up as a hobby. "Are you all right?"

"I was fine before the Gestapo here started in on me." Wreath nodded toward Faye.

Julia smiled. *At least she knew how Faye could be.*

But Shane's look was stern. "J.D. said he had a child with him?"

"A little boy." Wreath ran back through the details of the encounter. "The guy didn't seem dangerous, though." Merely strange.

"You should have called the sheriff," he scolded. "The owner out there skirts trouble most of the time."

"Theriot?' Wreath asked.

"You ran into him?" J.D.'s frown mirrored Shane's.

"He rushed right over," she said.

"To help?" Shane sounded surprised.

She gave a quick shake of her head. "He didn't want me to call the police."

"I suppose not," J.D. murmured.

"Did he threaten you?" Shane suddenly looked oh-so police-like, jaw jutting, shoulders thrown back.

"It all happened quickly," she said. "There was this German shepherd puppy in the middle of everything." She looked at the four of them, their faces painted with concern. "It sounds like a bad comedy."

"It's not a laughing matter," Faye said. "You should be safe at a flea market."

"My bike will turn up, but I'm upset about the little boy. He was panhandling. That's not right."

"I'll ask around," Shane said.

Tension hung in the air, and Wreath turned to Faye to ease the mood. "I did pick up good ideas while I was there. Maybe we can take some of Theriot's business."

Faye let out a sigh. "Wreath, we try to keep you safe, and you fret about the store."

"I'm fine. Landry's the safest place possible."

Shane walked to the front window and looked out. "Even small towns have a criminal element," he said. "It's mostly petty—like your bike, shoplifting—but there are bad people."

"Like Big Fun," Julia said in a somber voice.

Wreath's legs felt like they were melting.

"I checked for you, J.D.," Shane looked uneasy. "Procell's been charged with manslaughter; they're trying to put a case together. The system runs slow in rural parishes."

"Does that mean he could get out?" Wreath wasn't successful in keeping her voice calm. She'd been interviewed by the district attorney's office, the questions like something off the TV shows Faye loved. She didn't relish facing Fred Procell again.

"It's . . . unlikely." Shane's voice wasn't as forceful as it had been when he talked about Theriot. "But a witness has come forward."

"Witness?" Wreath said. "Who?"

"That word hasn't trickled down to my level. Clarice can probably find out, though."

"She's in Haiti!"

Each of the adults stared at Wreath, their expressions like the doctor who had taken her blood pressure when she had the flu. She could almost feel them gauging her emotions.

"We can contact Clarice if you'd like," J.D. said. "She's e-mailed Faye and me a couple of times to check on how you're doing."

"On her mission trip?" Wreath's voice sounded weird. *Will I always have a problem that requires watching?*

"Wreath!" Faye was exasperated. "You know how much Clarice loves you. She checked in a couple of times." She put on the smile she gave new customers. "Now can we talk about something more pleasant?"

"Good idea." Wreath would not spend her life running. Not from Big Fun or anyone else. Landry was her home now, these people family.

"Stay alert," Shane said.

"Gotcha." Wreath wanted to salute but Faye and J.D. looked so serious that she thought better of it.

Faye compressed her lips. "You need a phone. You could have called us today for a ride."

Her own cell phone might be nice. But if she took one from them, she'd be tethered. Maybe after she got used to all the changes.

"The fried pie lady was right there," she said after a moment. "Why should you have to make that trip?"

Julia walked over to Wreath and picked up her hand. "Because they care about you," she said. "When will you get it in your head that you don't have to do everything alone?"

"Alone? We're practically having a meeting of the U.N. right now." She hadn't seriously considered keeping the flea market incident to herself. That was a first.

"What happened to that quiet young girl in my civics class?" Julia asked with a hint of smile. "You used to be eager to hear our words of wisdom."

"Don't you two have a few miles to run or something?" Wreath asked.

"Already done," Julia said. "Can't you tell?"

"So that's what that smell is."

"Off to the shower." Julia grabbed Shane's hand. "Here if you need me."

Before the door closed, J.D. had leaned forward. "Wreath, I hope you'll be careful. I know you and Faye like to scout for bargains—"

"Treasures," Wreath said.

J.D. didn't smile. "That experience today could have been dangerous."

If Faye had issued the warning, or Julia, Wreath might have blown it off. But she didn't know her grandfather well enough yet. She studied him for a second, then stepped forward and gave him a quick hug.

"Thanks for looking out for me."

6

On Monday, Wreath rode to work with Faye and scoured every street for her bike.

"That old bike's long gone," Faye said. "Let's order you a new one."

"It'll turn up," Wreath said. "Trust me. This guy's no master criminal." At least she was fairly certain he wasn't.

"Or we could start car shopping."

"I don't want a car—" Wreath paused as they rolled to a stop sign. "There it is!"

Faye's head whirled toward the corner. "Are you sure—"

But Wreath had already jumped out of the car and dashed toward the bicycle, propped against a newspaper rack.

"What are you doing?" a boy's voice said when Wreath grabbed the handlebars—and realized the bike wasn't hers.

"Uh, sorry," she said to the middle-school kid who had been hidden by a big oak. "I thought that was my bike."

"Weirdo," he muttered as she headed back to the car.

"False alarm," she said to Faye.

"So that's what it looks like when you're careful." Faye drove on through the intersection. "Not only did you almost jump out of a moving car, you grabbed the bike before you saw the kid."

Wreath's face grew hot. "I did, didn't I?"

"You're prone to action, aren't you?"

Wreath watched the trees. "I've never thought about it." She shrugged. "Yeah, sorta."

"Was your mother like that?"

She looked out the window, unsure how to answer. A year ago, she had Frankie all figured out. But with each week—and each decision—she felt less certain about who her mother had been.

"Did she fight all her own battles?" Faye adjusted her mirror. "Or did you fight them for her?"

"We were a team." Wreath surprised herself by reaching over to touch Faye's arm. "The way you and I are."

Her bike was propped outside the Dollar Barn when Wreath left work Thursday afternoon.

For certain this time.

Leaned up against a wall, near the back, it was not in plain sight. Not waiting for the light, she stumbled over the curb and dashed across the street.

When she put her hand on the seat it was almost like greeting an old friend. Everything appeared okay, even the back tire, which sometimes lost air.

"Get your hands off my bike," a voice said behind her.

She jumped back as an arm shot around her and pushed the bike forward. The red-haired guy carried a sack in each hand.

"*Your* bike!" Wreath grabbed the seat.

He frowned when he caught sight of her face and pushed the bike out of her reach.

She stretched and clamped her hand on the seat. "This is my bike. You stole it."

"Prove it," he said, half dragging her as he rolled the bike toward the front of the store. He wore the same pants he had Saturday with a clean long-sleeved shirt. His bushy hair resembled that of a pro baseball pitcher J.D. rooted for.

"I've notified the police," she said.

"You seem the type." His words were clipped but that accent was strong.

"The clerk in there's a friend of mine." She tilted her head toward the Dollar Barn. "When we get to the front, she'll call them again."

At this he paused.

Wreath held her breath. Destiny was leaving in a week for the beach with her cousin. Maybe she'd be working.

"I don't have time for this," he said.

"Neither do I." Nor did she want him to know who she was. Not until she knew more about him. Wreath gritted her teeth and tugged. The bike fell over and dislodged the sacks from the guy's arms. An array of children's medicines flew out, followed by a bottle of grape soda and a small pink teddy bear.

"Now you've done it." He held onto the bike while trying to pick up the Tylenol and Pepto-Bismol. The latter had busted open and oozed onto the parking lot.

"*I* haven't done anything."

"Of course you haven't. Spoiled pretty girls don't ever do anything wrong."

"I'm not spoiled." Although Faye and J.D. sure tried. Wreath hesitated, not letting go of her bike. "Is that medicine for your little boy?"

He straightened. "I don't have a little boy."

"How about the one you shamelessly used to con people Saturday?" Her voice was mocking. "A puppy and a kid in the same scheme. Classy. And what's your connection with Fred Procell?"

His eyes flew open. "Shut up," he said. He picked up the Tylenol. "This is for a friend. Her kid's sick."

Wreath pushed down a stab of guilt, but let her anger win. "You'll have to take it on foot. My bike goes with me."

"She's got a fever."

"The child's mother?" Wreath asked, confused.

"The kid," he said and made a quick play for the bike. "Jack needs this."

She planted her feet and held on. "What kind of scam are you running?" She was not going to be bullied by this punk. She had to get information from him—without giving any up. "How dare you use a sick child! You should be ashamed of yourself."

For an instant she thought she'd pushed him too far but he merely rolled his eyes. "Thanks for the lecture, Mother Teresa. I'll pray about it."

"You should," she muttered.

"It obviously doesn't work," he said. "If it did, you'd be gone by now."

"I'm not leaving until I figure out what you're up to."

"Well, Dora the Explorer, we'll have to save that for the next episode."

"Aren't you clever?" she said. "Why didn't that flea market owner call the cops on you?"

His eyes flew to hers. "What are you blabbing about now?" But she'd glimpsed a thread of anxiety beneath his bravado.

"That Theriot guy turned the whole bike thing back on me," she said. "And, by the way, thanks for sticking me with that dog."

"Forget about the dog." He stepped closer. "What did Theriot say?"

She shrugged. "That you were panhandling again."

"Like he didn't drive me to it," he muttered. He moved a few inches toward her. "Stay away from him." His voice, even with the accent, sounded tough. "Do you understand? Don't get mixed up with him."

She kicked at his shin out of pure frustration. *Why did everyone want to boss her around?* "Let go of my bike, and I'll stay away from you too." Wreath planted herself over the front wheel, her hands gripping the handlebars.

"You're tough." The words sounded almost like a compliment. "I really was going to return the bike."

"R-i-i—ght. After you saved me from those dog people and that Theriot man."

He eyed her. "You did give that puppy back, didn't you?"

"No, I took it to work with me. She's minding the store— like I should be." She yanked the handlebars again.

"I'm not lying about Jack being sick," he said. "Do I look like I'd waste money on kid medicine?"

"Maybe you're a druggie," she said. Although his eyes were too clear for that. In fact, his muscular body looked *healthy*.

"R-i-i-ght." He mocked her. "And I chase it with Pepto-Bismol and snuggle with my teddy bear."

"Real funny." Wreath wavered. "I'll go with you to deliver the medicine, then I get the bike."

"No way."

"Help!" She tried a bluff. There was no one in the parking lot, and her cry lacked heat.

The guy let out a sigh. "Do you know anything about sick kids?"

"Not really." She nodded at the sack. "That Tylenol should help with the fever."

"The kid's been feeling bad for a few days," he said. "Now he's throwing up."

Wreath looked at the pink stain on the parking lot. "You'd better get more of that."

His head dropped. "Won't the Tylenol help?"

She frowned. "I don't think so."

"I'll have to hope it works." He got off the bike. "I'll walk back to the motel. Thanks for the loan."

Her guard flew back up faster than she could ride her bike down the hill by the library. "You're keeping that boy at a motel?" she asked. This grew more awful by the moment.

He threw an arm up in the air, the sacks in his other hand, and lunged at her. "Grrr!" he said. "I'm a monster."

Wreath didn't move.

The guy met her eyes, then put his purchases into one sack. Bending to pick up the broken bottle, he stuck it in the other bag and tossed it into a nearby Dumpster. With a wave, he strode off.

Wreath trembled as she mounted the bike. She, on her own, had retrieved it. Although she probably wouldn't brag about it to Law, Faye, or J.D. They would not approve of her methods.

As she coasted through the parking lot, she saw the guy. He walked fast as he made his way down the other side of the street, his head down, his shoulders slumped.

Why hadn't he bought more Pepto-Bismol?

She wheeled the bike back to the front of the store. It wasn't her fault the medicine bottle broke. He shouldn't have tussled with her.

Nor should he have stolen her bicycle.

What if the child got sicker?

It wasn't her business.

But people hadn't used that excuse when they helped her. They kept helping even when she pushed them away.

She skidded to a stop, jumped off her bike and rushed into the store.

Destiny was at the cash register, not a customer in sight. "You're here!" Wreath said.

"Hey, girlfriend. We still on for tonight? Mitch and Law and I will pick you up at eight? Pizza, the usual?"

Wreath scurried toward the pharmacy aisle. "Sure but I've got to run an errand first," she said over her shoulder.

Destiny followed her. "You sick?"

"It's for a friend." Wreath picked up a large bottle of the pink medicine. "You know anything about this stuff?"

"That's the same thing my last customer asked." She rolled her eyes. "Did you see that guy's hair?"

"Huh?" Wreath studied the label.

She looked over Wreath's shoulder. "He probably left before you got here."

"Oh, right," Wreath said and headed toward the toy counter, Destiny on her heals. "Y'all sell coloring books?"

Destiny didn't reply, and Wreath looked up. Her friend was chewing on her bottom lip.

"It's for a sick kid I met," Wreath said. "I'm kind of in a hurry. Keep me posted about the plans for tonight."

"You're acting odd."

Wreath pulled the crumpled cash out of her backpack. "No I'm not."

"Law said y'all had a fight about going off to college."

"It wasn't a fight." Wreath puckered her brow. "He mentioned that?"

Destiny broke open a roll of quarters and handed her the change. "He said he was trying to talk you into going to Tech with us."

Wreath sacked the items. "When'd you talk to Law?"

"Last night."

She tried to keep her face impassive. "I thought you were packing."

"I was. He came by to say hey."

Wreath replayed the evening before in her mind. Law had picked her up at Faye's and taken her to a supper at church. He'd seemed in a bit of rush when he left, but he hadn't mentioned going by Destiny's.

A woman in pajama bottoms and a surgical-scrubs top plopped items on the counter. "You ringing me up today or not?" she asked.

"See you later," Wreath said.

Destiny and Law had gone to kindergarten together. They'd been friends way before Wreath came along. It was stupid to be jealous.

Climbing on her bike, she set off on her mission.

7

Wreath pedaled hard down Main Street. She looked to the right and left. He couldn't have gone far in the few minutes it had taken to make her purchases.

But after several blocks, she was ready to give up. This was foolish. She needed to get home.

Faye would be worried, and probably with good cause. Wreath had veered into an unfamiliar neighborhood, a mix of rundown houses and shabby industrial businesses.

Cars were parked in front yards and litter lined the street. A big dog was tied to a porch rail. The house looked like it could fall down if the dog jerked at the rope much harder. Two men, wearing grease-covered overalls, sat in front of a tire-repair place.

Then she saw the red-haired guy, his face down, his steps quick, a few yards ahead of her.

"Chasing your boyfriend?" one of the mechanics yelled.

She ignored him and sped up, the sun on her face. The sunshine didn't seem to notice how shabby the neighborhood was.

As she caught up with the guy, he whipped around, the sack clutched close to his body. "Did you get lost on your way back to work?"

Wreath dragged her feet to keep from passing him.

"My luck gets better and better. Why couldn't I take a bike from a loser?" he said and turned back around and continued walking.

"Be choosier next time." She coasted alongside him.

"So, you're following me?"

"Very astute."

"You're a nut."

"Said the guy who threw a dog at me and stole my bike."

"*Borrowed* your bike. You said you'd steer clear of me if I gave it back. Which I did." He walked on. "And yet here you are."

"So what's the deal with you and that flea-market guy? He was watching you."

"Stay away from him." He looked around as the pie lady had done. "He's a mean SOB."

Wreath raised her eyebrows.

"That's the same way Jack looks at me when I swear," he said. "Sorry."

She held out the sack. "Here."

"What are you doing? Working on your bucket list? On a church scavenger hunt?"

"If I were looking for a chip on a shoulder, I'd be in luck." She thrust the bag at him again. "You're a colossal jerk."

"Ooh. Don't let Jack hear you talk like that."

"Did you leave him alone all this time?"

The guy glanced over at her uneasily. "I'm doing the best I can," he mumbled. He walked on, faster now.

Wreath gave the pedals a push and rolled next to him again. "More Pepto-Bismol. Take it."

"That's a big sack for a bottle of stomach medicine."

"I got Gatorade too. It keeps you hydrated, I think," she said. "I bought him a coloring book too. All they had were unicorns and princesses, so I went with the unicorns."

She summoned her nerve. She needed to know why he had been looking for her. Frankie used to say that not knowing was sometimes better than knowing. It had confused Wreath at the time, but right now she got it. Did she really want to know?

He cleared his throat. "You're not pouting, are you?"

The bike swerved. "I don't pout."

"Then why do you have that look in your eyes?"

"I need to know why you were panhandling."

He swatted at a mosquito that had landed on his forehead. "You better get going. This isn't the best part of town."

"I can't leave until we talk."

They stopped in front of a rundown motel—The Palomino, according to its neon sign of a rearing horse. "Rooms by the week. Vacancy." *No surprise there.*

The Corral, a bar with beer signs glowing, had a hefty array of pickups out front. It sat in the middle of a horseshoe of cinderblock buildings, a driveway on either side.

The motel office sat to the right of the entrance drive, its sign half burned out, leaving only the word *Off.* A drive-up window had a note taped to it.

"You left a child here?" She could not mask her alarm.

"We live here."

Her stomach knotted. She had stayed in a few of these places. Wreath despised them, the constant coming and going, the smells, the noise. Her mother, though, claimed to like not being tied down, said you met some of the nicest people on the move.

That's where Big Fun had come from, a motel up near Shreveport.

That was enough to sour her on cheap motels. And now that poor kid lived here. Wreath forced herself not to ride off.

The guy stared at her. "You're not going to throw up, are you?"

"Huh?"

"You look like you swallowed a bad piece of meat."

"I was thinking about . . . someone." Wreath waved the sack in front of his face. "Take it."

His eyes were watchful. "What's the catch?"

"There's no catch."

"People don't come around here"—he gestured toward the motel—"giving stuff away."

"I broke the other bottle, and I'm worried about the boy." She threw the sack at him hard and it hit him in the stomach.

He grunted but caught it.

"Bum?" a small voice said from the drive. "Whatcha doing?"

The child from the flea market, wearing a gray knit hat—*and Strawberry shortcake pajamas?*—dashed across the Corral parking lot and latched onto the guy's leg. Tears rolled down a pale, dirty face. A deep purple bruise glowed from his temple. "I didn't think you was coming back."

"Oh, Jack, I won't ever leave you." He scooped up the child, who was barefoot, soles filthy. He frowned. "How'd you get that bruise?"

Wreath had to rescue this child. But how?

Jack looked over at Wreath. "I was jumping on the bed."

"Jack." The guy—*Bum?*—frowned.

"I know it's dangerous." The child stumbled over the word and tears rolled down his face.

"What's dangerous is you wandering around out here." Bum's voice was stern. "You're supposed to stay inside with the door locked."

"I g-g-got scared." The words were almost hiccupped.

"What'd I tell you?" The guy sounded gruff.

"No boogie man can beat Bum up."

"You got that right." He fist bumped the boy. "I got you medicine—and a toy." He shuffled the child to his hip and pulled the stuffed animal out of the bag.

The child, eyes wide, snatched the toy, then looked at Wreath. "Who's that girl?"

The guy lowered the boy to the ground and dug through the sack. "She brought you juice."

"Is she our friend?"

"Not exactly."

"Sure I am." Wreath drew in her breath and hoped that whatever came next would not be too bad. "My name's Wreath."

"That's a funny name," the boy said.

Bum—*now that was a peculiar name*—made a choking sound and his neck turned a blotchy red. He looked as mad as Frankie had the time Wreath stepped between her and Big Fun in a fight.

"*You're* Wreath Willis?" His voice was low and angry. "So Miss Goody Two-Shoes is a liar." He ignored the child, who whined and tapped his leg with a stubby little finger.

"Why were you looking for me?" Wreath asked and got on the bike. Just in case.

"Bum has a funny name too," the child said, as though neither Wreath nor Bum had spoken. "It's not his real name. It's a knick-knack, a knick . . ." He quirked his head, his nose scrunched up. "What's it called again?"

"A nickname," Bum said with a glare at Wreath.

"One would hope," she said.

"I wasted days because of you. What's your deal?" His voice grew louder.

"My deal? I don't appreciate strangers coming to my job." The words were defiant although anxiety washed over her.

"It doesn't matter," he said. "I got the information I was looking for." He didn't as much as blink. "Not that it did me any good."

"What kind of information?"

He didn't reply.

Jack made a weird sputtering noise. His eyes went big, and he clutched the animal from the sack. His face was the shade of the belly of a fish caught on one of Big Fun's trips to the coast.

Bum's expression softened as it went from Wreath to the boy. "Come on, Jack."

"No!" Wreath scrambled off the bike and it fell to the ground. "You can't take him back in that place. Where's his mother?"

"She left." Jack's lip trembled, and Wreath reached for him.

"Get your hands off." The blotches of red worked their way up to Bum's face.

A series of shallow gags erupted from the boy, whose eyes had filled with tears again. "I don't feel so good."

"You poor thing." Wreath rubbed his back, the way Frankie had rubbed hers.

"If you don't get your hands off him this minute, I'm——"

"Going to kidnap me too?" Wreath knelt between Jack and Bum. "Or maybe call the cops?"

Jack was shivering, and Wreath put her arms around him. "It's okay," she said. "I won't let anyone hurt you."

"Uncle Bum says that," Jack said with a small smile. And then threw up on Wreath's new Converse All-Stars.

Uncle?

Bum's skin went paler than Jack's. He held up a hand, turned his face away from Wreath and gagged.

Wreath had seen plenty of vomit during her mother's illness. This was nothing. She set the sack on the ground and reached into her pack for a Baggie filled with wet wipes. "Let me wipe your face."

The child stood solemnly while Wreath cleaned his face. She pulled out a second cloth to wipe the dirt that seemed to stretch from ear to ear. "There!" Wreath tweaked Jack's nose. He was adorable. "All clean!"

The boy threw his arms around Wreath's neck. The lemon-y smell of the cloth mingled with the smell of kid sweat and puke.

"Thanks," Bum mumbled.

"Bum don't like barf," Jack said.

"Nobody likes barf, kid." Bum patted his head.

"Remember that time I ate those gummy worms and drank that milkshake and—"

Bum held up a hand again, his face still colorless. "Don't go there, Jack."

"We was at my birthday party," Jack said, "and Bum—"

"Jack!" Bum said and turned away to gag again. "Quiet!"

Wreath watched, oddly amused. When Bum turned back around, she stood. "Is he really your nephew?"

Bum didn't answer but pulled the Gatorade out of the sack and unscrewed the top. "Here, Jack, have a drink of this."

She grabbed his arm, and he winced. "You should wait a few minutes before you give him anything to drink," she said. "In case . . ." She glanced at the puddle on the ground.

"Oh, right." Bum shuddered.

"I'm thirsty." Jack's voice was both contrary and weak.

"Let's get you back inside." Bum picked him up.

With the child in one arm and the Gatorade and sacks in another, he took a step toward the building and turned. "I'll catch up with you later about that other matter," he said. "Um . . . thanks."

Wreath debated. *Was the child safe?*

Jack squirmed. "I want her to come too."

"Come on, Jack." The words held a hint of desperation.

And then Jack threw up again.

Bum, face contorted, held him at arm's length. The Gatorade and packages flew to the ground. "You have got to be kidding me," Bum said and gagged again.

Wreath pulled out a few more wet wipes, a good substitute for a sink in her experience. "Let me."

She reached for Jack.

Bum did not argue.

8

Wreath wiped the boy's face and arms as she lifted him, and Bum bent to pick up the supplies. His hair had come loose over his face like a red curtain. It really was a pretty color.

"You're nice," Jack said, patting Wreath's face. "Like my mommy."

Bum grew still. "Jack, hush," he said in a quiet voice.

"He was being swee—"

"You too. Shhh," he hissed. "You've got to get going."

He reached for Jack. The child, in turn, clutched at Wreath's neck like a vine clinging to a tree in the junkyard. "I want her to come—"

"Jack!" Bum's voice was low and harsh. He craned his neck toward the street, then looked at Wreath. "You shouldn't have come here."

She glanced around, surprised that dusk was settling on the dingy parking lot.

"Is it the mean man?" Jack asked.

Wreath dabbed at his face with a cloth she still held. "Don't be frightened," she said gently, then looked at Bum. "What are you teaching this child?"

"I don't have time for one of your lectures." Bum's jaw was hard, and he seemed to survey the street. Then he exhaled. "Follow me. Don't look back."

She knelt to pick up the medicine, but Bum tugged at her shirt. "Leave it."

Grabbing the Pepto-Bismol despite his words, Wreath followed. Bum never let go of her shirt as they scrambled toward the drive. They made it into the breezeway before a voice called out. "Hey!"

"Go to the office," Bum said to Wreath. "Hurry. You don't want him to see you here."

"I don't like him." Jack burrowed his face into Bum's shoulder. "He's not nice."

Wreath risked a quick look and saw a black pickup, door standing open, parked on the edge of the street.

"Turn around," Bum growled and steered them into the dim office, about the size of a utility shed. An old lawn chair, its seat drooping, sat to the side. A plastic table held a stained coffee pot and three chipped mugs.

A counter made of fake wood sat to the right, a scratched Plexiglas window separating the space from the lobby. A door on the other side was closed.

Bum tried to put the boy down, but he wouldn't let go. "Can you hold Jack for a sec?" he asked. "I'll be right back."

Wreath's heart pounded as she reached for the child. "That's what you said when you handed me that dog." She threw Jack a smile.

"I need to see what he wants," Bum said. "Stay put for five minutes." He hesitated. "Please."

"I don't feel good," Jack said with a whimper.

Wreath caved. "Come here, little guy."

He avoided Wreath's arms and slid to the floor.

Bum was already heading back outside. The door, swollen out of shape, swung not-quite-closed.

"I need to use the bathroom," Jack whined.

Wreath looked around. A "Back in 15 minutes" sign was taped to the check-in desk, although it looked like a permanent fixture. Behind the desk, barely visible through the plastic shield, was a big calendar, the days crossed off. Like the one in Lucky where Wreath had stayed those few miserable days before graduation.

She patted Jack's shoulder.

"I need to use it bad." The child wrapped his legs around each other.

Wreath peeked outside through a grimy window. Bum was leaned up against the passenger side of the pickup talking into an open window. She couldn't see who he was talking to.

"Use it!" Jack said from behind her, the declaration filled with a panicky squeak.

"Hello?" Wreath called out.

Jack squinted. "Who you talking to?"

"The person who works at the desk," she said. "Hello?"

He wrinkled his nose. "He's the mean man."

"What?" She looked down.

He gave a slow nod. "He goes through that little door," he said in a whisper, pointing to where the counter raised and lowered. "But if you go back there, you'll get in trouble. 'Cept sometimes a lady works there. She's mean too." Jack put his hands down to his crotch. "I think I'm going to pee on myself."

"Don't do that! Where's the restroom?"

"Ain't no restroom in here."

She decided it wasn't the time for a grammar lesson and looked around. "Where is it?"

He pointed toward the door. "Out there." Another squirm. "In mama's house."

Wreath took another look out the window. Bum was nodding, still propped against the truck.

She turned to the child. "Lead the way."

9

Bum fought the urge to look over his shoulder.

He didn't want Jack to come running out of the motel. Or, worse, that girl, Wreath. Why had she misled him at that furniture store? It'd taken him days to figure out Fred Procell was in jail.

At least that was a relief.

"You hear me?" Theriot's voice was hard, as usual. Bum knew better than to lose focus around him.

"I got it," he snapped. Blood seeped through his sleeve where Wreath had grabbed him.

Theriot took the toothpick out of his mouth, glanced at it, and tossed it onto the street.

"I'll water the dogs and make sure no one's snooping around," Bum said.

"And the envelope?"

"That wasn't part of our deal." His teeth were clenched.

"You didn't tell me you and your kid would be panhandling either. Or that your sister hadn't been in touch." He spit onto the gravel parking lot. "If you want a roof over your head, our deal will be what I say it is."

Bum sneaked a look toward the office. Jack needed a safe place to stay. At least Bum could protect him here. The street would be another matter.

"All right. I'll pick the envelope up at the desk tonight and drop it tomorrow. And we get another week."

Theriot cackled like an old woman. "We'll see how it goes. If you bail on me, your sister owes me double and you and the kid will be locked out."

"If that's the deal, you have to let us set up out at the flea market, make a few bucks."

Theriot stared at Bum.

Bum stared back.

"I don't have to do anything." Theriot put another toothpick in his mouth. "But seeing's how Starla left you and your kid in the lurch, you can have a little space on the other end. No panhandling." He chuckled. "Bad for my image."

"Right." Bum turned and walked back toward the motel. He was almost past the bar when Theriot spoke again.

"And don't think I didn't see that girl." He snorted. "The one from the flea market."

Bum clasped his hands and cracked his knuckles. He couldn't keep from turning.

"Does she know where Starla is?" Theriot said.

Bum stepped back toward the truck. "She doesn't know about anything, and I'm certainly not telling her."

"She better not be turning tricks on my property."

Bum wanted to punch him. "She's not like that." What explanation could he give for Wreath's presence? "She came to invite us to her church or something." She might as well have, with a sermon on this and a lecture on that.

"Keep her away from here," Theriot said. "She threatened to call the cops Saturday. I won't put up with that crap."

"She won't be back," Bum said and walked quickly away. He sidestepped the small pool of puke and wished he could rub Theriot's face in it.

At the office, he banged the door open with his shoulder. "Sorry it took—" The lousy excuse for a lobby was empty, and his pulse galloped.

"Jack?" he called. "Jack!" He never should have trusted a stranger. No matter how pretty she was.

Bum lifted the Formica piece of counter and slipped underneath, even looking in the closet behind the desk where he and Theriot exchanged envelopes. Jack was nowhere to be seen.

Banging his head as he ducked back into the lobby, he ran to the back door. "Jack!" he shouted and flung open the door into the courtyard. The hum of the ice machine was all that greeted him. "Jack," he screamed, not caring if Theriot heard. "Jack!"

Bum would have liked to throttle his sister at that moment. And that girl.

He charged through the courtyard and tripped over a pothole.

A couple of neighbors drank beer on the steps of their cottages—although that word was a stretch—and eyed him suspiciously.

The man-boy who lived in the second room watched him coming. "Where you going, Mr. Bum?"

"Checking on Jack." He sprinted on past.

"He's with that pretty lady."

Bum didn't know whether to be relieved or terrified.

By the time he got to Room 22, he felt like one of Theriot's strays, desperate and mad. He jerked open the storm door and turned the cheap knob. When he pushed, his shoulder banged against the wood. The door was locked.

"Open this door!" He slammed his palm against it with such force that the cheap wood shook and his hand stung. "Jack!"

He heard Samson barking.

Rearing back, he lowered his shoulder and rammed the door—right as it flew open, propelling him into Wreath.

She flew backward, a washcloth waving in her hand. Bum's arms flailed. Wreath, who didn't have time to break her fall, slammed into the floor and hit the corner of the dresser with her head. A big breath whooshed out of her. Her eyes were closed when Bum finished falling.

The dog yelped and fled behind the bed.

For an instant there was an unnatural silence in the room, Bum's weight pressed against Wreath's soft frame.

Then a series of barks and a giggle erupted from the bed. "That was silly," Jack said.

"Hush, Samson," Bum said. "Jack, shut him up." That was all he needed. For Theriot to be reminded about the dog.

Jack wriggled to the other side and gently hoisted the dog by its stubby front legs, murmuring to it. The dog quieted. That kid was nothing if not resilient.

Bum lifted himself off of Wreath, anger and worry fighting inside his gut. "What were you doing in here?" He pushed the door shut, and it closed with a click.

Jack scooted to the foot of the bed, face flushed red. "I had to pee." The voice was less exuberant than it had been moments before.

Please don't let her throw up.

Wreath, her eyes closed, remained on the floor. She raised one arm, then the other.

"She don't look so good." Jack's head hung over the edge of the bed.

"Doesn't," Bum muttered. "Doesn't look so good."

Wreath's eyes flew open. "You nearly kill me, and you're worried about grammar?"

Samson growled and ambled over on three legs. His back leg was still bandaged.

Wreath's long brownish hair tumbled around her shoulders, and she brushed it back from her face as she tried to sit up. She looked cute—and either very mad or in a lot of pain. Probably the latter, judging by the knot rising on her temple.

Bum looked at the bed. "Did she hurt you, Jack?"

Jack's eyes were as round as the disc they threw in the courtyard, Samson on his lap. "Wreath's my friend." The words held devotion, as though they'd known her for years.

Jack's new best friend put her head in her hands and moaned.

Remorse filled Bum, but he shoved it to the side. "Why did you take her from the lobby when I told you not to?"

"Her?" Wreath's face eased up toward the child.

"I think you hurt *she?*" Jack said and crouched for a better look. The face was crinkled, a couple of feet from Wreath's.

"Bum called you *her.*" Wreath interrupted. She put her hands on the floor and crawled toward the bed. The dog went into a barking frenzy.

Head and shoulder aching, Bum shot to his feet and extended a hand to help her. "Jack, take Samson into the bathroom."

"No!" Wreath's voice was raspy as she grabbed the ratty bedspread and pulled herself up, her breathing shallow. She touched her temple and looked at the blood on her fingers.

"Is you going to throw up, Wreath?" Jack said as Wreath half sat, half fell onto the bed.

Bum felt like he was watching a slow-motion video. Wreath had not only tracked down the bike, she was on the verge of figuring out the truth. Or at least a piece of it.

Wreath seemed to summon all her energy as she lurched to where Jack sat and yanked off the knit cap. The child's curly blond hair sprang out in every direction. Why hadn't Bum braided it like Jack asked?

"You're a girl." Wreath said.

His niece nodded with a grin, as though Wreath had handed her a present. "Jaclyn Marie," she said, and honest-to-God fluffed her hair. "Most people call me Jaclyn, 'cept sometimes Bum."

"I can help you, sweetie," Wreath said, her voice low, then met Bum's eyes in the mirror. "We need to get out of here."

"You're not going anywhere." Bum grabbed her hand, which was clammy.

She yanked back and rubbed her left wrist. Her eyes were moving back and forth. "Stay away from me, you pervert."

He frowned. "You're the one who locked herself in a room with a strange child."

Jack climbed off the bed and clung to Bum's leg. "You said always lock the door." Jack's voice had shifted to a wail. "She got me a washcloth when I was 'bout to throw up again."

The dog crawled toward Wreath on its belly. "It's okay," Wreath said, scratching between its eyes. Her own gaze did not leave Bum.

That mutt would barely let Bum touch him—and Bum was the one who had risked everything to save him.

Wreath staggered and put her other hand on the bed to steady herself. Her gaze went from Bum to Jack to her backpack, lying on the broken-down armchair. "Stay away from me or I'll scream," she said, her voice unnaturally calm. "Jaclyn, hand me my pack, please."

The child whimpered in harmony with Samson, who slunk under the bed.

"There's nothing to be afraid of, darling," Wreath said. Her breath sounded shallow. "Hand me my pack."

"You got blood on your face," Jack said. "Lots of blood."

Bum caught Wreath right before she hit the floor for the second time.

10

Bum pulled a second threadbare washcloth from the shelf and ran cold water over it. As he wrung it out, he looked at himself in the mirror, his red hair as frayed as the old mop in the utility closet.

What a screw-up.

He criticized his sister but he was no amateur when it came to mistakes. Not only had he swiped a bike—a nice girl's bike—but he'd knocked her out in a rundown motel room.

How long before someone called the cops looking for her? That'd get them kicked out of the room for sure. And no telling what Theriot might do.

"Hurry, Bum," Jack called. "She's moaning."

Wreath said something he couldn't understand, her voice as thin as Jack's had been when she vomited. As Bum turned back toward the room, Wreath grabbed Jack by the arm and jerked on the door, which hung at an odd angle.

"Stop!" Bum rushed out of the bathroom, waving the washcloth. He was definitely ready to surrender. "Sit down." His voice sounded gruffer than he intended.

"You're crazy." She looked toward Jack. "Don't be scared. Everything's all right."

"Bum's nice." Jack nodded over at Bum reassuringly. "If you're sweet, he'll give you candy."

"Get away from her!" he yelled. Bum charged toward them, and Samson hobbled out from under the bed, tangling Bum's feet. Flinging himself in the direction of the door, he grabbed Jack's ankle. Wreath still held her arm.

Jack began to scream, and a stricken look came over Wreath's face. "I'll come back for you, Jaclyn," she croaked. "I promise."

And she fled through the door, bouncing off the doorframe.

Bum, scrambling on all fours, got to the door in time to see her career across the courtyard, half running, and half falling. He took a step forward and then drew back, forcing the busted door shut.

The dog gave a bark that sounded like a scold and crawled back under the bed.

"Wreath forgot her backpack," Jack said.

11

Wreath climbed onto her bike, still on the sidewalk in front of the Corral. Her head spun faster than the wheels, and she was fairly certain she would join Jack—*Jaclyn!*—in today's vomit club.

She fingered the knot on her forehead, the blood sticky. The bike swerved.

Once she got to Faye's, she'd never leave. Ever.

The bike wobbled as she reached for a tissue.

She'd left her pack in the room!

With her money. And her journal. And all her supplies. Even in the worst days of running she hadn't gone off without her pack. She never was separated from her journal. It was the only truly personal item she owned.

Wreath looked over her shoulder. Her legs trembled so hard they nearly banged against the bike.

No sight of Bum.

Nor anyone else, for that matter.

In the early evening shadows, the street looked empty—and creepy. Spanish moss hung from the big trees. A few houses had left garbage cans out by the street, and litter was strewn everywhere. A cat, gray like heavy fog, streaked across the street a few yards away, chased by a big tabby.

Coasting until she was out of sight of the office door, Wreath put her foot out and propped herself up.

Should she call the police? Was that really where they lived? And where was Jaclyn's mother?

The Palomino sign popped on, the noise and flash making Wreath's head hurt worse.

Going into that room had violated one of Frankie's main rules, admonitions Wreath had listed in her journal before her mother died.

> *Dear Brownie: Frankie says the world is a good place with bad people. Be wary of strangers, especially men. Don't get trapped in small spaces. Avoid narrow halls and stairwells. Make sure there are two exits. Look for a way out when you go in. Never let a man hit you.*

Wreath let the truth sink in.

She had failed once more at being a normal girl.

She shuddered. That room had looked like someone had turned a storage closet into a home. There was a double bed, unmade. A pallet was spread on the floor.

The bathroom had a rusty metal shower stall with a plastic curtain. The microwave looked like it was about to fall off the edge of an orange counter in what had once been a kitchen. There was an ugly stain on the bloated piece of tile where the roof had leaked.

Poor Jaclyn, living like that. And forced to pretend to be a boy. The world had let her down.

Bum had been frantic when the door crashed open. Scared, no doubt, about being found out.

She touched her head again. *Ouch.*

Wreath turned around. She'd march back and demand her pack and find out why a girl was masquerading as a boy. If he *was* Jaclyn's uncle, did Wreath have the right to rescue her? She'd seemed happy, both at the flea market and at the motel. However, children could be too trusting.

As Wreath's bike rolled a few feet forward, a pickup roared down the street and did a quick U-turn. She moved into the shadows and watched it pull up to the drive between the motel office and the bar.

Then it went into reverse and the driver whipped around and parked between two other trucks at the Corral.

A man got out, yanking a small German shepherd out of the back seat. He attached a leash to a choke-chain collar, jerked the chain, hard, and headed toward the driveway into the courtyard.

Wreath got off the bike and tried for a better look. The animal and the man had disappeared. But she knew what she had seen. The man in the pickup was the dog-seller from the flea market. That was the puppy Gretel. *Gret-Gret.*

She turned the bike toward home and flinched as she got back on. She pumped the pedals weakly.

Guilt about leaving Jaclyn grew with every block. Where was the girl's mother?

12

Law's truck sat in the driveway, and Wreath groaned as she rolled her bike around it. She'd forgotten their plans.

Faye's car wasn't in the carport, a small blessing.

A cheer erupted as she opened the back door. Her friends were watching a reality show and giving high-fives all around. Not one of them had blood on their face or puke on their shoes.

Wreath glanced at the spotless kitchen tile, watching as a drop of blood splattered. "Hey, y'all," she said. Her voice sounded like she hadn't used it in a while.

"Hey!" Law jumped up, a grin on his face. Then he froze. "Whoa. What happened?"

"Nothing." The room spun when Wreath shook her head.

"That's a lot of blood for nothing," Mitch said. He wore a Beat Bama T-shirt and an LSU cap. No doubt where he was heading in the fall.

Law rushed toward her. "Do you need a doctor?" He steered her toward the couch and slipped his arm around her shoulder.

"OMG!" Destiny, in a pair of ridiculously short cut-offs, rushed to sit next to Wreath. "What did you do?"

"It's not as bad as it looks." Wreath couldn't summon the energy to say more.

"I'd like to see what the other guy looks like," Mitch said.

Wreath gave a little laugh, and Law exhaled. "A laugh," he said. "You had me scared. So what happened?"

"It's kind of a long story. Where's Faye?"

"She just left for J.D.'s about ten minutes ago to watch an old movie or something," Destiny said. "We'd better call her."

"No!" Wreath yelped. "There's no need to mess up her evening."

"My parents would kill me if I got hurt and didn't tell them."

"Faye's not my mother." Wreath's eyes grew when she touched the knot. "Could you maybe get some ice?"

"Whatever." Destiny headed toward the kitchen.

"So *does* the other guy look worse?" Mitch asked.

"I'm not sure. How bad does this look?"

Law shifted from side to side, like Faye inspecting a piece of furniture at a garage sale. "Not terrible. Not great either." He put his fingers up to her temple and touched her lightly. "You sure you don't need a doctor?"

"It's barely anything. Let me change, and I'll be ready to go out." But she wobbled back onto the couch when she tried to stand.

Destiny reappeared with a bag of frozen peas. "That's quite a bruise," she said and bypassed Law's outstretched hand. "I got it." She held the package on Wreath's face. "This should help the swelling go down."

The cold felt good against her damp skin, and Wreath closed her eyes.

"No napping," Law said. "You might have a concussion."

"It's not a concussion. I bumped my head." She paused. "I don't think I can eat anything."

"But this is almost my last week here," Destiny said.

"You're only gone for a week," Mitch said.

"You're the one who said we should get pizza tonight."

Law's stomach growled at the words, and. Wreath reached up to take the peas. "I'm sorry I messed it up. Y'all go on."

"I'd better stay here," Law said.

Destiny looked from Law to Mitch and tugged at the hem of her shorts. "I'm going to be gone a whole week!"

Wreath looked at them. She was doing it again. Messing life up. "Are you letting them drive your new truck, Law?" she asked. "Get something to eat. I'll catch up with you tomorrow."

His brow wrinkled. "I forgot we were in my truck. You're not going to pass out, are you?"

"Faye won't be late," she said. "I won't doze off until she's here to check on me."

"Make up your mind, dude," Mitch said and winced when Destiny elbowed him. "Sorry, Wreath. My stomach overtook my brain."

She forced herself to get off the couch. "Just for that, you're buying next time." She hoped she didn't throw up before they left. Following Law to the kitchen door, she tried not to wince when he gave her a hug. She was going to be sore.

"Later, gator," Mitch said.

Law gave her a peck on the cheek and murmured that he hated to leave her.

Destiny hung back when the guys stepped outside "This wouldn't have anything to do with that sick kid, would it?" she asked in a low voice.

"Maybe."

"Are you involved in something bad again?" She wrinkled her nose, and Wreath noticed she was wearing the perfume Law and his grandparents had given her for graduation.

"Destiny!" Mitch yelled from the driveway. "Come on! We're starving."

Wreath nudged her toward the truck. "We've still got your going-away supper Saturday."

Law walked back toward them.

"Here I come," Destiny chirped.

"You sure you don't want me to stay?" Law said.

She wanted to say *yes* but couldn't. "There's no reason for you to miss out on the fun," she said instead.

"See you tomorrow after work?"

"Tomorrow."

Tomorrow she would have fun.

First she had to figure out how to help Jaclyn. And get her pack back.

13

"I'm not prying," Faye said the next afternoon in the workroom at the store.

Wreath knew what that meant.

"But tell me what happened to you again?"

This was the fifth time today Faye had *not* pried. Wreath had pretended she was asleep when Faye got home Thursday night. The coward's way. From the moment Faye laid eyes on Wreath in the kitchen today, she'd sniffed around like a hound dog on the trail of a bear.

"And don't give me that rigmarole about tripping and bumping your head," she said now.

Saying she'd gotten knocked down in a stranger's motel room would freak Faye out.

"You're not acting like yourself. Let me take you to the doctor."

"It doesn't hurt," Wreath said after a moment. The headache had mostly vanished.

Frankie didn't believe in running to the doctor. Not the time Wreath fell off a ten-foot slide in the government housing projects in Shreveport. Nor when she twisted her ankle running from a mean dog in Vivian. Even though it *had* swollen up bigger than the cantaloupe her mother bought that same day from a guy by the road.

Frankie almost yielded when Wreath stepped on a nail in the backyard in Lucky but, after inspecting it, she declared it wasn't rusty and should be all right with a dab of ointment and a Band-Aid.

Faye was studying her face when she looked up.

Wreath had hoped to put the explanation off until closing time, but that wasn't going to happen. She needed Faye's help with what to do about Jaclyn—and how to retrieve her backpack. Riding to the motel after work was too risky.

Although an encounter at the Palomino might be better than her impending confession to Faye.

"So your bike was parked in broad daylight outside the Dollar Barn?" Faye would have made a great prosecuting attorney.

"Yep. That guy from the flea market came out and I got it back."

"Just like that?"

Wreath recalled the skirmish, the medicine, the child at the motel. "More or less."

"Wreath?" Faye's worry was palpable. "He didn't hit you, did he?"

"No!" She'd seen guys who hit women. Bum didn't seem mean. In fact, he was gentle with Jaclyn. "He's a stupid guy. Made a dumb spur-of-the-minute decision."

Faye inspected Wreath. "I don't want you to live in fear. Nonetheless, that business with . . . I guess with Fred showing up, then your bike being stolen . . . there's a lot of meanness in the world."

"I need advice," Wreath said in a rush.

"That's progress." Faye gave up a quick smile. "I knew you'd tell me sooner or later. This time it wasn't even a day."

She'd vowed only weeks before not to keep secrets from Faye. She'd skated close with the bike-recovery tale. "That guy, the one who stole my bike, the one with the kid? They're in trouble, but I can't figure out what." Wreath fidgeted with her hair. "I don't know whether to get involved."

"Wreath, he's a thief," Faye said. "You don't want to get mixed up with someone like that."

"What about the child?"

"Did he seem afraid or like he was being abused?"

"That's the thing." She lowered her voice. "He's a girl."

Faye's face wrinkled in confusion. "*He's* a girl?"

"A little girl pretending to be a boy. Jack is Jaclyn. All curly-haired precious girl. She's his niece."

Faye put her hand to her head. "Why is a girl staying with her teenage uncle?" She paused. "Or is that a front?"

A front? Faye and J.D. loved their police dramas overmuch, in Wreath's opinion.

"I think she's Bum's niece, but I need to make sure."

"Bum?"

"That's the name he goes by."

Faye flinched. "How old is this Bum character?"

"Slightly older than me, I'm guessing."

"If Jack—Jaclyn—is his niece, what happened to her mother?"

"I don't know," she said.

"We need to call Shane."

Wreath held up her hand. "What if he is her uncle? What if the police take her away?"

This fear Wreath had long lived with, that a bureaucratic stranger would snatch her and toss her into the system. She didn't want that for Jaclyn unless she was in danger.

"It looks suspicious," Faye said.

"But do we have the right to blow up their lives?"

"We have the right to help a child. A responsibility even." Faye tapped her fingers on the worktable. "So they live in Landry?"

"Temporarily, I think."

"Dare I ask where?"

Wreath shuffled her feet. "At a place south of town. A kind of . . . motel."

"And you know this because he told you, right?"

"I went there," she said with a gulp.

Faye shook her head. "You are going to cause me to have a heart attack."

Another thing to worry about.

"I can't figure out what this guy's hiding," she said.

"You've just described the way I felt when you showed up here." Faye sprang up and started straightening the counter.

"You didn't trust me either," Wreath said.

"Like you feel about Bum?" Faye gave her head a shake. "What a horrid name."

Wreath sat on her hands to keep from fidgeting. "What else can we do, besides calling Shane?"

"Wait for Clarice?"

"She won't be back for nearly a month. And I hate to drag her into this."

Faye steepled her fingers. "She's an expert," she said. "You should have heard the speech she gave to my women's club."

Wreath leaned forward.

"As I recall, the child must appear to be in harm's way, malnourished, or not in school," Faye said. "That's when you know to call the authorities."

"I don't think Jaclyn's old enough for school. Bum seems to care about her and to provide food." *Probably doing without himself.* "They even have a pet." She turned up her nose. "But living in that motel . . . what a mess. And the dog's been injured."

"It's hurt?"

"Its leg is. But it's not scrawny. It looks like a foot stool."

"How much time have you spent with this dog—and its owner?" Faye's look was pained.

"Not much," Wreath mumbled. "So what do we do?"

Faye lifted her shoulders in a graceful shrug. "This part of Clarice's talk I remember well," she said. "People have a right to raise their children as they want, even if we don't agree with them. As long as they don't put them in danger."

"What if something awful happens?"

The room was quiet. "You're not going back to that motel, if that's what you're thinking."

"I left my backpack there."

Faye's eyes narrowed. "At the same time you got a head injury? If you ever do something—"

"I guess I could look for them at the Junque Mart. See if they're there again."

Faye shook her head so hard that her carefully styled hair flew loose. "Absolutely not."

"But my diary's in my pack . . . and my money. Even my notes on the store's summer displays."

"Why not ask Shane to get it back?"

Wreath grimaced. It was hard to explain to Faye when she barely got it herself. "I need to find out if Jaclyn's in trouble before I call the police." She leaned forward on the table, her head tilted back. "Would you go out to the flea market with me? I could show you that red rocker."

They both knew this was not about finding an item to sell.

"I'll take you," Faye said in a brisk voice, "but you better not do anything stupid."

"You'd really do that for me?" Wreath's voice was dry.

"Let's say I've become more flexible this past year."

As much as she didn't want to, Wreath had to ask. "Will J.D. be okay with us going?"

"He won't love the idea," Faye said. "He warned me again about that man—Theriot. He's well known in Landry for all the wrong things."

"Would J.D. go with us?"

A tender look flitted through Faye's eyes. "What a lovely proposal," she said. "But he and a group of men from church have a project in the morning. Building a wheelchair ramp out where your *cousin* used to live."

Wreath felt her face grow hot. "That was dumb, wasn't it?"

A year of running, hiding, pretending to live with a cousin.

"You did what you thought you had to."

"Jaclyn's like me," she whispered.

"That didn't escape my notice. What if I had turned you away?" Faye shook her head. "What a tragedy that would have been."

"You saved me," Wreath said softly.

"I was talking about a tragedy for me." Faye cleared her throat. "I needed you more than you needed me."

Wreath met her gaze, held it. "Thank you."

14

The crowd at the flea market was as big as last weekend's. And Wreath's certainty about her quest shrank with every car that pulled into the lot.

"Now I see where all the downtown traffic is," Faye said.

Wreath scanned the crowd while she paid.

A woman in jeans and a T-shirt was in the announcement booth when they drew near. The dog-seller still peddled puppies and Wreath veered down another aisle to avoid him.

"Where were they?" Faye asked first thing.

"Uh, over there." Wreath pointed to the booth. A group of youngsters in matching Western outfits were clogging on the stage. The noise level was as high as before, but Wreath's heart sounded even louder to her ears.

Faye nodded and followed as she led her toward the spot where Jaclyn and Bum sat last week. When a child laughed, they both jerked around—to see a toddler on a man's shoulders. A woman followed with a smiling child in tow.

"It doesn't seem fair." Wreath spoke right into Faye's ear. "Some children have everything, others . . ."

"I don't understand either." Faye moved around Wreath. "That's why we have to help."

Wreath's heart turned over at the words.

"Let's step into this booth so we're not conspicuous," Faye said.

She almost laughed. "In this crowd? It'd take a clown on stilts to stand out, and that's only a maybe."

Faye turned toward the booth. "I like that little red rocker," she said. "Let's see what he'll do. You look for the guy while I bargain."

As Faye struck the deal on the chair and a couple of pieces of pottery, Wreath peered at the crowd. Bum and Jaclyn were nowhere in sight. *What was she supposed to do?* Jaclyn needed help, although Wreath wasn't sure what kind. And her journal in her backpack was her most important possession. She had to get it back.

No amount of finagling would get Faye to that sleazy motel.

Handing the chair to Wreath, Faye clutched the pottery and insisted on forging through the crowd the other way. "They're probably not here since they were made last week," she said. "We might as well look around."

Made?

Wreath bit back a smile and followed as Faye steamed onward. Her grip on the rocker tightened with every step, and she looked from one side to the other.

She stumbled when someone brushed against her, and the impact dislodged the rocker. It banged against her hip and fell onto her foot. "Sorry!" she said and bent to pick it up.

A man knelt with her, and the crowd parted around them. "Where is she?" Theriot asked, his breath hot on her ear. It was almost like they were in a room alone together.

Wreath jerked back.

Toothpick between his lips, he wore a different camouflage shirt but the same evil smirk.

Wreath rose without answering. Faye, about three booths away, had her back to them. She inspected a vintage tablecloth and pointed at the fabric. The booth operator was nodding. A spot, probably, or a tear.

Taking a step away from Faye—Wreath had no intention of leading this fiend to her—she found her path blocked by a wall of camo. "Do not ignore me, girl." He gripped her arm. "Where *is* she?"

Wreath jerked away, and his fingers pinched hard before she broke loose. "I don't know what you're talking about." The space felt tight and Wreath's head hurt again.

"Tell me what you know about Starla."

Holding the small rocker up against her chest, Wreath debated and took a few more steps away from where Faye stood. "Listen, mister," she said with her best Frankie imitation. "I don't know who you're talking about."

"I saw you here last week."

"Along with ten thousand other customers." She held up the rocker. "Don't worry, I won't be back."

His voice was dark and rough. "Why'd you go to the Palomino?"

"Hey, Wreath!" Faye yelled. Wreath kept her back to Faye and ignored the call.

Theriot grabbed her arm again.

"Wreath?" Faye's voice had gone from greeting to question, and she moved more quickly toward them.

"Do not interfere in my business," Theriot pasted an ugly smile on his face as he stepped aside. "If you're helping Starla run, you'll have more than one bruise on you."

Faye, owl cookie jar in hand, was within a couple of yards. She frowned.

"She know where Starla is too?" he asked.

"We don't know any Starla," Wreath said.

"You're a good liar." He withdrew the toothpick, looked at it and threw it down. "I see why you and Bum get along."

Faye had set aside the cookie jar and was pushing her way toward Wreath. "What's going on?" She looked from Wreath to Theriot. "Get away from her."

"I was telling your friend here about our merchandise." Theriot pointed down the aisle, past the booth with the tablecloth. "There are nice old bottles down there at the end, ma'am."

Looking over Faye's head, Wreath drew in a breath.

Theriot laughed, an ugly raspy sound. "I've acquired a new vendor." He pulled out a tiny wooden case and extracted another toothpick. "Maybe we need to work together."

Bum and Jaclyn were near the end of the row, the girl once more disguised as a boy. Bum was lining up something on a blanket, while Jaclyn sat with her legs crossed, head in her hands.

Theriot gave Wreath a quick look and walked toward the podium. "Don't forget to try the funnel cakes," he said over his shoulder.

15

Faye planted her feet in the middle of the aisle. "What just happened?"

"I'm not sure. He bumped into me, got too close. He was asking about someone named Starla."

"Let's get out of here. I shouldn't have brought you back."

"Bum and Jaclyn are here." Wreath pointed. "We can't leave now."

Faye glanced over her shoulder. "That man is dangerous."

"That's why we have to get Jaclyn out of that motel."

When Faye hesitated, she plowed on. "We can escape through that exit at the end if we need to."

"Your grandfather will not be pleased with me," Faye said and took a step toward Bum.

This end of the market was sparse, heavy on the junk. A few people wandered by but the aisle was not jammed like the one near the stage.

A small collection of bottles and knickknacks were spread around Bum on the dirt floor. He appeared to be peddling an antique soda bottle to a young couple. His sales pitch was delivered in that swamp accent that got under Wreath's skin.

"This will look great in our kitchen," the woman said with a smile. The man watched Bum.

Hair down and wild, Bum smiled back, his straight, white teeth at odds with the disarray of the rest of him.

The woman dug in her purse, pulled out a couple of dollar bills and handed them over.

Jaclyn looked up at the exchange. Her hair was stuffed under a cap. Her face was clean and not as pale as it had been. She sat on a dingy blanket, likely from the motel room, and presented the customer a small smile.

When she saw Wreath, she jumped up like she was on a pogo stick. She definitely felt better. "Bum, look! It's Wreath! Is you okay, Wreath?"

Wreath shifted the rocker and reached out to hug Jaclyn, but Bum stepped between them, bringing Wreath up against his hard chest. She wasn't sure for a split second if it was her heart or his she felt beating.

Faye stepped into the cramped area and wedged herself between them. Her scowl would have made most of Wreath's friends crumple. Bum merely glared back.

Jaclyn had edged to the front and reached for Wreath's hand. Her eyes looked bright and clear. "Is that your granny?"

"Jack!" Bum said. "That's not polite."

The nervous strain of the past few minutes erupted from Wreath in a burst of laughter. Faye did not seem as amused, her gaze still focused on Bum.

"Should I 'pologize?" A tiny furrow appeared between Jaclyn's eyebrows.

"It's okay," Wreath said. "This is my friend, Miss Faye."

Bum took a step away from Faye and scuffed his tennis shoes at the ground. He looked like a bull penned up at a parish fair. He wore a pair of ragged jeans, and he was clean, although he hadn't shaved. And that hair . . .

"What a cute child." Faye threw Wreath a look. "Are these friends of yours?"

Who knew Faye could be subtle?

Before Wreath could answer, Faye stepped further into the booth and looked down. "What's your name?"

Jaclyn looked at Wreath, and a cloud of doubt replaced her smile. *Poor thing.* She didn't know what she was supposed to say.

"This is Jack," Bum said.

"Jack?" Faye said. "You're awfully pretty to be called Jack."

So much for subtle.

"My dog's name is Samson," Jaclyn said. "He had to stay home today." A shadow ran across her face. "He can get us in trouble."

"Jack!" Bum said.

"Samson's a strong name," Faye said, then glared at Bum.

Bum straightened his shoulders. "I take care of Jack."

"I know who you are. You're the scoundrel who made off with Wreath's bike." Wreath vaguely remembered that stern voice from early days at the store.

Bum took a step away.

Score one for Faye.

Jaclyn was not intimidated. She pulled on Faye's blouse. "Does you have a dog?"

"No," Faye said. "I had a cat a long time ago."

Wreath didn't know that. Faye didn't seem like a pet person.

"Does you have a house?" Jaclyn asked.

"I sure do. Wreath and I live together. You can come visit us sometime." She smiled down at the child. "Wreath buys candy for our guests. She loves to share."

"I like candy." Jaclyn beamed. How had Wreath not realized she was a girl? "My mommy likes candy too. Or I think she does." She looked at Bum.

"Jack . . ." His voice was gentle but firm.

She kept on talking. "I thought I saw my mommy. I was wrong."

"Does your mommy live in Landry too?" Faye asked.

"Yes," Bum said, then ran his fingers through his hair.

Wreath pretended to study one of the old bottles. Faye was a pretty good detective.

"She runned away," Jaclyn said.

"Ran," Bum corrected. "She was called away, but the word is *ran*, Jack. You know that."

"Well, I hope she comes back soon," Faye said.

"Thanks, ma'am." Bum spoke with such deference that he looked like one of the ushers at church.

"Wreath bumped her head," Jaclyn said. "She bleeded."

A small sound escaped Bum. It might have been a groan. Faye's forehead wrinkled. *Uh-oh.*

Red splotches appeared on Bum's neck again, and sweat trickled down his temples. "Get lost," he mouthed when he met Wreath's eyes.

"Nervous?" she mouthed back.

He gave his mop a quick shake and spoke. "It was a misunderstanding, ma'am."

"Is that so?" Faye knelt to eye level with the child. "She didn't happen to drop her backpack, did she?"

"She did," Jaclyn said proudly. "We brought it today in case we seed her."

"*Saw* her," Bum said. "Your pack's there, under that blanket."

"We didn't steal nothing from it," Jaclyn announced. "Stealing's wrong."

"Aren't you a smart one?" Faye said.

Bum reached down and picked up the pack. "Well, here it is." He dangled it from two fingers. "You probably have something to do."

Wreath reached for the pack with a saccharine smile, but he yanked it back with a sly smile of his own. His eyes met hers. "I enjoyed reading that diary," he said. "You're a good writer."

Wreath charged at him. "That's an invasion of privacy."

"You mean like you and her coming here asking questions?"

She could have sworn she heard Faye chuckle. She jerked the pack out of his hands and ignored the speculative gleam in Faye's eyes.

"Bum, is you and Wreath mad at each other?" Jaclyn's lower lip jutted out.

He drew in a breath and stepped back. "We're just teasing." His voice was several degrees warmer. His gentle manner with the child exuded masculinity, even if he was rough on the outside. The Cajun accent made Wreath feel like she was wearing a sweater on a summer day. She couldn't figure out why it got to her.

"Bum's right." Wreath stepped toward the aisle. "We'd better go."

"Just a moment." Faye pulled a magnifying glass out of her pocket. "Tell me about those old soda bottles," Faye said. Six bottles, green and brown, were lined up on the grass.

"You know what they are?" Bum's eyes widened, and he picked up one of each color and held them before Faye.

"Uncle Jo and Aunt Ida bottles," she said. "You don't find many of these."

An odd look flitted across his mouth.

"Don't you think they'd look good with that summer display you're putting together, Wreath?"

Bum tilted his head.

Jaclyn fidgeted, not interested in the shop talk, and reached for Faye's hand. "I threw up," she said as though it were an accomplishment.

"She's much better." Bum sounded slightly distressed. He displayed the pair of bottles, his hands extended. "I can make you a good deal on these."

Faye, her hand on Jaclyn's small shoulder, assessed the array of bottles, a few battered kitchen appliances, and an assortment of rusty tools. "Do you have wholesale rates?"

Wreath frowned at Faye. Other than the bottles, this was junk.

Bum looked about as surprised. "Um, sure."

"What would you take for the lot?" Faye's eyebrows rose.

"The lot?" Bum glanced toward Wreath and back at Faye, who gestured around the small space.

"Everything." Faye paused. "Keep in mind we have to make a living too. We'll give you a hundred dollars, not a penny more."

Had Faye had a stroke? There wasn't twenty dollars' worth of sellable stuff here.

"Sure?" The question in Bum's voice almost made Wreath smile. Faye had that effect on her too.

"We'll take it all." Faye pulled out five twenties, and Bum almost snatched the bills. "We'll need you to carry it to our car."

"Excuse me," Wreath said and pulled Faye aside. "I thought you didn't want me near him."

"I need more time with the girl. Besides I don't dare send you to the parking lot alone. Not with Theriot around."

"But he's involved with Theriot." Wreath clutched her pack. The situation was spiraling out of control. She so preferred control.

"I'll have the girl, and he won't let anything happen to you," Faye whispered. "You can't carry the rocker and all of this."

Bum was frowning a few feet away. "Jack better come with me," he said.

"I want to stay." Jaclyn's declaration was part whine, part defiance.

"Don't dillydally." Faye held her keys out. "And be cautious."

Wreath grabbed the keys and bottles and gingerly picked up a handful of rusted cooking utensils. She put them in a battered cardboard box that sat on the grass.

Bum watched for a moment before packing the rest of the items. He hoisted the box of shabby merchandise onto one shoulder and reached for the rocker. "Let me have that."

"I got it."

"Bum's strong," Jaclyn said. "He knows how to fight."

At this, Faye raked her gaze over him. Bum groaned once more. "Jack!"

"He says we's not supposed to fight. 'Specially not girls."

"We're supposed to love one another," Faye said.

"My Mommy loves me."

"Oh, I know she does," Faye said.

Bum squirmed, then surrendered. "Lead the way," he said to Wreath. "Jack, stay put."

"I'll keep a close eye on her," Faye said.

"We won't be long," Wreath said.

16

Wreath and Bum didn't speak until they reached Faye's car.

She looked everywhere but at him. Except for the occasional glance.

"Here it is." She tapped the hood.

"You expect to carry all this in that thing?"

"We do it all the time." Wreath opened the trunk and pulled out an old blanket. "We'll wrap the rocker in this so it won't get dinged up."

"It's already chipped."

"That's patina," she said, "which is different from messing it up."

"If you say so." He changed the angle on the rocker until it wedged in and banged the trunk shut. "So you and that woman do this a lot?"

"Yep." People strolled by, although no one appeared to pay attention to them. Wreath stepped up until she was nearly chest-to-chest with him. "Now tell me why you were looking for me."

He ran his fingers through his overgrown shrub of hair but didn't step back. "I found out what I needed to know."

"You're kidding, right?" She jabbed her finger into his chest. "You don't breeze in, stir up someone's life, and run out the back door. Tell me."

"I shouldn't have gone to the store."

"Why are you making Jaclyn dress like a boy?"

At that, he had the grace to look uncomfortable. "It's only for a little while. The people I deal with aren't as interested in a boy as they might—" He broke off. "It's complicated."

"Really?" Wreath's voice was heavy with sarcasm.

"Lots of kids stay with aunts and uncles during summer."

"Not in a motel room."

"I keep an eye on her for my sister."

"What kind of trouble are you in?" she demanded.

He glared at her. "Leave it alone, Wreath."

"I can't." The words drifted away on the dusty parking lot.

"This whole thing has turned into a freaking disaster," he said. "You're not the kind of person I thought you were." He tilted his head. "Someone told me you might know how to get in touch with Fred Procell."

The knot in Wreath's stomach was bigger than those turkey legs roasting in the distance.

Bum kicked at the ground, and a puff of dry grass settled on Wreath's shoes. "What are you? Seventeen? Eighteen? You're too young for him."

"You think me and—" Wreath shook her head so hard her neck ached.

"He lived with you up in Lucky."

"Who told you that?"

"Theriot." Bum stepped closer. Although he did not touch her, she was locked in the grip of his stare. "Do you know where my sister is?"

"What? I don't know your sister."

"She dated Fred Procell off and on." He frowned when he said the name. "She told me he was chasing after a chick in Landry, someone he'd known in Lucky."

"You think I was Big Fun's girlfriend?" Even the question made her want to throw up.

"He always did go for the young, pretty ones, according to Starla."

Wreath stared. "Your sister's name is Starla?"

"You know her?" With the hopeful question, he was the devoted brother, and Wreath fought off feeling sorry for him.

"Theriot grabbed me today and asked about someone named Starla. I don't understand any of this." She stopped, put her hand on Bum's arm. He flinched and pulled away. "Why does he want her?"

Bum looked like warm misery when his eyes met hers. "She's . . . involved with him too." He cleared his throat. "So Big Fun wasn't, you know, after you?"

"He wasn't trying to date me." Wreath slumped against the car door. "Murder me is more like it. He was my mother's boyfriend."

"They broke up?"

"Permanently." She hugged her arms around her middle. "My mother died."

She saw a moment of pity in his eyes. She hated pity.

"He didn't . . ." Bum cleared his throat and started over. "Fred didn't—" He paused again.

"Kill her?" Wreath shook her head. "Although he didn't help her get well." She thought about that day Frankie slipped away forever. Big Fun had flirted with a neighbor while her lifeless mother was loaded into the ambulance. "My mother got sick."

Bum's hand hovered over her hair for a moment. Then he let it drop. "I'm sorry."

Wreath drew in a breath. "And now your sister's missing." *Was she dead too?*

He nodded. "Starla comes and goes. She dumped Jaclyn on me and my folks and took off." His eyes turned toward the ground again. "She got mixed up with Big Fun and Theriot and forgot to come back."

"Big Fun killed a woman." The sick feeling grew in Wreath's stomach, and she met his eyes. "He's in jail."

He gave a nod. "I'm sure Starla's alive. She and Theriot hooked up after Procell went to jail. Then . . . I don't know. I've got to keep looking, get her out of this mess."

"She left her little girl," Wreath said. "She must be in trouble."

He stared toward the flea market. "I came here to talk sense into Starla and take her home. Ran right up against Theriot." His voice was so low Wreath could barely hear. "He baited me into going to see you. He's good at that . . ."

"At?" She cocked her head.

"At baiting poor dumb things like me," he said. "He wants her back, says she skipped out, owes him for the room and other stuff. Drugs probably." Bum shook his head. "And he's crazy jealous. He counted on your connection with Big Fun to help him find Starla."

"But you didn't stay that day at the store."

"I didn't think you could possibly be the girl he was talking about," he said. "Linda at the Palomino told me later that Big Fun had gone to jail."

"Why didn't you go back home?"

"I have Jaclyn, no money, no place to stay," he said with an ugly laugh. "Theriot let us stay in Starla's room, demanded I pay off her debt this summer." He looked down at his knuckles. They were cut and scratched. "I hoped she'd show up."

"Where do you think she is?"

"I'm not sure," he said. "Wherever she is, she's doing something she shouldn't."

Wreath quirked her head. "Why are you telling me all this?"

17

Bum kicked the dirt again. If they stood here much
longer, there would be a crater beside the car.

A shiver ran up Wreath's spine. Maybe it was the story
he was telling.

"You're the only decent person I know." He grabbed her
arm, not hard like Theriot had, but urgently. "If something
happens to me, promise me you'll make sure Jaclyn's all right."

"Are you in danger?"

He shot her a disgusted look. "Anyone mixed up with
Theriot is in danger. And don't dare tell me to go to the
police."

"But—"

"They'll take Jaclyn, and I need to get Starla out of this
mess, not get her arrested." He looked up at the sky, a lone
cloud in sight. "Starla's an idiot but my niece needs her mother. I've got a plan."

Wreath watched the sky too. The clouds, always drifting.
No way would she leave that child in jeopardy. "This plan of yours.
What is it?"

"You be there for Jaclyn. I got the rest."

"That's it?"

"You're better off not knowing."

She considered that. "If you need us—me or Faye—we'll help," she said after a moment. "With one exception."

Bum grimaced.

"You can't put Faye or J.D. in danger. *I've* brought too much trouble to their door already." She shook her head sadly. "I want to help Jaclyn. She shouldn't have to pretend to be a boy, shouldn't have to live in a place like that." She shuddered. "It's creepy."

This time he met her eyes. "And this Faye woman? She can be trusted?"

At this Wreath smiled. "She's the best."

He turned his head, like a crow looking at a piece of bread. "Most people don't like their boss that much."

"She's a friend, too. I live with her." She pulled out a card from the store, grabbed a pen and scribbled. "Here," she said. "I put our home address and number too."

When she laid the card in his hand, he rubbed her wrist for a split second, and she looked up startled. Their eyes locked.

"Are you for real?" he asked.

18

Law sat in front of the hardware store talking to J.D. when Faye and Wreath drove up.

"Need a hand?" He jumped up, an easy smile on his face.

Wreath studied him for a moment. In his park uniform, he looked even more tan, and his beautiful dark hair had been trimmed. "You got a haircut," she murmured.

"I decided it couldn't wait till school." He gave his bangs a shake. "It was getting shaggy."

"Looks nice. *You* look nice." She wanted to grab him and never let him go.

"Wreath, will you show Law what to unload?" Faye had hopped out of the car and J.D. already had his arm around her shoulders.

"So the flea market is as good as everyone says?" J.D. said.

"It's interesting." Faye moved even closer.

"At least no one assaulted you today," Law said.

Wreath rubbed her arm. The memory of the hulking Theriot lingered. "We escaped unscathed." She threw Faye a look. They had talked about Bum and Jaclyn on the drive to the store and agreed to tell J.D.—and no one else—the whole story.

But with Law, fresh and clean and cheerful, standing there, Wreath felt like a colossal cheater.

"They sell hardware?" J.D.'s banal question allowed Wreath to step away from Law with a gulp of relief.

"They sell everything," she said. "New and used tools, bedding plants, hanging baskets, lawn mowers."

Faye jumped in. "Furniture. Glassware. Clothes. Pretty much everything we have in our store."

"It's kind of scary," Wreath added and tried not to notice how Law struggled with the rocker as he got it out of the trunk.

"Is that why my granddaughter's so solemn this morning?" J.D. gave her a quick hug and picked up the sack of small items. He headed into the store behind Law.

She was always surprised at how he could read her. *Did a blood connection automatically make you closer?*

Law rested the rocker on its side. "Where you want this?"

Wreath motioned toward the front of the store. "I want to do something patriotic in the window. I'm planning an Independence Day sale."

"I thought we were going to the lake that day." He glanced over to where Faye and J.D. unwrapped pieces of glass. "Remember? You can't devote your life to the store."

Wreath moved the rocker and lowered it with a thump. "I hardly think working a holiday is devoting my life to the store." She gathered three cobalt blue glasses off a nearby shelf and lined them up on the seat, adding a crisp white doily underneath them. "Besides, this is fun."

He put his hands on his hips. "Red, white, and blue," he said slowly. "You're creative."

"You don't make that sound like a good thing."

"I guess it depends on what you want."

She looked at him. *You,* she wanted to say. *I want you.* She faked a grin. "I told you. I want to have fun, but I have to help here too. I owe them everything."

"Girl Scout." He touched the bruise on her forehead. "You're coming tonight, aren't you? We're driving to Alexandria for a movie and a burger."

"Wouldn't miss it." Wreath drew back to study his face.

"I'm glad you're not going off to Florida or somewhere this summer," he said.

"Think how I feel about you and Destiny and college."

His gaze shuttered. "I'm due at the park." He headed toward the door with a quick good-bye, then turned back. "We still have one of those puppies . . . if you change your mind."

He was such a nice guy.

19

Faye used a wire pad and cleanser that afternoon and strained to get the rust off an iron skillet she'd bought from Bum.

"Faye?"

She looked up and pushed her hair off her forehead with her arm.

"Why'd you buy all of that?" Wreath asked.

Faye kept scrubbing. Dirty water and suds dripped. "I like those old bottles. Very regional." She tilted her head. "I'm surprised you weren't more interested in them."

Wreath picked one up and rubbed her fingers over the lettering. "The antique bottles I understand, but why'd you pay so much for the other stuff?"

"You know why," she said quietly.

"Because they're in trouble?"

"That child reminds me of you. I can't bear to think she might be hungry."

Wreath twisted her mouth. "You didn't know me when I was little."

"I know you now. And I'd bet a year's sales that you were cute, smart *and* trusting."

"We don't know if we can trust Bum with that money. What if he buys drugs or runs off?"

"At least we tried to help."

"You tried."

"You did too. You didn't call the police when he stole your bike—or when he mysteriously wound up with your backpack." Faye dried her hands on a red towel. "You have a soft spot for that child. I understand that." She gave Wreath a questioning look. "I hope you aren't developing a soft spot for her uncle."

Wreath lined the bottles up on the workroom counter. "No way."

"That was an awfully long visit to the parking lot."

She flushed and pulled out a chair. "It's not like that," she said. "But Bum's got a load of secrets."

"Sounds familiar." With that, Faye sat down at the table where the two had held some of their best conversations.

Where Faye had thrown cups, where Wreath had smashed a few of her own. Where Wreath had quit, then begged for her job back, where Faye had laid her off. Where Law and Mitch had served Wreath Thanksgiving dinner.

Where secrets had been shared and memories made.

Faye reached for one of the bottles, held it up to the light. The old glass was wavy, with a few small bubbles trapped in it. "I told J.D. what happened." She sat the bottle down. "And we agree on two things. One: We have to help that girl. Two: You mustn't put yourself in danger."

20

Wreath was ready before Law arrived to pick her up. "You're wearing a new—*brand new*—dress?" Faye said from across the kitchen. "I'm proud of you."

"I bought it with graduation money." Wreath tugged at the hem. "Do you think it's too much? We're getting burgers for Destiny's going-away supper . . ."

"You look precious." Faye stirred a pan on the stove. "But no burger's as good as my spaghetti." She chose a spoon from the back of the counter and dipped into the pan. "See what you think."

Wreath tasted. "Umm. Maybe I should have eaten here."

Faye swiped at her with a dishtowel. "You need to go out with your friends, have some fun."

"That's what Law says."

"J.D. and I love having you around but your friends won't be here much longer. We're almost to July."

"Don't remind me."

The doorbell rang, and her heart jumped. Tonight she would have fun.

"I love that sound," Faye said. "Can't believe how dull this house used to be."

Wreath hurried into the living room and threw open the door with a smile. "What are you doing at the front—"

Except it wasn't Law.

Bum stood there, holding Jaclyn's hand. He was dressed in jeans and a long-sleeve black T-shirt. His hair was surprisingly clean and brushed. Jaclyn wore a stocking cap, jeans, and a shirt with a bulldozer on it. *Almost all boy.*

"Oh. Hi," Wreath said.

"I tried to call," Bum said. "Okay?" The word was a belligerent plea.

"Hi, Wreath," Jaclyn said. "I'm not sick any more, and Bum's gotta go do something 'portant."

"I wouldn't be here if it weren't important," Bum said, "but I've got to . . . take care of something and wondered if you might . . ." He nodded down at Jaclyn. "For an hour or so." He looked everywhere but at Wreath. "She's better." He glanced up. "She won't vomit on your shoes."

Wreath gave a weak smile. "I'm sorry. I sort of have plans."

"I knew this was a bad idea." He tugged on Jaclyn's hand but she didn't budge.

"It is a good idea." Jaclyn stomped her foot.

"Oh, precious." Wreath knelt.

"Wreath?" Faye entered the living room and her face broke into a smile. "Well, if it isn't our new friends."

Bum's face turned brighter red than the tomatoes at the flea market.

Jaclyn smiled. "Is this where you live?" Her voice was filled with what sounded suspiciously like awe.

"As a matter of fact it is," Faye said. "Would you like to come in?"

"Yes, ma'am."

Bum grabbed at her, but Jaclyn hopped over the threshold. "I was checking with Wreath on something," he said.

Jaclyn was already rubbing her hands on the white carpet. "This is soft."

"We can't stay," Bum said.

"You said I could stay with Wreath a little while."

"I said *might*." Bum's jaw was stiff. "Wreath's got something to do."

Jaclyn's bottom lip trembled.

Wreath looked over Faye's shoulder at the antique mantel clock. Law would be here any minute, with Mitch and Destiny. She really didn't want to be standing in Faye's living room with Bum.

On the contrary, Faye seemed at ease. "I don't believe I've ever known a person named Bum," she said.

"It's a nickname," Jaclyn proclaimed.

"So I presumed." Faye smiled.

"My last name's Bumgardner," he said.

"Do you have parents, Mr. Bumgardner?" Faye said.

Now what?

"Yes, ma'am," he replied, looking at the floor.

"Them's Mamaw and Papaw," Jaclyn chimed in.

"*They are* Mamaw and Papaw," Bum said.

But Jaclyn had turned toward Faye. "They live in Tibbydoe." She stumbled over the name.

Bum threw his hands up. "Jack!"

"Thibodaux? My goodness!" Faye exclaimed, as though Bum didn't look ready to blow a gasket in her living room. "Don't you love South Louisiana?"

"I love McDonald's," Jaclyn said.

Faye grinned. "My friend Mr. J.D. is partial to their sausage biscuits."

Wreath stepped toward Bum. "I can't help you tonight, but I'd be happy to another time."

Faye motioned toward the couch, the fancy one covered in brocade. "Let's sit down and visit a moment," she said. "Although first I need to check on our supper."

Jaclyn looked around with what could have been glee. "Somethin' smells good."

"We ate before we came," Bum said, his voice soft. "Remember?" He sounded almost like he was begging.

"That was only peanut butter crackers. This smells like s'ghetti."

Bum's eyes closed.

"Wreath, do you think you could help me in the kitchen for a moment?" Faye asked.

"Can I come too?" Jaclyn asked.

"We'll be right back, sweetie," Wreath said. Then, when they were out of earshot, "What should we do?"

Faye clasped her hands. The room was quiet except for the bubble of sauce on the stove and the murmur of voices from beyond the wall—childish chatter and Bum's low response.

Only trouble would have brought Bum here tonight. That much Wreath knew. "That poor little girl," she said.

"Why don't you suggest that J.D. and I keep her this evening?" Faye's brow quirked. "Something tells me Mr. Bumgardner will hear it from you more easily."

"But you and J.D. have plans."

"We're eating and watching a police show on TV. It'll be good having her around. We'll switch to cartoons, read a book, something fun."

Fun.

"What about your detective career?" Wreath bit back a smile.

"I'll practice by interrogating Jaclyn."

"Faye!"

"You know I'm kidding. If I'm not mistaken, Jaclyn's going to be a new fan of my cooking." She motioned toward the living room. "Let them know everything's all right."

"And you're not afraid of where this could lead?"

Faye seemed to ponder the question. "A little," she admitted after a moment. "But we can't turn our back on a child in need."

"Thank you," Wreath said softly and hurried toward the living room. She had barely reached the carpet when a loud knock sounded on the kitchen door.

"Go on," Faye said. "I've got this."

"Good news," Wreath said and listened to Faye greeting Law in the other room. "Miss Faye hopes you'll stay for supper, Jaclyn." She looked at Bum. "If it's okay with your uncle?"

Bum looked more miserable than he had when Jaclyn threw up. "I don't know." He sounded as troubled as he looked.

"She loves little girls." Wreath pulled the cap off and ruffled Jaclyn's hair. No matter how nervous Wreath was about this evening's plans, Jaclyn was bound to be more scared.

"Really?" Jaclyn asked, eyes big, expression somber. Then she arranged her hair and straightened her shirt. Her baby teeth shone in an unexpected smile.

"You told Faye?" Bum's frown was bigger than Jaclyn's smile.

"I can't keep secrets from her," Wreath said.

"Can I trust her?"

"With Jaclyn's life," Wreath said quietly.

Jaclyn roamed to the far side of the room and picked up a brass frog on an end table. Law was chatting with Faye in the other room, although Wreath could only catch a word here or there.

"Is she ready?" Law asked.

"Almost," Faye said.

Then they faded away.

Bum moved close to Wreath, his musky smell apparent. "I don't want that scum Theriot to know Jaclyn's a girl," he whispered. "Or any of those lowlifes around the Palomino."

"I got it." Wreath spoke into his ear, close enough that his hair almost tickled her nose.

He looked up at the ceiling for a long moment. Then he gazed directly into Wreath's eyes. "If I don't trust you . . ."

Jaclyn grabbed Wreath's skirt. "Are you eating supper with us, too, Wreath?"

Wreath got on her knees and put her hand on Jaclyn's bony shoulder. "Not this time, but you'll love staying with Miss Faye and Mr. J.D."

"Who's J.D.?" Bum's voice was accusatory.

"He and Faye are engaged." She lowered her voice. "Want to know a secret, Jaclyn?"

The girl nodded, her round eyes amber, like Bum's.

"Mr. J.D.'s my grandpa."

"Goodie!" Jaclyn clapped her hands.

Bum looked startled.

"Wreath?" Law called and walked into the living room. "Oh." He took a step back, his expression almost comical. "Faye didn't say she had company."

"This is my friend, Jaclyn," Wreath said, standing. "And . . . her Uncle Bum. Faye's keeping an eye on Jaclyn while Bum goes to work."

"What's your name?" Jaclyn's expression was full of curiosity.

"I'm Law." He smiled at her but shot a look in Bum's direction. "You go to Landry High?"

"I'm not in school," Bum said.

"Well!" Wreath said because she couldn't think of anything else.

Law turned, his expression quizzical. "The others are in the car," he said. "Guess we'd better get going." He headed back toward the kitchen, pausing. "Nice meeting y'all."

Jaclyn's eyes were wider still. "Is that your husband?"

Bum groaned.

"He's my friend." Maybe her boyfriend before summer was over.

A car horn sounded two quick times.

"That's probably Mitch," she said. "I've got to go."

"Sorry we interrupted." Bum's voice was sharp.

Wreath ignored him. "Come on, Jaclyn." She held out her hand. "You can watch Miss Faye cook."

She started toward the kitchen, then turned. "If Bumgardner's your last name, what's your first name?"

His gaze met hers. "I don't know you well enough to tell you that."

Wreath made a funny sound. "You're trusting us with your niece."

"Nice try."

The car horn sounded again.

"Wreath!" Law called from the kitchen. "You coming?"

"Thanks again for keeping the kid," Bum muttered. "I swear this is all going to be over soon."

"Take care of yourself," Wreath whispered. "We'll take good care of Jaclyn."

21

Law peered at Wreath as they walked down the driveway toward Mitch's car. "Who's that guy?"

She looked back at the house without answering. *Would Jaclyn be all right?*

"Hello? You with me?" Law's tone was strained.

"Of course." Wreath clicked her heels. "Right here!"

"You're acting strange lately." He reached for her hand, gave it a quick squeeze and dropped it. "Sort of distant."

"I've got a lot to think about," she said. "You leaving, college–"

"That guy back there?"

"Huh?" Wreath skidded to a stop, the car a few yards away.

"Who's the guy?"

"We met him and his niece at the flea market." *Where did misleading end and lying begin?* "Faye bought some merchandise from him today."

"That kid's a girl? She looks like a boy."

"It's a crazy story," Wreath said. "They're going through a rough time."

"Aren't we all?" Law took a step away, and her hand fell like a tree branch in a strong wind.

"What's wrong?" she asked.

"It's a crazy story," he mocked. "Mitch and Destiny are waiting."

"Stop, please," she said. "Tell me why you're upset."

His steps slowed. "My dad called today."

There was a beat of silence.

"The call—collect, of course—came on my mom's phone and she handed it to me without any warning."

"What'd he want?"

Law shrugged. "I hung up—which made my mother mad. Then her loser boyfriend showed up."

Before Wreath could reply, the horn honked again. She jumped, and Law growled. "Cut it out, Mitch."

Mitch stuck his blond head of hair out the window and laughed. "Destiny did that. She's wound up."

Destiny clamored over the seat and poked her head out too. "I'm starving. What took you so long?" She looked at Wreath. "Cute dress."

"Thanks." She tugged at the hem.

"Wait no more." Law opened the door. "Let the fun begin." His voice did not match his words.

Wreath slid into the backseat. "I'm sorry I was distracted," she whispered. "You want to stay here and talk about your dad?"

He shook his head. "We can talk later," he said, then scooted forward. "Let's have some music, dude."

Mitch turned the radio up.

"I wish you guys were going to Florida with me for the Fourth," Destiny said. "This is our last summer to hang out."

"From what I hear, we'll still have summers in college," Mitch said with a grin.

Destiny made a face. "Who knows where everyone will be? Away at summer school or working somewhere else? This is our last *real* summer."

Wreath's heart thudded. "It's going to be different," she said.

"Not for Law and Des," Mitch said. "Tech'll be like advanced high school. They'll probably have classes together and everything."

"It's a great school," Law said. "But Destiny's known me since I was five years old. She'll ditch me as soon as we reach Lincoln Parish."

"No, I won't!" Destiny swatted at him. "I'm glad you'll be there." She looked toward the back seat. "What do you think college will be like, Wreath?"

"I don't have a clue." No one in her family had been to college as far as she knew—unless maybe J.D. had. Wreath had to remind herself that she'd been a good student and successful salesgirl for months now—and had friends. Even if things felt strange at the moment.

"They say the dorm's a blast," Mitch said. "It'll be like having our own apartment. No curfew. No parents telling me to make my bed."

A twinge zapped through Wreath. She'd never had a parent fuss about her room. Until a month ago, she hadn't had a room.

"You sure you want to miss out on the dorm, Wreath?" Destiny said.

"I'm just happy to have a room at Faye's." They probably couldn't understand how much she meant that.

Law reached across and patted her knee, the way Jaclyn patted Samson. "We'll get Wreath to Tech before it's all over, won't we, Des?"

"Sure," Destiny said.

"Dream on," Mitch said. "Wreath's got a sweet deal. Besides, what would Aunt Faye do without her?" He met her eyes in the rearview mirror and winked.

"You're lucky. You get to keep your job," Destiny said. "My dad said he doesn't want me to focus on anything but school for the first year."

"Yeah, I'm lucky," Wreath muttered and blamed her lousy mood on Bum for showing up like he had.

"You've turned that store around," Mitch said. "You probably don't even need to study marketing."

"Can you even study that at RPCC?" Destiny asked.

"Probably intro courses," Law said.

"Are classes super hard?" Wreath asked.

"For me probably," Mitch said. "Not for you three brainiacs. I'm the only one in this car happy just to have a diploma."

They all laughed.

Wreath stared out the window, and the car grew quiet, except for the radio, playing a rap song that gave her a headache. Or had the headache originated with the doorbell?

"How was work today, Law?" Destiny asked.

"Fine."

Finally a good topic. Wreath smiled. "You should see the cute puppies he found," she said. "They're adorable."

"I know, right?" Destiny said.

Law turned slightly. "Destiny's dad said she could have the last one. I took it by yesterday. I thought I mentioned it."

Wreath's face grew warm. "Must have slipped your mind."

Destiny started singing along with the radio, and Mitch joined in.

Law fidgeted in the seat next to her.

If this was what a summer of fun looked like, Wreath should probably pass.

22

"I'm not happy with this plan," Faye said.

Wreath rolled her eyes. "It'll be fine. It's broad daylight on a Monday."

J.D. frowned.

"Why don't you let your grandfather drive you?" Faye said.

"You two need to watch the stores." Wreath rearranged her ponytail. "I won't be long."

"This makes me uneasy," J.D. said.

"Be careful," Faye added.

"Don't worry so much." Wreath rode off with a jaunty wave. "See you at home. Jaclyn's going to love the outfit."

Faye let out a sigh and J.D. draped his arm around her shoulder. "You as anxious as I am?" he asked.

She gave a quick nod, tempted to lean into J.D. and let the concerns slip away. "Despite everything, she has to do things on her own." She sighed. "Wreath doesn't totally trust us."

"Don't you mean she doesn't trust me?" J.D.'s voice was low and somber. "I'm the one who let her down."

Faye drew back and looked into his steady eyes. "The world let her down."

"You think she'd leave us again?"

"No . . . at least not by running away. But she is distracted."

"Is it that Lawson Rogers fellow? I'm afraid he'll hurt her."

"Like John David hurt Frankie?"

He didn't answer.

"J.D., you couldn't have changed any of that. Frankie was young when she took off."

"Why didn't Frankie's mother contact me? I had a right to know I had a grandchild."

"She was probably afraid, the same way we are. Afraid that someone would hurt her daughter—who was little more than a child herself."

"Will Wreath ever turn to me when she needs something, tell me what's on her mind?"

Faye put her arms around him. "I doubt most teenage girls tell their grandfather their secrets. We have to give her time."

J.D. picked up her hand. "Is it cliché to worry that Law will break Wreath's heart when he leaves for school?"

"I'm more concerned that a cute little girl named Jaclyn is going to." *Or a fellow named Bumgardner.*

23

The rundown motel looked almost cozy today. The green of the trees framed it, and the sky was blue. Wreath scanned for Theriot's truck or his lumberjack frame. Not around.

She pedaled through the breezeway and into the courtyard. Bum's reaction to the food was unknown but she would blame it on Faye and make him take it.

The same people lounged on their tiny porches. A young man with the look of an overgrown child bounced a tennis ball against the wall and jumped when it flew back toward him, then ran after it.

He paused to give Wreath a wave. "Bum had to go to work. He won't let me play with Jack when he goes to work." He swung his foot at the tennis ball but missed. "I like to play."

"Half-Pint, get back over here," a woman on the steps said. "And, you." She nodded at Wreath. "Move on along. Bum isn't here."

"Do you happen to know when they'll be back?" she said. "I have something for Jack."

"Jack's here." The young man beamed. "See? He's playing peek-a-boo."

"Half-Pint!" the woman said. "Get in this house right this minute."

Wreath looked at the cottage where Bum and Jack stayed, in time to see the curtain flutter. She turned to the woman, who tamped a pack of cigarettes and carefully drew one out. "She's alone?" Her voice was almost a squeak.

"*He* is not alone." The woman pulled a lighter out of her pajama pants pocket. "I've got an eye on him."

The curtain moved again, and Jaclyn's little face popped up and lingered.

The woman noticed too. "Get away from that window," she hollered so loud that Wreath flinched. Frankie might have had her flaws, but at least she hadn't been a shouter.

Jaclyn disappeared again.

The yelling brought the young man called Half-Pint to the front door. "We've got cable," he said. "Do you have cable?"

"No—" Wreath stopped. "Yes, actually, I do have cable." For the first time in years.

"You need to get on out of here before . . ." The woman drew on her cigarette.

"Before what?"

The woman studied the glowing end. "Didn't your mama teach you to mind your own business?"

"She did," Wreath admitted.

"Then what are you doing over here?"

"I need to drop this off."

"What is it?" the young man asked.

"Half-Pint! Don't make me get the belt."

Wreath tensed. "It's groceries," she said and reached into the bag in her basket. "I'm Wreath. May I give your son some cookies?"

The woman ogled the package of chocolate-chip cookies. "I suppose it wouldn't hurt nothing."

Wreath held up the cookies and smiled toward the door.

"I like cookies." He scampered down the steps like he was chasing the tennis ball again. He snatched them from her and tore into the bag.

"What do you say?" the woman said.

"Thank you, Miss Wreath."

"I'm Linda, by the way. This is Troy, but everyone calls him Half-Pint." She stubbed out the cigarette and threw the butt into the grass by the porch, where it joined dozens of others, plus an assortment of soft-drink cans and a candy wrapper. "Jack, you got company," she yelled and gave a Wreath a curious look. "Don't stay too long."

Wreath was already pushing her bike toward the end cottage. *A child shouldn't be left alone like this.*

"He don't like to leave the kid," Linda called. "He usually isn't gone this long."

At least that was something.

As Wreath stepped onto the porch, Samson barked. Jaclyn said something, and the door, a little out of kilter, flew open. The dog pushed the storm door ajar and jumped on Wreath, his tail wagging. From the front, you couldn't tell he was hurt.

Jaclyn didn't step over the threshold, but a smile moved up her face like a perfect sunrise. "I didn't know you was coming to my house today."

A lump lodged in Wreath's throat. Why hadn't Bum asked her and Faye to babysit?

"Whatcha thinking?" Jaclyn asked and pulled at the knit hat she wore.

"I'm thinking how cute you'll look in this outfit." She lowered her voice and pulled the gift bag out of her pack. "Miss Faye made you something."

"What is it?" Jaclyn's eyes were round as the silver dollars Wreath's grandmother had collected.

"You'll have to open it and see," Wreath said. Only Faye would have come up with an outfit that could help Jaclyn pass for a boy but still look girly.

"What else'd you bring me?" Jaclyn peered into the grocery sack, which had fallen open.

"I brought snacks. You hungry?" That wasn't the question she wanted to ask but seemed gentler than, "Have you had anything to eat today?"

Jaclyn nodded. "Bum made me lunch 'fore he went to work."

"Great!" Wreath forced cheerfulness into her voice. "Want to join me out here for dessert?"

The girl took a step toward Wreath, then pulled back. "I'll get in trouble."

"We'll sit right here." She patted the concrete, where the dog was sprawled. "We won't leave the porch."

"Bum said the bad man might get me."

Looking over Jaclyn's shoulder, Wreath could see the jumble of the dark room. A news show blared on television. The words *terrorism* and *bombing* drifted over the child's head. The lump threatened to choke her. "We could have a picnic inside," she said. "Would that be OK?"

Jaclyn started to nod but stopped and appraised Wreath. "I'm not s'posed to have anyone inside ever." She chewed on her lower lip. "But you's been here before, and Bum says you're nice." She gestured, like an adult showing someone into a grand house. "We have to keep the door closed."

Wreath had been taught similar precautions. She and her mother moved so much that she never got close to other families. And Frankie didn't want her bringing children to the house when Big Fun or one of his kind might be around.

The reality of Jaclyn's life made Wreath's heart hurt.

"How about leaving it open a crack, to let some fresh air in?" she said. "Does that sound reasonable?"

"You talk funny," Jaclyn said. Then, without pausing to take a breath: "I ain't never been on a picnic before."

"Well, you're going to like it." Wreath's voice trembled. *This child. This child. She deserves a different life.*

"Did your Mommy take you on a picnic?" Jaclyn watched as Wreath pulled a beach towel out of her pack and spread it on the musty bedspread.

"My granny did." *Funny.* That memory hadn't surfaced in forever.

"Miss Faye?"

"Oh, no, sweetie, she's my friend, not my granny."

"Who's your granny?"

The stinging in Wreath's eyes increased. "She lives in heaven."

"My granny lives in a trailer." Jaclyn turned up her little nose. "Her house stinks."

Wreath made a production out of pouring a paper cup of orange Gatorade and handed her a small plastic bag of sliced apples. "For our first course, we'll have fruit."

She giggled and scurried closer, trying to see down into the pack. "Then what?"

"Cheese and crackers?"

A quick rap sounded on the door, and it flew open. The dog barked, and Wreath spilled Gatorade on the towel.

"What's going on?"

24

Samson's bark turned to a growl, and Jaclyn dashed behind Wreath.

Theriot's big frame blocked the motel room door. His expression was obscured by the bright light outside. "What's that mutt doing in here?" He grabbed the dog's face and made it squeal. "I'm going to kill Bumgardner."

When he let go, Samson slunk under the bed with a weak growl.

Theriot glared at Wreath. "Where is he?" He looked toward the bathroom, then at the alcove that doubled as a kitchen. A bag of microwave popcorn, probably what Jaclyn ate for lunch, sat on the counter.

Wreath handed Jaclyn a piece of cheese and a cracker and moved more fully between her and Theriot. Thank heavens she hadn't taken Jaclyn's hat off. "Bum's not here."

"But you are. And not supposed to be. Neither is that dog."

"We're having a picnic," Jaclyn said.

"I'm watching Jack while Bum's at work." She handed the child a piece of apple. No reason for Jaclyn to know how frightened Wreath was. And she wanted Theriot to know that people were paying attention to what happened in this room.

"Did he tell you what he was doing today?" Theriot said.

Wreath shook her head.

"You better not be lying."

"'Cause lying's wrong," Jaclyn said. "Bum told me that."

"That's right," Theriot said. He stepped closer to the bed and popped a cube of cheese into his mouth. "Where's Starla, little boy?"

"We don't know." That was delivered with a tremor. "We'll find her, though. Bum says so."

"He does, does he? That's not what he told me." He pulled a toothpick out of the little wooden tube and stuck it into his mouth.

"Please!" Wreath laid her hand on Jaclyn's back.

"I'm scared, Wreath." Tears had pooled in her eyes.

"Wreath?" Theriot stepped to where he nearly touched them. "My, my, my. You're the gal Fred was tangled up with."

"I don't know what you're talking about."

"Hmm."

Wreath made a fuss over handing Jaclyn a drink. "Do you want me to give Bum a message?"

"As a matter of fact, I do." Theriot leaned against the door-frame and crossed his arms. At least he was no longer right up on them. "Tell him he was supposed to call me last night. And he has one day to get rid of that dog or he and the kid'll be sleeping on the street."

He stopped on the porch and swiveled his head around. "You want me to give Big Fun a message?" Then he strolled down the steps without waiting for Wreath to speak.

"He's not nice." The tears ran down Jaclyn's dirty cheeks.

"No, he's not."

"Uncle Bum'll keep us safe. Always and always."

Wreath rubbed her back again. *One could only hope.*

25

J.D. picked up the phone on the second ring. "Hardware," he said. "May I help you?"

"Uh, J.D.?" Now that Wreath had him on the phone, she felt shy.

"Wreath? What's wrong?"

"I'm fine," she said quickly. She patted Samson on the nose and looked at Jaclyn, asleep on the bed, her little mouth wide open. "But I might need a ride."

"I'm on my way." She could almost see him grab his keys and wallet from the cash register drawer. "Where are you?"

"I'm still at the Palomino, out by—"

"I know exactly where it is."

"I'd like to bring little Jaclyn with me. And her dog too." She chewed on her lip. "Are you all right with dogs?"

"Haven't owned one since your father was a boy, but I've always been partial to dogs. Your grandmother favored cats."

Wreath filed that away.

"I'll be there in ten minutes, maybe less."

"Is Faye around?"

"She's next door at the store. Should she call you?"

She shook her head, which was pointless. "Tell her not to worry. And, please, park by the curb. Don't pull in, okay?"

"You sure you're not hurt?"

"I'm fine." She felt better already. "J.D.?"

"Yes?"

"Thanks a lot."

As Wreath hung up, she glanced outside once more. Theriot was nowhere in sight, but his truck was parked by the office. It almost blocked the driveway. The sun was moving along to mid-afternoon. How long would Bum be gone?

She hated to wake Jaclyn, a trail of tears still visible on her face. Wreath, though, did not intend to stay in this room.

She placed her hand on the frail leg and gave it a gentle shake. "Wake up, sunshine." Frankie used those words every morning that Wreath could remember. The sound of them made her feel closer to her mother. Perhaps they would soothe Jaclyn.

The girl rolled over and stuck her thumb in her mouth.

"Sweetie, wake up."

Jaclyn crawled under the covers, dislodging Samson. "I want Bum."

"He's still at work, baby girl."

"I'm not a baby."

"Of course you're not," Wreath said. "That's why I hope you and Samson will help me at the shop for a while."

Jaclyn propped herself on her elbows, pausing midway to brush her hair out of her eyes. "What shop?" Her voice was whiny but her eyes were wide open.

"The one Miss Faye owns." Wreath drew in a breath. "Mr. J.D.'s giving us a ride in his big truck."

A suspicious look hovered. "He's nice."

"Yes, he is." Wreath scratched Samson under the neck. "And he likes dogs."

Jaclyn sat up and adjusted the shirt Faye had sewn her. Wreath had let her put it on after Theriot left and the door was locked. "Samson's going too?"

Wreath made a shocked face. "We can't leave Samson alone while we go have fun."

"How will Uncle Bum know where to get me? He'll be sad if I'm not here."

"What if we leave him a note?" Wreath could ponder later what kind of an uncle left a small girl on her own all day. She knew the answer: one who was desperate.

"What about supper?"

"Miss Faye will cook us something good. Bum can come too if he doesn't work too late."

"He always works late," Jaclyn said. "Half-Pint's mama feeds me supper sometimes–if she's got any food."

"We'll tell her you're going with me."

"Half-Pint doesn't like it when I'm not here to play."

Wreath grew still. "He doesn't hurt you, does he?"

"He hit me with the tennis ball one time."

"I bet that hurt." Wreath tried to figure out how to proceed. "Did he throw it at you?"

"No, silly," The giggle was girlish. "It bounced off the motel and right into me. Him and me both started crying."

"Jaclyn . . ." *How to say this?* "You must be careful with big boys, okay?"

She nodded solemnly. "Bum says boys and girls is different. He told me that little girls shouldn't let anyone but their mama touch them."

"Sounds like Uncle Bum is pretty smart." Although that was a lie. From the looks of this room and a child left locked up all day, Bum was as stupid as his sister.

"Bum don't go to school," Jaclyn said. "He quit going after mommy left."

Figured.

"Precious, we need to get moving," Wreath said.

"I hope Uncle Bum's not mad when he comes home. Sometimes he don't like to talk."

Wreath knew the feeling.

Faye was standing in front of the store when the truck pulled up. Jaclyn and Samson were in the back seat, and Wreath sat next to J.D.

"Wreath says I might spend the night tonight!" Jaclyn climbed over J.D. and leapt out of the cab as she talked. "Samson too!"

"That sounds lovely," Faye said. One eyebrow inched up at the mention of Samson.

Wreath pulled the dog out of the back seat. "Sorry to spring this on you," she said in a low voice. "I didn't know what else to do. They were alone in that seedy motel."

"This is exactly what you should do." J.D. gave Faye a quick hug. "Isn't it?"

"Absolutely," Faye said.

"These is pretty," Jaclyn picked up a small pot of zinnias and stuck her nose in the middle of a bloom.

J.D. walked over, picked up a watering can and showed her how to water the plants. Her face lit up.

Wreath felt a pang in her stomach.

"Bumgardner left the child alone?" Faye's voice was low.

"A neighbor was *watching* her."

Samson squirmed out of Wreath's arms and peed next to the bench. Then he settled in a patch of sunlight near Jaclyn.

"That Theriot guy came by their room." Wreath shuddered. "I hate to think of Jaclyn in there alone with him."

"What did he want?"

What *had* Theriot wanted? "He was checking up on Bum, I guess."

"You think he was watching you?"

"I doubt it, but he was mad that I was there. Seemed suspicious. And he blew up about Samson. Said they have to get rid of him or be kicked out."

"Maybe J.D. could keep him until they get settled."

"That could be years."

"He still doesn't have any idea where his sister is?"

"Not that he's told me," Wreath said. "Jaclyn acts like her mother's coming home. Poor little girl. She must be scared to death."

That's why Wreath had to help.

26

Bum stumbled into the courtyard, so tired he could barely walk. Anxiety over Jaclyn made his pulse race. He'd been gone way too long.

Maybe Linda had heated up that can of ravioli for her.

His stomach growled. It was only a small can, and Jaclyn needed all of it.

While the doors to most of the ramshackle cottages stood open, no one was outside. Televisions were turned up loud, and he could hear voices. None, though, had the high-pitched drama of Jaclyn's.

He quickened his pace almost to a jog.

The door to their room was closed, as expected, but there weren't any lights on. Jaclyn usually turned every light on if he was even a few minutes late.

"Jack!" he yelled as he stepped onto the porch. He wiped at his face to make sure no blood remained. "Jack!"

"The kid left with your girlfriend."

Bum swiveled so fast he felt like he'd been on a Tilt-a-Whirl ride. Pain shot through him. *Wreath had been here?*

Theriot stood in the shadows. He chewed on a toothpick. "Fred Procell won't be any too happy about that." Theriot took the toothpick out and studied it. "But if you do your part, who says he ever has to know?"

"Where's Jack?" Bum threw his last energy into the question.

Theriot shrugged. "Do I look like that kid's keeper?"

Bum clenched his fists and moved toward Theriot. At another round of pain, he winced.

"Oooh, weeee," Theriot said. "You ran into trouble today."

"Nothing I couldn't handle." Although he might have a broken rib.

Theriot held out his hand. "Fork it over."

Bum fished into his pocket and surrendered the wad of crumpled cash.

"You're worse than your sister. Can't you even fold money?"

Not when I am carrying a dog.

With his back to the courtyard, Theriot thumbed through the cash and gave a satisfied smirk. "Maybe we don't need Miss Starla after all. You're a lot better at collecting than she was."

"So we're even?"

Theriot drew back. "Hardly."

"You said if I collected today . . . plus, I mowed this paradise." Bum tried to sound tough. His body ached from the fist in the stomach and the sorrow of seeing another dog chewed up. His plan had to work.

"That girlfriend of yours has raised the ante," Theriot said. "You should have left her out of this."

"She's not my girlfriend." Bum took a step toward Theriot, despite his weakness. "And she doesn't know anything."

"That's what Big Fun said right before she got him thrown in jail."

"I swear to you, she doesn't know anything."

"Seems like she's mighty wrapped up in your business."

"She's some sweet thing who got messed up with Procell. I don't want her poking around either." He had to convince Theriot that Wreath didn't matter.

"If you don't help me rake in a big haul this weekend, you'll hurt way worse than you do today." He kicked at Bum. "I'd hate to see that boy of yours left all alone for good."

Bum leapt down the steps and slammed against Theriot. He couldn't keep from wincing, but he grabbed Theriot's collar anyway. "Stay away from Jack."

Theriot's breathing quickened. "Get your hands off me."

Bum held on tighter, his knuckles busting open again. Blood trickled down his arm.

Theriot exhaled, his breath hot and damp on Bum's face. "You've got spunk, I'll give you that. Use it to help me out, and we'll be good."

"What's that mean?" Bum did not relax his hold.

"It means working my big event Saturday night and the Sunday collection plate."

"You can't keep adding jobs."

"Interest rates are rising." Theriot gave Bum a shove. "Now get cleaned up before anyone sees you like that."

Fumbling with the door, Bum didn't respond. How he'd let himself get dragged into Starla's messes, he'd never know.

"And like I told Miss Wreath, that mangy mutt goes or you go. I thought I made that clear." He threw his toothpick on the dirt. "You need to quit rescuing everything that comes along."

The note, on a sheet of paper torn out of a notebook, lay on the floor inside the room. He almost didn't see it for his amazement at how the room looked.

The bed was made, clothes folded into neat stacks, the shade on the lamp straight. Even the dishes were washed. That wasn't easy since the old faucet wasn't connected.

The room even smelled different. Not prissy but . . . fresh.

Don't step on me!!! The lettering was bold, not goofy bubble writing. *Jack is good. We have gone to see Faye. Jack can spend the night. All is well, no thanks to you. P.S. We have Samson. He's in the doghouse, so to speak.*

Wreath knew not to give too much away—and she'd said first thing that Jaclyn was okay. The stupid joke at the end almost made him smile. Then he caught a glimpse of himself in the mirror.

His lip had swollen, his hair looked like an Amazon-sized pot scrubber, and he was pretty sure he was going to have a black eye. Just his luck that the weasels who owed Theriot wanted to take their frustration out on him.

He glanced down at his knuckles.

This time, when he'd seen that little dog, he'd hit back. Then grabbed it and dropped it at the vet's office. Not that he'd left his real name and address, of course. That was cheating but how else could he have helped that animal?

It took every ounce of willpower not to let out a sob as he flopped onto the bed.

27

At daybreak on Tuesday Wreath sat up, confused.

"Mama?" she whispered.

The dog at her feet whimpered. Wreath fingered the soft sheet and rolled over to see the child next to her.

Of course. She was at Faye's. Frankie was dead. Jaclyn was snoring.

And apparently Samson needed to go outside.

At least he hadn't gone on the carpet, which Faye had sworn would get him exiled to J.D.'s house.

An idle threat since Wreath saw Faye sneak him a piece of meat, which he ate on the white carpet. J.D. had acted disappointed that the dog wasn't shipped off to his house overnight.

Jaclyn, despite a reassuring late-evening call from Bum, would not be separated from Samson. She'd fallen asleep snuggled up to the dog—and she staked a claim to the middle of Wreath's new bed. This must be what it felt like to have a little sister.

Wreath slipped into a pair of denim cutoffs and a Modest Mouse T-shirt she'd bought at a thrift store. She ran a brush through her hair and twisted it into a knot on her neck.

The ceiling fan stirred the air, and Wreath pulled a sheet around Jaclyn. "It's going be okay," she said softly. Then she petted Samson. "Let's go outside."

While the dog explored Faye's backyard, Wreath sat in the porch swing and drifted back and forth. The sun had not quite made an appearance but the birds were ready. They chirped so loudly it almost sounded like a bird clock the store had stocked last spring.

A wave of longing for Frankie cascaded through Wreath. Some of her loneliest moments in the junkyard had come in the dark minutes before dawn.

A mosquito buzzed in her ear. *Nothing like a mosquito to bring you back to the present.*

Faye's yard was big enough for two houses. It always felt serene, ringed with stately azalea bushes, their blooms gone for weeks. A collection of tall, skinny pines were scattered near the bushes, their acidity good for the flowers, according to Faye.

A crape myrtle anchored the corner where Wreath's room was—her own room—and a birdbath sat near that, a popular hangout for blue jays and sparrows during the summer.

A big oak sat on the other side of the yard, its trunk too big to put your arms around. It had been there when Faye and Billy chose the lot. A faded photo in the den bore witness to its history. It stood like a watchman, impervious to storms or evil men.

A similar collection of oaks lined the courtyard of the Palomino, their trunks big and sturdy too. Nothing felt safe about them.

The door to the patio slid open. Faye, in white robe and terry-cloth slippers, stood barely visible in the morning darkness.

"Hey," Wreath said. She was still not used to waking up in a house with Faye.

"We opening early today? Or you pretending to be a rooster?"

"Our guest woke me up." She nodded toward Samson.

"Bless his heart." Faye stepped closer. "And how's his buddy?"

"Slept all night without a whimper—as long as I let her have the middle of the bed."

Faye let out a small laugh. "Always good to grab the best real estate."

Wreath patted the swing. "Want to sit down?"

"I'd better get the teakettle going first." Faye bent to pet Samson, who had waddled up to sniff her feet. "Have you had your coffee?"

"Not yet. I was enjoying the morning quiet."

"Doesn't sound all that quiet to me. Who needs an alarm clock with those mockingbirds?"

"And the blue jays."

Faye slid the door open and paused. "I don't suppose there's been any more word from Mr. Bumgardner?"

Wreath's small laugh sounded loud in the morning air. "You can't stand to call him Bum, can you?"

"It's a terrible name."

"He's supposed to pick Jaclyn up at the store later. He was vague on when that would be."

"They need to get out of that motel."

She gripped the edge of the swing. "He wouldn't even consider J.D.'s offer to stay over there. He's stubborn."

"Imagine that. A stubborn teenager."

Wreath quirked up one side of her mouth and threw Faye a *touché* look. "Even if he does stay with J.D., that's a short-term fix. What happens to Jaclyn if her mother doesn't come back?"

28

"Bum?" The voice was low and urgent.

He pulled the pillow over his head. Had anyone ever died of a headache?

"Bum!"

Oh, my God that hurt. "Just a few more minutes, Jaclyn," he mumbled.

Jaclyn! He bolted upright, swamped by pain.

"Bum, open the door now!" No wonder Jaclyn was attached to Wreath. They shared that bossy attitude.

Wreath? What was she doing here?

Half falling out of bed, he pulled on the tattered cargo pants and grabbed the long-sleeve shirt he'd worn yesterday. He slipped his scarred feet into the tennis shoes and jerked open the door. "What's wrong? Where is Jaclyn?"

Wreath stared at him, a small frown on her lips. "She's fine. Much better than you apparently."

"What time is it?" He ran his hand through his hair, his fingers caught in the knots.

"Do you even known what day it is?"

He squeezed his eyes closed, then glared at her. "It's Tuesday."

"Very good. It's about seven o'clock."

When he picked up one of Jaclyn's ponytail holders and smoothed back his hair, she shook her head. "A little late for that."

Then she brushed past him into the room.

In her shorts and T-shirt, she looked clean and pretty. He felt dirty and gross. "Did you leave her by herself? She'll be scared."

"You mean like you did yesterday?"

Guilt—or was it hunger—danced in his stomach. He'd eaten a few slices of apple he'd found in a plastic sack in the kitchen but saved the rest for Jaclyn. The bag of popcorn they'd shared for lunch yesterday had been his last meal.

He had hoped to snag a few bills for food from Theriot's stash but the goon had been lying in wait for him.

That was a new approach. Things had heated up.

"Hey, you there." Wreath snapped her fingers.

Bum met her eyes and had the urge to pull her toward him.

She stepped away.

"Jaclyn's with Faye—and so is Samson. Faye's making pancakes for breakfast, then they're working on a sewing project." Wreath's happy face was so different from the squalor of the room that his hunger disappeared. "When I left, your niece was babbling about making Samson an outfit."

"Thanks," he mumbled and sat down on the bed. His legs were shaky.

"Is that blood?" Wreath asked and reached toward his arm.

Bum jerked back. "Don't touch me."

His terse words didn't stop her. "Your hands!" She ran her fingers along his battered knuckles. "Were you wrestling wild animals yesterday?"

"In a manner of speaking." He was nearly overcome by her touch.

But when she tried to push up his sleeve, he moved. "Can you give me a minute? Then I'll get Jaclyn."

Wreath's eyes were as big as Jaclyn's when he brought her a Happy Meal. "You got bit by a dog. You need to see a doctor."

"It's nothing." The dogs hadn't been nearly as bad as the humans. "He nipped me when I wasn't looking."

He stood and walked toward the laundry basket of clean clothes in the corner, then remembered they'd been folded when he got home. He looked around, lost.

"In there." Wreath nodded toward the particle-board dresser. "Top drawer."

When was the last time someone had folded and put up his clothes?

"What if that dog has rabies?" Wreath said.

"It doesn't." Or at least Bum hoped it didn't. "Tell me again why you came over? I told you I'd get Jaclyn this morning."

"Faye was worried." Wreath's face grew red with the comment. "We want to talk about keeping Jaclyn when you're working. This is no place for—"

"I got it."

"We want to help her."

"And me?" He felt weirdly jealous.

"You? I'm under strict orders to bring you home for breakfast—and the Samson style show." She smiled. "You can't beat a deal like that."

When Wreath looked at him like that, he almost had hope. If anything good came out of this mess, he'd be the first to apologize to his sister.

29

B um strolled beside Wreath and pushed her bike with
his right hand. He'd insisted, and she made a big deal
out of how much she appreciated it.

Right. Her chatter was awfully close to pity.

He held his left arm up against his body. That bite on his
left hand was red and bruised, and his right hand was puffy.
It had taken his best bluffing to convince Wreath he'd had a
minor skirmish with a stray.

The sun was up good now, and birds made a ruckus. He
tilted his head back and let the light shine on his face. He
could walk for miles like this with Wreath.

"I know what you're thinking," she said.

No you don't. "I was just, uh, listening to the birds."

"Don't you love the way they sound first thing in the morning? They don't care where they are. They just sing."

"I'll take your word for it. I'm not usually up this early."

She laughed, a cheerful little sound. "You're missing the—"

He held up his swollen hand. "You'd better not say it's the
best part of the day." He was surprised to find himself grinning.

"I'm just saying that birds are happy whether they're out in the woods or in Faye's subdivision."

"Or over by a dumpy motel?"

She gave a quick nod. "I take comfort in that, don't you?"

"I never thought about it." He wiped his forehead. "Mostly I think about how hot August is going to be."

Wreath gave a small sigh. "That's a month away. Can't you try to enjoy today?" She threw him a look. "Summer's going so fast."

He looked up with a snort. "We must be in different time zones."

"Probably not," she said and studied him. "Lousy seasons never go fast. . . but they do go."

She was so cute when she went all motivational on him. But Bum wouldn't tell her that. "It's too early for such deep thinking," he said instead.

"You sound like Faye."

He turned toward her. "I like this Faye woman more and more."

"Faye's the best," she said. "Everyone should have someone like her in their life. I'm happy to share."

He realized she was telling the absolute truth.

Bum swallowed and tried not to stare into her sparkling eyes. Wreath might be the most alive person he'd ever met.

"We'd better walk faster or Jack will eat all the pancakes," he said. When they set off again, their shoulders bumped against each other. Neither moved away.

The quick tap of a horn sounded from behind them, and Wreath jumped.

Her face felt like she'd fallen asleep in a fire-ant bed as the pickup pulled up next to the curb. The passenger window glided down. "Need a ride?"

"Law! What are you doing here?"

"Wondering the same thing about you."

"Bum and . . . Jack are having breakfast at Faye's. Want to come?"

"I just came from there." Then he grew quiet and fixed an unfamiliar stare in Bum's direction.

"You remember Bum, don't you?" Wreath said.

"Sure I do." He quirked his head and seemed about to say something else, then silently ran his hand through his thick, under-control hair.

"He had to work late, so we kind of kidnapped his n—"

"What she's trying to say is there's nothing going on between us," Bum snapped.

Wreath bit back a groan.

"Didn't think there was."

"Sure you did," Bum said. "Wreath's great. I wouldn't want someone making a play for her if I were you."

"Shut up, Bum!" Wreath said through gritted teeth. "Right now."

"I'm telling the truth."

"You're being a jerk," she said, then turned her bike toward the truck. "We'd love a ride, Law."

"I'll meet you there." Bum ambled off.

Law hopped out of the truck and lifted Wreath's bike into the bed. "What's his problem?"

"His sister ran off, left him with that kid and overdue bills, I guess."

They slid into the pickup, and he put the key into the ignition, not looking at her. "I'm not seeing enough of you lately." He nodded toward Bum, who was already nearly a block ahead. "Is that why?"

"Not exactly," Wreath said. "I want to help the child."

"And the uncle?"

"I want to help him but not in that way."

"You mean as a friend? Like you and me."

"He's nothing like you."

"You didn't call me back last night." Law started the truck. "It stung to find you out for a daylight stroll with that guy."

"Oh, Law, I'm sorry. I got tied up with Jaclyn. Then Faye and J.D. and I got to talking. Faye didn't tell me you called." She drew in a breath. "Want to do something tonight?"

A look that could only be called *uneasy* settled on Law's face. "I, uh, I have plans for tonight." He swallowed and pulled away from the curb.

She fidgeted. "You and Mitch got a guys' night out?"

"Not exactly." He gave a small cough. "Destiny's taking me for supper as a thanks for hooking her up with Jake."

"Who's Jake?"

"You know. The puppy from the park." He cleared his throat. "Want to come with?"

Her stomach knotted. "Is Mitch going?"

"I, uh, don't think so. Mitch has a family supper."

"Destiny might not want me to tag along."

"You're making too big a deal out of this. We're all friends."

"She'd probably rather have you to herself since she's leaving for Florida." Wreath took a deep breath.

"Said the girl walking down the street with a guy."

She looked at him out of the corner of her eye. "Point to Team Law."

"What's come over you?"

That question irritated her. "What's come over *you?*"

Law threw up his hands. "I'm trying to understand you. I like you, and I want to spend time with you."

She felt defeated. Nothing was going right. "I'm helping Bum and Jaclyn during a family crisis."

"I think I get that." He reached over to touch her hair. "You're good-hearted, Wreath."

"I am not." For starters, she had not one good-hearted thought about Destiny right now. She was jealous of her only girlfriend.

"Besides, I know there's nothing going on with you and that dude," Law said. "He's not your type."

She stiffened. "What's that supposed to mean?"

Law shrugged. "Did he even finish high school?"

"He quit to help his sister. It's been hard."

"You had it harder than anyone, and you didn't quit."

Wreath had judged Bum like that at first but he worked hard to take care of Jaclyn. *Had it been like that for Frankie when Wreath was little?* She wished she could remember—yet was glad she couldn't.

"I don't know why he made the choices he did" was all she said.

"It's hard to understand people sometimes." He nodded toward the sidewalk where Bum walked, head down, left arm cradled against his chest. "Is there something I can do to help?"

"Not that I can think of." She patted his leg. "You're a good guy, Law Rogers."

"You're not so bad yourself. Now let's see if we can talk Bum into accepting a lift."

30

Wednesday was barely underway when J.D. handed Wreath a cup of coffee from the hospital's pot. It had been less than a day since she and Bum had encountered Law on the street. It seemed like a week.

The clock said three o'clock. Three in the morning. The hospital's waiting room had a flickering fluorescent light that made a buzzing noise like a bug zapper.

"It's not from Starbucks," J.D. said, "but it's better than nothing."

"Thanks for getting up in the middle of the night," she said. "I'm sorry Bum was rude."

"He's scared, and there's nothing that can unravel a guy quicker than that."

"You'd think he could accept help without such a fuss."

J.D. gave a small smile. "One could hope."

"I mean it's not like we're trying to run his life."

"Clearly not."

"He's too stubborn for his own good."

"Very likely."

"Why can't he see he needs help to make his life better?" She paused and looked into J.D.'s kind face. His eyes crinkled at the corners. "Why are you looking at me like that?"

"I'm happy to know I'm not the only one who wrestles with such questions."

Wreath met his eyes but couldn't go where they led. Not yet. "If he's not healthy, who'll take care of Jaclyn, right?"

"Right."

A woman in scrubs stepped from the hallway and gave a tired survey of the waiting room. "Mr. Bumgardner?" Wreath jumped up and waved. J.D. stood quickly too.

The woman's face was sober as she reached out to shake J.D.'s hand. "I'm Dr. Manzant, the ER physician." She glanced at the tablet computer in her other hand. "Your grandson's a lucky fellow."

"Oh, he's not my grandson," J.D. said. "He's a friend."

"Well, it's a good thing he has friends like you. That bite was definitely on the unruly side. I'm relieved the others healed as well as they did."

J.D. threw a glance at Wreath.

She gave her head a quick shake.

Dr. Manzant squinted at the computer screen. "So you're close to Mr. Bumgardner?"

"We're getting acquainted," J.D. said. Wreath was so happy her grandfather was with her.

"He signed the release." The doctor sounded like she was talking to herself, then looked at J.D. "He has given me permission to discuss treatment with you—although he wasn't happy about it."

"Will Bum be ok?" Wreath interrupted.

"That depends on the dog who wanted a taste of him. I need to confirm that the animal had its rabies shots?"

J.D. exhaled. "We believe so."

The doctor frowned and directed her focus to J.D. "Where is the animal now?"

"It was injured. That's why it bit him," Wreath said. "He dropped it at an animal clinic in Landry." That he had told them on the drive to the hospital.

The doctor looked at her computer and back at J.D. "We see cases from all over Rapides Parish," she said, "and are in regular contact with authorities . . ." She fell silent.

"I'm afraid I don't understand," J.D. said.

The doctor glanced toward the admissions desk where J.D. had promised to pay Bum's bill. "I'm an animal lover myself." Her voice was quiet. "But with this dog's aggression, I must recommend it be euthanized."

"It had its shots!" Wreath said.

"Most of Mr. Bumgardner's bites are healing well but—"

"Most? It's not only his hand?" she said.

Dr. Manzant's voice was husky. "That dog could seriously hurt a child. Mr. Bumgardner must have a strong constitution or we'd have seen him a few days ago. At least he kept the bites clean."

"We didn't know," Wreath said, and J.D. put his big weathered hand over hers.

"Young men aren't the most forthcoming," Dr. Manzant said. "He said he kept it a secret, didn't want the animal to get in trouble."

Wreath doubted that was the only reason.

"Frankly, if he weren't eighteen, we'd be looking at a Child Protection report." She glanced at the screen again. "Are there children in the home?"

The stale coffee leapt back up in Wreath's throat. J.D. gave a slight nod. "Only one. She is staying with friends temporarily."

The doctor typed something.

"Whatever dog did this doesn't live with them," Wreath said. "Their dog's afraid of people."

"A skittish dog can be dangerous."

"Samson didn't bite Bum," she insisted.

Pieces of what happened had unfolded over breakfast at Faye's but Bum refused to say where he'd encountered the dog. "Dogs snap at people all the time," he'd said. "This one had been attacked and didn't like me walking down his sidewalk."

"What do you mean attacked?" Wreath had asked.

"He got into a fight with another dog."

"So he ran out and bit you?" She had shaken her head. "Something's off about that story."

Bum absently dragged his fork through a pool of syrup, his plate otherwise empty. "You've got to be the most stubborn girl ever. You make Jaclyn look like a pushover."

"You're way more stubborn than I am."

"I am not."

"Children!" Faye said.

"If Bum's arm falls off, I'm twisting the other one until he admits I was right," Wreath said.

He let out a rusty laugh. "If my arm falls off, I'll admit I should have listened to you."

Now, looking at the doctor, Wreath was glad she'd bullied Bum into coming to the hospital. Where would she be if Law hadn't hauled her out of the junkyard when she had the flu?

She'd made Law promise to keep her secret. What right did she have to demand that Bum tell her everything?

"We bandaged his ribs too," the doctor was saying. "Keep him off ladders for a while. He got pretty banged up with the fall."

Wreath chewed her lip. J.D. looked out the corner of his eye.

"No more ladders," Dr. Manzant repeated. "And no more dog bites."

By the looks of his lip and knuckles—and probably other injuries Wreath didn't know anything about—a dog might be the least of his troubles.

31

Wreath climbed into the back seat of J.D.'s truck. Maybe if she forced Bum into the front, he would talk about his problems.

Her stomach churned at the thought of multiple dog bites—and multiple secrets.

The sun was at almost the same spot it had been when she'd sat on Faye's patio yesterday. The resemblance ended there.

The hospital parking lot was filling up with assorted employees in scrubs and a stream of people walking in the door marked for outpatient surgery. An ambulance's swirling red-and-white lights disrupted any feeling of early-morning calm.

"You sure you don't want to sit up front?" Bum's voice was impatient.

"I'm good."

"Everybody buckled up?" J.D. asked.

"All set." She added his question to her stash of grandfatherly clues. Although Frankie was a good mom—the best—she'd not been much of a caretaker. Having J.D. express such small measures of concern made her feel . . . safe.

Bum slumped down in the seat and looked over at J.D.

When he spoke, his voice was hesitant. "Do you think we could go by that McDonald's?" He pointed across the street.

"You must be feeling better," Wreath said.

"Good idea," J.D. said with a nod. "I'm peckish myself."

Bum moved closer to the door. "I, uh, I don't have any money with me."

"My treat," J.D. said. "In fact, I know a good café a couple of blocks from here. Homemade biscuits."

"No!" Bum straightened his back. "I'd rather go over there."

Wreath could see her grandfather's crinkled brow in the rearview mirror. "Maybe the drive-through?" he asked.

Bum's lips were pursed. "That'll work," he said after a moment.

J.D. pulled into the line of cars waiting for a turn at the squawky box. The sound of orders sputtered back toward the truck.

Bum leaned forward and peered across J.D. into the restaurant.

"See someone you know?" Wreath asked.

He shifted again, still staring. He did not answer. The truck rolled forward, and he twisted sideways.

"Something wrong?" J.D. said.

He drew in a breath. "I must have been mistaken."

Wreath leaned forward and put her hand on his shoulder. He looked in need of comfort. "What you getting, Bum?"

He pulled back, and his tone was peevish. "Why are you being so nice to me?"

Wreath pulled back too. "Because you're so charming."

He almost smiled. "Thanks for driving me to the hospital, sir," he said. "But did you have to bring her?"

J.D. glanced at Bum. "I made this trip for my own boy a couple of times."

Wreath's heart felt funny.

"Was he accident prone too?" Bum asked.

"He fell off a ladder or two in his day." J.D. emphasized the words *fell off a ladder. Or two.* "Happens to teenage boys."

"You have any more kids?"

"Just the one." J.D.'s voice barely carried to where Wreath sat.

Bum gingerly adjusted his bandaged arm and turned to look at Wreath. "So that's your dad, huh?"

She stared out the window. "It's almost time to order," she said.

"Wreath's father was a good boy." The words floated out, quiet. "He died way too young. I sure don't want to see that happen to you."

"I don't either." Bum looked away from J.D.

"May I take your order?" the garbled voice said.

The entire truck seemed to give a sigh of relief.

But the peace was broken as they pulled up to the window. "Starla?" Bum sounded dazed.

"You okay?" J.D. asked.

Wreath looked past the cashier to a young woman assembling breakfast sandwiches. A young woman who bore a slight resemblance to herself.

Bum craned his neck, the rest of his body still.

"Does Starla look like me?" Wreath asked.

"Jaclyn thinks she does." His hand was on the door handle. "I don't see it."

J.D. turned back to the window to take their food.

And Bum jumped out of the truck.

"Bum!" Wreath lowered her window. "Bum!"

J.D. exhaled and sat the sacks of food on Bum's seat. He arranged orange juice and coffee in drink holders, then pulled the truck into a space in front of the restaurant, as calm as if selling a geranium to a customer.

"Let's give him a minute," he said and handed Wreath a biscuit.

"You take such good care of everybody." Her voice was uncertain as she watched through the front window of the restaurant. Bum walked slowly as he approached the counter.

J.D. rubbed his eyes, his food untouched. "I left you on your own for seventeen years. That's not what I'd call taking good care of someone."

She draped her arms around his neck from behind. "That wasn't your fault."

He patted her hand. "I didn't take good enough care of your father either."

"My dad got killed in a wreck. You weren't to blame."

"And after he died . . ." J.D. cleared his throat. "I was not the kind of father John David deserved, nor the man your grandmother deserved. Drank too much. Argued with anyone who'd look at me. Nearly ran the hardware store in the ground."

Her throat felt dry. "I don't believe that."

"It's true."

"But you seem . . . perfect."

He surrendered a tiny smile. "How'd I get so lucky to have you in my life?"

She watched Bum lean over the counter. He spoke to the cashier and pointed to the kitchen.

"Do you think life's unfair?" Wreath asked.

Now Bum and a young woman in a striped uniform were talking. Her visor shielded her expression.

"I used to."

"And now?"

"It's easier now that I have you and Faye. It seems like things work out but not always on my schedule."

"Does that make it better or worse?"

He chuckled and took a sip of orange juice. "You are so much your father's child. He loved to ask questions, wanted to figure everything out."

Wreath smiled, too, which struck her as odd.

"I believe we owe life more than it owes us," J.D. said. "If we do our part—with an assist from the Mighty One, things work out."

Bum's face was grim. The skinny woman shook her head and pointed toward the kitchen.

Bum barreled out the door, wiping at his face. *Were those tears?* The woman had returned to the grill, her back to them.

Wreath tightened her grip on J.D.'s shoulder. "I'm glad you're my grandfather," she said.

And leaned back to wait for the bad news.

32

Faye slipped her feet into her slippers and smiled when Jaclyn rolled over with a snore.

She looked like an angel. A small, dirty-faced angel.

Samson had jumped off the bed a moment ago and whined as he headed for the hall. Faye was glad for the excuse to get up.

She hadn't slept since Wreath appeared in her room at midnight with word that Bum had called. He was running fever, complete with chills, and only had "kiddie" medicine.

"Do you think we should check on him?" Wreath asked.

"I told him that he needs a doctor." Faye had pulled on her robe. She had inspected the dog bite on his hand when he'd walked in the door for breakfast the morning before. "That's the last time I let a teenager keep me from using my good sense."

What was it with these kids?

"I'd better call J.D.," Wreath said.

The simple statement made Faye feel like she'd come over a hill too fast in her new car. Being awakened in the middle of the night for such an errand would undo years of scar tissue around J.D.'s heart.

"I'll keep Jaclyn if you want to ride along," Faye said. "Bum will probably need to go up to Alexandria. I doubt the clinic here is open."

"I should have made Bum go earlier." Wreath pulled her hair back into a ponytail. She had the thickest, prettiest hair, gorgeous even when she'd tumbled out of bed. Faye's hair had never looked that good, even when she was a girl.

That bedhead was going to drive the other girls in the dorm crazy. When the time came for her to live on campus. Which wouldn't be for a while. Hopefully.

J.D. dropped Jaclyn off on their way out of town. Bum carried her in, despite his hurt arm. Wreath hovered nearby and protested when he started to lay her on the couch.

"She might be scared if she wakes up alone there," Wreath said. "Put her in my bed, and make sure Samson's with her."

"Why don't you put her in my room?" Faye said. "The dog too. We'll keep each other company while y'all are gone."

"Are you sure?" Wreath whispered.

Now Faye smiled again. Wreath was right. Jaclyn liked the middle of the bed.

She left the door ajar and headed toward the patio door. "Come on, fellow," she whispered. "And thank you for not peeing on the carpet."

While Samson sniffed around the yard, Faye went to the kitchen, in need of a strong cup of tea. Her boring old house had been transformed into a place she enjoyed. A place where she felt needed.

Why had she and Billy not opened their home sooner? They had gotten caught up with the furniture business and bridge games and the silliness of life. They'd not been devoted to kindness—to the world around them, probably not to each other.

That was her greatest regret.

She poured the hot water into the cup, the tea infusing it with color.

Beyond the ranch-style walls, she had a boutique, in quite solid shape despite Wreath's worries, and a good-hearted fiancé who made her heart beat in ways she thought were long erased.

Thank goodness Wreath came along when she did.

Thank goodness Wreath came along.

33

Wreath could barely keep her eyes open Wednesday afternoon. Faye and J.D., content together, looked like they'd been on vacation instead of up all night.

Jaclyn was playing "salesman" with a collection of items that ranged from "that couch there" to an order of imaginary fried chicken. Samson chose the most expensive chair in the store to stretch out on. Bum had gone back to the motel, avoiding his niece.

"My bad," he said when he had gotten back into the truck at McDonald's. "That wasn't Starla after all."

"Did that girl know your sister?" Wreath asked.

"Why would you think that?"

"You seemed to have a lot to say to each other."

"You were spying on me?"

"You don't have to snap at me."

"Here." J.D. handed Bum his food, manner still calm. "You've had a long night."

Bum wolfed down his breakfast and slumped against the door like he was asleep. Wreath had done that enough to know he was faking.

He sprinted from the truck to the motel room after instructing them to tell Jaclyn he would get her as soon as he woke up from a nap.

By the time Wreath and J.D. got to Faye's, Jaclyn had been fed, bathed, and was wearing a cute little skirt with her boyish T-shirt.

"Where'd that come from?" Wreath asked.

"Miss Faye and me made it."

"I made an executive decision," Faye said "She's all girl, and she deserves pretty clothes."

Wreath opened her mouth but Faye held up her hand. "Don't you worry. We'll keep her safe."

34

J ulia burst in the back door of the store Thursday with such force that a row of old postcards fluttered to the floor. "Sorry!" She practically danced over to pick them up.

"Aren't we looking happy this afternoon?" Faye said. "Did you win the lottery?"

"I've got news!" She twirled around.

Wreath always felt out of control when people *had news*. But Julia looked so happy. "They gave you the senior art classes?" Wreath said. "Yay!"

Julia's face grew serious. "No, they said I'd be teaching social studies again."

"Did you sell a big painting?"

"Nope. Guess again."

Faye put her hands on her hips and surveyed Julia from head to toe. "Are you getting married?"

"Shane proposed?" Wreath's eyes went to Julia's ring finger, which was bare.

"Okay, not quite that kind of news." Julia said. "I got into the Savannah College of Art and Design! I'm going for my master's degree."

"Online?" Wreath asked.

"On campus. I got in. It's a miracle!"

"You're leaving?" The disappointment practically poured out of Wreath's question.

Some of the joy left Julia's face.

"That's wonderful news." Faye said. "Guess I'll be the only non-coed around these parts."

Wreath felt wooden. Who would help her with her artwork and school and give opinions on Wreath's store decorations? She depended on Julia.

"I know I said I'd help when Wreath's in class, but—"

"We'll make a lot more money selling your artwork when you're famous," Faye said.

"Shane said you'd understand." Julia clasped her hands. "You do understand, Wreath?"

"Are you and Shane breaking up?"

"Never!"

"I don't get it," Wreath said. "You're leaving but you're staying together?" If Frankie was gone for ten minutes, her boyfriends moved on.

"He knows this is my dream. And we can Skype, and he'll come visit, and I'll come home."

"Weird." With Bum's secrets and Law leaving and Faye getting married, there was too much to deal with. "Weird," she repeated.

"My goodness, Wreath!" Faye made no effort to hide the scold. "Shane's the kind of man who encourages the woman he loves."

Julia's head bobbled like one of the high school girls about to go on a prom date. "He's a sweetheart," she said. "Since he's a deputy, some people think he's gruff. But he's a big ole teddy bear."

Wreath thought of Bum carrying Jaclyn into Faye's house, despite his hurt arm. Was he a guy who would support someone's dreams? Law was. He'd cheer her on, even though she was staying in Landry.

"There's something else." Julia hesitated.

"No," Wreath said under her breath.

"Wreath?" Faye frowned.

"Did I say that out loud?" She scrunched her eyes. "Sorry."

"Want to stomp your feet too?" Faye sounded more like the woman Wreath had first met a year ago.

"It's okay." Julia didn't even look bothered. Many adults would have backhanded Wreath by now.

"What's the *something else?*" she asked.

Faye quirked her brow. "Probably that Julia will be glad to leave after the way you're acting."

"No way!" Julia said. "Nothing Wreath can say would make me miss her less."

A frown settled on Faye's face. The lecture on manners would start before the back door closed.

"The something else is—" Julia twisted her hands. "It's probably obvious. I won't need the garage apartment anymore."

"Not a problem," Faye said with a wave of her hand.

Like losing the rent from the apartment wasn't a big deal with their small budget? Like a new tenant could possibly be as cool as Julia? Like every danged thing in Wreath's life wasn't going crazy?

Julia walked over to Wreath and touched her cheek. "I'll be back, Wreath. And we'll always be friends."

Wreath nodded. "I'm sorry I'm being such a brat." She blinked back tears.

"Is that the phone?" Faye asked. "If you'll excuse me for a moment—" She scurried off like one of the mice that lived in the attic.

"The phone didn't ring," Wreath said.

Julia met her eyes. "She's not the most subtle woman I know, but she'd walk through fire for either one of us."

Until she left, like everybody else.

"I kind of hoped you'd get this more than most." Julia's voice didn't sound at all like a teacher's. "You're artistic. And ambitious." She sniffed. "It's probably a dream but I have to give my art a try."

"I'm not ambitious."

"Of course you are. What other teenager would transfer in and grab the valedictorian spot? Or run a store for a lonely widow? Or try to help the guy who stole her bike?"

Julia wound a strand of hair around her finger. "You're the reason I had the courage to do this. When I watched you last year, I knew I was wasting my life. I had fallen back on stupid excuses." She eased down into a chair and patted the one next to her. "Wreath Willis didn't make excuses. She saw what she wanted and went for it."

Wreath felt an unwelcome sob rising in her throat. "I wish I hadn't been so persuasive."

Julia grinned.

"I'm happy for you . . . I think." If she said it enough, she might convince herself.

"You'll get used to the idea. And I'll be back."

"I thought when everything got in place it stayed that way."

"Rarely," Julia said. "But sometimes changes are better than we can imagine." She clasped her hands. "Like Shane and me. I never expected to meet someone in Landry of all places. If I'd run off last summer—like I almost did—I wouldn't have met him, wouldn't have this wonderful man in my life." She winked. "For that matter, I wouldn't have gotten to know wonderful you."

"You realize you're over-the-top, right?" Wreath flashed a teeny grin.

"I'll remind you of that when you fall in love."

Wreath fidgeted with the linens. "Aren't you afraid of growing apart?" She shrugged. "Maybe getting hurt?"

"Until I met Shane." Julia walked around the table and helped straighten the display. "I was too young to know what I wanted." She held a soft feed sack towel against her face. "You're a beautiful young woman with life spreading out in front of you. Don't be afraid."

"I really am happy for you."

"I believe she means that." Faye walked up and gave Wreath's shoulders a squeeze.

"I guess I'd better get used to change," Wreath said.

Faye reached for the soft towel, reached over and dabbed at Wreath's eyes.

In a moment, they were all laughing . . . and crying.

35

The glass case was filled with new diamond rings.

"What do you think about this one?" The clerk—Tomas, he'd said with a handshake—held up a diamond with two small emeralds, sparkling green. He was a twenty-something hipster who beamed at the Friday business.

"It's beautiful," Wreath said. What would it be like to wear a ring like that and pledge to love one guy the rest of her life? Bum's wild hair came to her mind. Then Law's enticing smile.

"Is it what Faye would like?" J.D.'s voice was doubtful. "It needs to be just right."

Wreath's face grew warm. She was here to encourage, not daydream about herself. She had relented about the short trip to Lafayette because it mattered so much to him—and, truth be told, she wanted to get out of town.

"Thanks again for helping me with this." His voice was calmer than it had been as the salesman showed them an array of gaudy-awful rings. "Faye says you have the best taste of anyone she knows."

"She exaggerates," Wreath said.

"This ring is exquisite," Tomas said and pointed to another diamond. "Any woman would be charmed by it."

Wreath couldn't hold back a small snort. "Faye's not the charming type."

Her grandfather burst out laughing.

Tomas lifted the ring off its black display cloth and put it back into the glass case.

"I wanted to get the ring today," J.D. said, "so Faye can show it off when you plan your end-of-summer shindig."

Did everyone's grandfather use words like *shindig*?

He met her eyes, his twinkling. "Or is it a hootenanny?"

Would her father have been charming like this?

"I didn't know we were having a *hootenanny*." She had to smile. "But I like the sound of it. First we have to get through the July Fourth sale tomorrow. I've got red, white, and blue Popsicles to hand out."

"My social calendar was a lot duller a few months ago," he said. "Seems like we have one occasion after another to celebrate."

"Granddad . . ." The word hung in the air for a minute. J.D.'s mouth made a small *O*. She was surprised too but liked the way the word sounded coming off her tongue. "Thanks for bringing me with you."

"My pleasure." His eyes crinkled at the corners.

Tomas was polishing a case, not rushing them at all. "You have a lovely store," Wreath said. "The cases at our store are always dusty."

The clerk cocked his head. "You're in retail?"

"Nothing as grand as this. A conglomeration of things up in Landry. Retro furnishings. Vintage clothes."

"You work at Durham's Fine Furnishings?"

"You've heard of it?"

"She practically runs the place," J.D. said proudly.

"I love your website," Tomas said "I'd kill for that Art Deco set you posted a few days ago."

Wouldn't Faye get a kick out of this? Wreath had tried to talk her out of buying it. "Too frou-frou." But Faye loved the style.

"It's still there," Wreath said. "We found two end tables and a lamp to go with it too. You should come see it."

His mouth drooped. "I work weird hours." He leaned over the counter. "You know how store schedules are."

"Let me know when you can come, and I'll open for you," she said. "We have great products that you won't find anywhere else."

"It's eclectic," J.D. said. "Their displays are worth the drive."

Wreath looked over to see if he was teasing. He was serious.

"I'll try," Tomas said. "First I have to help you find a ring."

"We need something elegant but fun. Somewhat sassy. But not flashy." Describing Faye was tough. "She's classier than most women—and strong-willed."

"My granddaughter's got her pegged," J.D. said. "And she drives too fast."

The clerk smiled at Wreath. "You probably should slow down," he said.

"I'm talking about my fiancée," J.D. gave a soft laugh.

"I prefer to be chauffeured," Wreath said with a wink.

"We must find the perfect ring," Tomas left his shelter behind the case. "We need to look at our one-of-a-kind antique jewelry."

"One-of-a-kind, just like Faye," Wreath said.

"Does she have a favorite color?" he asked.

"Red," they said in unison.

Tomas moved from case to case, talking to himself, pulling out a ring, looking at it, shaking his head.

Wreath approached the counter, but he held up his hand. "Not yet," he said, and she wandered back to a tray of fresh cookies. J.D. lingered at a display of men's jewelry, another surprise. Other than a sturdy watch, he never wore jewelry.

"Voilà!" Tomas had moved beyond the one-ring-on-the-counter-at-a-time and arranged—not in a straight line—six stunning antique rings. He'd forsaken the plain black cloth for a piece of red silk. He'd also omitted price tags.

"Look at that cameo!" Wreath rushed to the counter. "It's gorgeous."

Tomas smiled. "It's Victorian, came from Mississippi. You'll never see another one like it."

"It's nice," J.D. said, "but how about that one?"

Tomas grabbed his heart and looked as though he might keel over. "That's my absolute favorite. Primo garnet with diamonds. White gold band." He looked at Wreath. "From an Evangeline Parish estate. Certified provenance."

And Art Deco.

"She'd love it." Wreath picked up the ring. Its weight felt good in her hand.

"It looks like her," J.D. said.

"And no one in Landry will have one like it," Wreath added. "How much is it?"

When Tomas said the price, Wreath decided Faye's store needed to start selling jewelry.

"That's really more than we wanted to spend." Wreath didn't know what J.D. had budgeted, but she was scandalized. "Could you do any better?"

Tomas raised his eyebrows. "I'll call the owner."

J.D. looked bemused as he walked off. "You're quite the businesswoman, aren't you?"

"I suppose people don't haggle much on fertilizer and bedding plants, but most things can be discounted," she said and almost danced around the store. "Faye will love that ring!"

Once more J.D. meandered over to the men's case, where there was an assortment of signet rings, heavy bracelets, a necklace or two, and a row of fancy pocket knives.

"You like jewelry?" she asked.

"I'm more of an overalls guy myself." J.D.'s voice was hesitant. "I saw something in there that reminded me of someone."

"Alrighty!" Tomas returned from a room to the side. "The owner is in a generous mood."

"I bet he is," Wreath muttered, then raised her voice. "Could you gift wrap it?"

J.D. put his arm around her shoulder. "You are something else."

※

When Tomas handed the sack—the store's logo lettered in gold on cream—to J.D., Wreath fished a Durham's Fine Furnishings card from her backpack.

"Come up and look around," she said. "When Faye sees that ring, she'll probably give you that grouping."

He shook J.D.'s hand and gave Wreath a half hug. "I don't think I've ever had a grandfather and granddaughter in here shopping together before," he said. "You two are precious."

Wreath headed toward the door, feeling a rare tear in her eye.

"I'll be right there," J.D. said. "I want to check up on caring for this and a couple of other minor points."

"Sure." Wreath sat on a classic bench, painted gold, of course, in front of the store. Was J.D. buying Faye something else?

When he came out five minutes later, he only carried the one bag, though. "What a nice fellow." They climbed into the truck. "Now, how about a peanut-butter milkshake?"

Wreath looked over at him. "So Faye told you I've discovered peanut-butter shakes, huh?"

"Not that I can recall," he said, almost as though talking to himself. "That's what John David always wanted."

"Oh." Wreath's reply was quiet, and she stared ahead.

"Sometimes it feels like I've gone back in time," he said, "that I have part of my boy back. So, ice cream?"

She nodded. "Will you tell me other things my father liked?"

36

Bum sat alone on the cottage steps, staring at the end of a lit cigarette when Wreath rode up Sunday afternoon. The door to the room stood open. He wore a long-sleeved white T-shirt and had a blue bandanna on his head. His hair sprang out from underneath.

The combination almost looked like a costume from Landry's Fourth of July festival the day before.

A crumpled white sack sat next to a soft-drink can on the porch. A twenty-dollar bill lay under a rock. Three dirty bottles, one green and two amber, were lined up next to the door.

Wreath climbed off her bike. It had been nearly five days since they had taken him to the hospital, and he looked pale. "I didn't know you smoked," she said.

"I don't." He glanced toward the office. "What are you doing here?"

"Checking on you." She pulled the cigarette from his hand, dropped it on the ground and ground it out with her tennis shoe.

"J.D. just left. Did you two get your shifts mixed up?"

"My grandfather was here?" Warmth flared inside her.

Bum picked up the paper sack and dropped it back on the porch. "He brought me something to eat." His face flushed. "And tried to give me that money."

"Looks to me like he succeeded."

"I was afraid I'd wind up with another busted lip if I didn't give in. He's as stubborn as you are."

Wreath grinned. "It surprises me how alike we are."

"Aren't most kids like their families?"

"Beats me. I only found out J.D. was my grandfather a couple of months ago." She plopped down. "What'd your sister really say the other night?"

Bum cast another furtive look toward the front of the motel. "I told you that wasn't my sister. The pain meds fried my brain."

"I saw the look on your face."

His voice lowered. "You shouldn't be here, Wreath. Go on back to your safe little world, your safe little boyfriend."

Wreath propped herself on her hands, legs outstretched. "Impressive," she said. "Definitely an A-plus. You must have studied extra hard in jerk class."

He picked up the muddy green bottle and one of the amber ones. "I got these for Faye for being so nice to Jaclyn." He glanced at her. "I suppose I should give you one, too, risking life and limb to check on me."

She reached for one of the antique bottles. The glass was thick, the words raised off the surface. *Aunt Ida* with *Shreveport* on the bottom. It felt heavy in her hand. "Nice."

"You shouldn't be here, Wreath. Just because Big Fun's in jail doesn't mean the world's all sweet and shiny."

"I'm careful," she said. "I checked for Theriot's truck. If it'd been out front, I'd have gone on by."

He rolled his eyes. "Stealthy of you."

"So what'd your sister say the other night?"

"Hush," he hissed.

"Nobody's paying attention."

"Someone's always paying attention around here." He voice was almost a whisper and he nodded toward the closest open door, the room where Half-Pint and his mother stayed. "Linda's probably already called to let Theriot know you're here."

"Aren't you being melodramatic?"

"I don't even know what that means," he said.

"Of course you do. You live with a five-year-old girl hidden as a boy."

"Linda provides Theriot information and, um, a few other things for free rent for her and her boy."

Wreath grimaced. "My mama knew people like that. I worry about Jaclyn. She shouldn't be exposed to that."

"That's one reason I'm letting her stay at your house so much."

"It's Faye's house."

"Whatever."

"If only Half-Pint had another place to go," Wreath said. "What's wrong with him?"

Bum tapped his temple. "He had encephalitis as a kid. He's a year older than me but he's got a kid's mind."

"With a man's body," she said.

Bum drew back. "I watch out for Jaclyn. And he'd never hurt her."

"Does he go to school or some kind of program?"

He shot her an incredulous look. "Sure, a limousine picks him up and he makes baskets and sells them online. He's secretly a millionaire."

"N-i-c-e. You're improving. A-plus-plus."

"*Schools* and *programs* don't work for everybody, Wreath."

"He needs training—and someone to interact with. He's got a sweet personality."

"His mother's not a fan of the system. She says he'd just be getting babysat, and she'd have to get him up every morning and find transportation."

"Aren't there buses for disabled students?"

"You're missing the point, Wreath. She doesn't want the hassle."

"I feel bad for him."

He pulled the bandanna off and ran his fingers through his hair. "He nearly talked J.D.'s ear off. With Jaclyn gone, he's out of sorts." He picked up the brown bottle and studied it. "Why are you here again?"

She cleared her throat. "I thought you'd want to know how Jaclyn is. She wants to know when you're coming to see her."

He frowned. "You could have called the room or left a message at the office. This dump don't have much but we do get free ice and phone messages."

"I needed the exercise."

"Here I was, feeling all warm and fuzzy, thinking you wanted to check on me."

She stood and put her hands on her hips. "You shouldn't be smoking, your bandage needs changing, and you probably should by lying down."

"Now there's the Florence Nightingale I was looking for. And, yes, I had three-and a half years of history and know stuff like that."

She made a soft sound of dismay. "You quit school your senior year?"

His nod was so scant as to be barely noticeable. "I bailed when things got dicey with Starla. Not that my grades were all that great anyway."

"That stinks."

"It's the Bumgardner way," he said with a shrug. "Neither one of my parents graduated. Starla never got past eighth grade. She kept repeating it till she got old enough to drop out." He gave a dry laugh. "And she's obviously doing fine."

"Education's important. You could always go back."

"I'm never going back." His voice was low and intense.

"Not even for your GED?"

"I thought you meant to Thibodaux." He broke a cigarette in half. "I'll think about school someday. I'll find a place to start over. I'm not going back home."

Half-Pint walked out on his porch, yelled a hello and waved. Then he ambled toward the back door of the Corral.

"He goes to a bar?" Wreath had a sick feeling in her stomach.

"The bartender gives him leftover snacks," Bum said, "and Cokes."

"Life's unfair."

"Pretty much."

37

B um nodded at the woods that separated the motel from a highway. "You up for a walk?"

"Back there?" Wreath considered. "That looks like a place serial killers live."

"You're more likely to run into a serial killer right here." He gave the courtyard a sweeping glance, stood and reached for her hand. "The woods are kind of peaceful."

Wreath hesitated.

He dropped his hand. "Is the city girl afraid of a little nature?"

She nearly burst out laughing. "Yeah, that's right," she said, "I don't like spiders and snakes."

"I thought you'd be tougher than that, the way you come in here all avenging-angel like."

"You don't know anything about me, do you?" But she was pleased that he didn't seem to know she'd lived in the woods for a year. Most days it felt like the first thing people heard about her.

"I know plenty about you. You're soft-hearted when it comes to bossy little girls and gimpy dogs. You seem smart.

You're pretty. And Jaclyn thinks you hung the moon, sun, stars, and possibly a few streetlights."

"I *seem* smart?"

"I gave you a definite on pretty. I can tell that at a glance. I'll let you know about smart when I get to know you better."

"I was valedictorian of my class." Why had she needed to tell him that?

"Figures."

She looked away for a second and fidgeted with the bottle. This was a guy Frankie would have found intriguing. Wreath shouldn't.

He picked up the twenty and stuck it in his pocket, then swung one of the antique bottles in front of her face. "Aren't you dying to know where I got these?"

"I guess."

"Don't overwhelm me with excitement." He looked around again. "If we're going, we have to run. I don't want anyone to see."

Her curiosity won. "Lead the way."

"See? I do know you." He pulled on her hand. "C'mon."

"Don't you need to close up?"

"Nah. The only one who'd come in would be Theriot. Locking the door doesn't keep him out."

As they talked, they got further from the row of cottages, dashing around piles of trash. Wreath made a face. "Are you sure about this?"

"You have to look below the surface, Wreath." He tugged on her arm. "You'll like this place." A look of something almost like embarrassment skittered across his face.

He turned slightly and stepped off the asphalt drive. "Stay on the trail as much as possible. There's a lot of poison ivy."

"And everyone knows that poison ivy is the perfect complement to multiple dog bites." But she followed, although she suspected neither J.D. nor Faye would approve.

After only a handful of steps, the brush became thicker. At first the sunlight shone through, then it looked like the beam from a tiny flashlight. The trees provided a canopy.

Bum guided her down a makeshift path that got narrower until it was almost nonexistent. "You're not claustrophobic, are you?" he asked.

"I don't think so." She didn't mention she had lived in a VW van for a year.

"Good." His voice held approval, which mattered more than she wanted.

After they'd gone about half a football field into the woods, Bum stopped and put his uninjured arm out, like a crossing guard holding a child back from a busy street. "This is where it gets tricky."

"That's encouraging," she said.

Bum winked—which hit her like a punch in the gut—and picked up a big stick propped against a tree. Still pushing vines away, he took a step down into a small hole. "You have to look close to get your footing." He reached his good arm up toward her.

Wreath took his hand without hesitation and climbed down a steep embankment, crude stairs carved out of the hill. "Wow," she breathed. "What is this place?"

"Pretty cool, huh?"

"It looks like a grotto."

He frowned. "What's that?"

"A cave." She smiled. "It was one of my vocabulary words in literature last year. I wanted to design one at the store, but Faye thought I was taking on too much."

Bum shook his head. "You get involved in a lot, don't you?"

"I never really thought about it." Her life felt small to her, compared to Destiny's or sometimes even to Law's. "Maybe." She leaned her head back and looked at the awning of green. "How'd you find this?"

He met her gaze. "Hiding Jaclyn and Samson from Theriot."

She stepped forward, the layers of leaves and pine straw underneath softer than Faye's white carpet, then followed him into what looked like a cave, its walls green with moss and vines, light glinting off the occasional object. Her mouth dropped.

The sides of the enclosure were lined with old bottles, their bottoms sticking out like art-deco trim. "There must be hundreds of them," she said. Wreath ran her fingers on the bottom of one. A sense of awe had almost frozen her tongue.

"Minus a half dozen or so." His voice turned defensive. "They'll just rot out here."

"Bottles don't rot." Her voice was soft. The space was hushed, like church right before the pastor started preaching. "This place. It feels sacred."

"Or spooky." He patted a big rock that cropped out from the side. "Have a seat on my special chair."

"Now that's a line I've never heard."

He stepped back. "I'm not hitting on you."

"Who said you were?" Wreath drew in a deep breath. The damp smell was lush. The sounds of birds and traffic were muffled by the green ceiling. Nature had woven a tent overhead, creating a space so secret it reminded Wreath of her campsite at the junkyard.

"Why'd you bring me here?" she asked.

He raised and lowered his right shoulder. "You're the only person I've met who I thought might think this was special."

The shelter almost felt like a womb, safe and secure, impenetrable from bad men and sad children. Bum was quiet, his big body and unruly hair strangely at home. She tilted her head and was not prepared for the next words that flew out of her mouth. "I was homeless," she said.

Bum scrunched up his face. "That sucks. You and your mother?"

She laid back on the rock, looking at the shades of green. "Just me. After my mother died. I needed to hide."

His face, leaning over hers, went hard. "Big Fun."

"I made a plan for when Frankie—my mama—died." She ran her hand along the rough moss wall. "He found me anyway."

"Did he . . . hurt you?"

She squeezed her eyes shut. "Mama kept him away as long as she could. He hurt her instead."

"Why didn't y'all leave?"

"No place to go. No money. A lot like you. Once Mama got sick, she said her brain felt cloudy."

"I don't get why women get hooked up with him."

"Me either." Wreath sighed. "What did your sister see in him?"

"She thought he was cool." He cleared his throat. "My parents' house wasn't exactly a safe place. She was lonely. Afraid."

Wreath made a strange croaking sound, like the frogs that had once scared her. "Frankie said Big Fun could make her forget her troubles for a while . . . then deliver 'em back by the truckload."

Bum snorted. "She sounds like my sister."

Hands propped on her knees, Wreath tried to bring Frankie's face to mind. Some days recently the picture, once so clear, was like the fuzzy old TV they had in Oil City. "Mama was a good person," she said after a few silent moments. "She got derailed, as she put it. Once my daddy got killed and I was born, she couldn't get back on track."

Bum didn't answer, but she could tell by the way he held his head that he was listening.

"She did a lot of things right." Wreath clutched at the rough surface of the rock, her nails pressing against the stone. "And . . ." She leaned back and looked up where she imagined heaven to be.

Still Bum was quiet.

"She did a lot of things wrong." She felt tears begin to leak down her face.

Bum shifted and pulled her up against him. He smelled like the cheap soap from the motel.

"I shouldn't have said that," Wreath hid her face on his chest. "She did her best."

Bum fished out the wrinkled bandanna and gently pushed her head back. His touch as he wiped the tears felt as light as a dragonfly. "She must have been special to have a daughter like you."

Wreath stared into his eyes. Then she leaned forward and kissed his cheek. "Thanks."

He gave an almost undetectable nod. She could hear his breathing close to her face.

Drawing back, she put her fingers in his hair.

"Now what?" he asked.

"Now you have to tell me about those dog bites."

38

Wreath was wedged between Law and Bum in Law's pickup Saturday morning.

With knees pressed together and torso rigid, she stared at the wall of trees whizzing by on the roadside and tried not to brush up against either of them.

The word *awkward* must have been invented for moments such as this. No one was talking. More than a week had passed since Law had gone out with Destiny, and she was due back from Florida this afternoon.

Wreath had worked hard to spend as much time as she could with Law and managed to act cheerful when Destiny Skyped them from a beach house. A beautiful dark-haired cousin hammed it up in front of the camera and prevented any real conversation, which suited Wreath fine. Law had been animated and gave a full report on puppy Jake, who he saw regularly.

Time with Law had opened up since the strange bottle-cave experience with Bum, who had vague *things* to do and left Jaclyn and Samson at Faye's several nights.

Today's ill-tempered road trip evolved after Law mentioned seeing Bum hitch a ride on the highway toward Alexandria. Annoyed at his recklessness—*serial killers pick up hitchhikers, and Jaclyn needs him!*—Wreath called the motel, ready to rip into him. But she softened while on hold. Hadn't she blindly accepted rides with Clarice in the early days?

If Bum needed to get to Alexandria, Wreath would help him.

The concept was better than the reality.

The only conversation came when they pulled out of the Palomino parking lot at ten o'clock sharp. Bum stared out the window as though the front of the Corral captivated him and muttered that he didn't need Law to give him a ride.

"He's happy to take his truck for a drive." Wreath swiveled in the seat. "And we don't usually get to go places on Saturday. Right?"

Law twisted his mouth a fraction of an inch. "Sure thing."

"This is a colossal waste of time, and I've got to get back before dark." Bum's voice sounded like Jaclyn's when she got tired.

Law added a sigh and fooled with the radio, cranking up a Trace Adkins song so loud that a bullhorn would be required for further discussion. Bum's scowl, already etched into Grand-Canyon worthy lines, deepened. He crossed his arms. "I hate country music."

Wreath winced and looked at Law out of the corner of her eye.

"Find a station you like, man," Law said. "It doesn't matter to me."

"Law likes all sorts of music," Wreath said.

Bum shifted his legs toward the door and stared out the window.

Wreath adjusted the station with a sigh and looked at Law. "Thanks for taking off today." Her voice was barely audible over the radio, now blaring a Top 40 hit.

"No sweat. I want to be with you when you take your tour."

Bum straightened. "What tour?"

"A thing at the community college, no big deal," Wreath said. "Where should we drop you? That McDonald's near the hospital?"

"Good as any place." Bum might as well have grunted.

"That's helpful," Law said.

"Give me a break," he said.

"Believe me I'm trying."

Wreath exhaled. "Let's all chill. Why don't we drop him near the hospital, and then we can look around the college—unless you want to see it, too, Bum."

"What use do I have for a college tour?"

"Excellent point," Law said.

Wreath slumped. Sitting between them was like getting too close to the pit bulls Big Fun had kept behind the trailer.

Even the growling sounded familiar.

Bum's lies were catching up with him. If only Wreath weren't so nice. And that Law guy—why would he agree to drive to Alexandria to look for Starla?

He sucked in a breath as the McDonald's appeared, and he snapped his fingers. "Drop me here." Every ounce of his frustration was evident in his voice. "By the emergency entrance."

"Yes, sir," Wreath said with a smirk that managed to look cute.

"At the hospital?" Law's tone was skeptical.

"Isn't that where you look for missing people?" Bum asked.

"Do you think she's hurt?" Wreath sounded . . . concerned.

How did she hold onto that goodness? After that tale she'd told in the bottle cave, he wondered that she wasn't more like his worthless sister.

"Do you want us to go in with you?" Law asked.

And there was this guy. Bum wanted to hate him with his pickup truck and his high-school diploma and the way Wreath looked at him. But Law made it hard. "I'm good," he said.

Law met his gaze. "How about we pick you up here in a couple of hours?"

"I owe you a big one." Bum slid out of the truck and winced when he banged his arm against the truck door.

"Be careful." Wreath scooted to where he had sat, which put distance between her and Law. The movement eased the weight on Bum's chest enough that he could breathe again.

Law turned down the radio. "Good luck."

Bum gave a half-hearted wave and started toward the hospital entrance. He watched until they were headed toward the other side of the building. Then he headed across the busy street.

He knew where his sister was.

He didn't know how to convince her to take care of Jaclyn.

Wreath frowned as she watched the automatic hospital doors slide open. Bum hesitated and stepped back.

"You sure that guy's not scamming you?" Law pulled the truck around a row of parked cars and stopped.

"I don't think so."

"He's connected to Big Fun." Law cleared his throat. "I thought you wanted to steer clear of all that."

"You're right. I don't want to get close to it."

"But?"

"I'm afraid for Jaclyn."

"What if this Bum guy's using her to get close to you?" Law slouched down in the seat. "People use kids all the time to get money for drugs, that kind of thing."

"Bum doesn't use drugs."

"It's not always obvious."

"He's trying to reunite his sister and her little girl. He wouldn't use drugs around Jaclyn."

"You're too close to this. Maybe someone older needs to step in."

"Faye and my grandfather help."

He pulled back.

"What?" she said.

"You usually call him J.D."

She felt her face grow warm. "I guess I'm getting closer to him. Is that wrong, you think? I don't know him very well."

"He's a nice man, and he was your father's father. If you ask me, you should get close to him."

"Then why do you seem, I don't know, annoyed?"

"You're getting awfully attached in all this other stuff."

"Everyone's attached to Jaclyn." She twisted to look at him. "Why'd you bring Bum up here today if you're angry?"

"Because you asked me to." He screwed up his face. "But it seems like you're more attached to Bum than his niece."

Wreath opened her mouth to protest, then closed it. What if Law was right? Bum was the kind of guy she had always intended to avoid.

The silence hung heavy.

"We only have a couple of weeks before I leave for school," Law said. "You're always tied up with a project, some drifter and a kid, saving the store, your grandfather . . ."

"He's not a drifter! Besides, you work, too, and you've been busy with Mitch and Destiny—and that dog. You see Jake more than you do me."

"Only because you spend all your spare time rescuing Bumgardner." Law ran his hands through his hair. "Think about it. We didn't argue like this before he came along."

"Or Destiny and her dog."

"There's nothing going on with me and Destiny," he said. "We've been friends for years. We hang out. That's all." He looked at her. "Can you say the same thing about . . ." He nodded toward the restaurant across the street.

Bum was leaning into the passenger's window of a dented-up car. His left hand was on the top of the car, propping him up. In his right hand, he held a cigarette.

"Is there something going on with you two?"

"Not in the way you're talking about." Wreath's jaw was set. "Can we go look at the campus now?"

Law nodded, turned the radio up and they pulled away.

39

Bum watched the truck turn on the road toward the college, dropped the cigarette and ground it out with those stupid tennis shoes. He hated the raggedy things.

"I'm not," Starla repeated. "I can't."

"You mean you won't."

Her hand fluttered, and she lowered her voice. "Take care of things a little longer, please."

He slammed his hand against the roof of the car.

"Watch it, buddy." The driver played a childish video game on his phone and didn't look up.

"Bum . . ." Starla's voice held that same note she used to keep him from riling their parents. When she spoke again, it was a whisper. "We've got to work out a few things."

"Like how to score some weed or a few dozen pain pills?" He wanted to hit the car again, but who would take care of Jaclyn if he got beat up? And the engine was running. The jerk she'd taken up with would probably run him over.

"There's more to it than that." Her voice was still low.

"I don't have any money. Keeping a kid is expensive," Bum said.

"Those old people you told me about will probably chip in."

His head felt like it might explode. "We're not talking about buying somebody a birthday gift. We're talking about food, clothes . . . she needs to go to school in a few weeks."

"She's a baby. She doesn't have to go yet."

"She's five. That's time for kindergarten."

Starla waved a hand, as though school were as important as what topping to get on a pizza. "She'll catch up."

Why couldn't he have been born to a normal family? Law's parents probably had a college fund for him. And poor Jaclyn. How he wished she would never have to know what her mother was like.

"I can't do this anymore." Bum leaned further into the car, dumbfounded as the driver threw the phone into Starla's lap and glared at him.

"Quit harassing your sister, and take care of your own sickly kid."

"My own—? Starla, what—?"

"Let's get out of here." Her voice sounded panicky.

The driver punched the accelerator, leaving Bum on his butt in the middle of a parking lot—wondering why Fred Procell was out of jail.

And if Wreath knew.

40

The Rapides Parish Community College campus looked smaller in real life than online. Or maybe nothing would look right today.

She and Law had called a truce after the spat over Bum. Maybe that was the most for which to hope.

"Are you sure this is the main part?" she asked as they pulled into the visitor parking area.

"Like Destiny says, it looks like a high school."

Wreath, in the process of opening the truck door, stopped. "When'd she mention that?"

"That summer we took the computer class—me, Destiny and Mitch. We told you about that."

"No, you didn't."

He had the decency to blush. "I forget sometimes that you haven't always lived here."

Wreath stepped out of the truck while he talked.

"We've also come up here for events—'Movies in Moonlight,' a concert, those kinds of deals. It was kind of fun driving up here for those classes."

"Sounds like there's a lot going on here."

"You'll probably like it. Compared to Landry, it's practically New York City." He walked to her side with a sheepish laugh. "It's not so bad. It's just that I wanted you to . . . well, you know what I want."

"I'm not going away to college." She turned her back.

"I'm sorry I was a jerk, Wreath."

She stopped. "I'm sorry I was too."

He reached for her hand. "I bet you love those trees over there. They remind me of that dress you wore to prom."

Her peevishness disappeared quicker than the great blue heron by the campus pond. "They are that color, aren't they?"

She walked closer to the path lined with probably two dozen crape myrtles. Some of the blooms had fallen and looked like pink snow on the ground. "They're almost the color of that big rose bush behind the store too."

Law tilted his head. "Uh, yes?"

She smiled. "The one by the garage apartment where Julia lives."

"I haven't been back there much. I avoid alleys when possible." He looked at her. "I guess you heard that she's going away for her master's?"

"Unfortunately, yes."

Law swung their arms as they walked through the corridor of trees. "You okay with that?"

"She didn't exactly ask my permission. We had a cryfest the other day with Faye."

He put his arm around her waist. "You should have called me," he said. "My shoulders are your shoulders."

"I started to but . . ." Truth was, she'd gotten caught up with Bum. "I wish everyone could stay put." She stepped back, not enough to slip out of his embrace but enough to see his face. "Don't you?"

"Only you. I'm going to miss you a lot."

The afternoon sun shone on the campus. Light rippled off the water. The buildings, not historic in the least, looked almost stately instead of institutional. She couldn't quite picture herself here yet but that would come.

A big rabbit nibbled on grass near the edge, and Law pointed toward it. "That's a good sign."

"My lucky rabbit?"

"It means there aren't any predators around. He feels safe."

"That's the kind of place I want." She smiled and nodded toward a three-story building near the front of the campus, where a couple of students walked. "Do you think the library's open?"

"Looks that way."

"Ooh," Wreath said. "Nerd attack. Can we go in?"

He grinned and ruffled her hair. "You're the only person I know who gets excited about so many different things. I like that."

"Did you use the library when you took those classes?"

"Mostly to play computer games," he said, "while Destiny flirted with our classmates."

"You didn't flirt too?"

"I was too shy," he said. "Besides I was waiting for you to come along."

A wave of gratitude washed over her as they stepped into the cool, quiet space. "Ditto," she whispered.

Bum was waiting when they pulled up in front of the hospital. He stared at something in his hand.

As they drew closer, Wreath saw that it was an unopened pack of cigarettes.

He slid them in the side pocket of his cargo pants as they rolled to a stop and climbed in without a word.

"Hello to you too," Wreath said.

"Hey," he said.

"Hey," Law said.

"I guess you forgot you don't smoke, huh?" Wreath said.

"Leave me alone," Bum muttered. He sat so close to the truck door that Wreath feared he'd tumble out—if he didn't jump first.

No one spoke again until Law navigated to the edge of the parking lot. "Need to stop anywhere else?" he asked. "Food, anything?"

Bum peered past McDonald's. "Could we stop over there?" he asked. "It won't take a minute."

"Sure." Law turned on his blinker and eased out. "In the mood for a Big Mac?"

"Not McDonald's. That pet store over there."

This was different. "Something wrong with Samson?" Wreath asked.

"Nah. Need some preventative stuff."

"No worries," Law said and pulled across the highway. "Wreath and I'll wait here."

Within minutes, Bum was back in the truck, his hands empty.

"No luck?" Wreath asked.

He patted his cargo pants pocket, which rattled. "Found what I was looking for."

"Any other stops?" Law asked.

"Not for me," he said.

"I'm good," Wreath said and inched closer to Law. She was better than good after their afternoon. They had strolled through the library, then grabbed Natchitoches meat pies at a cute diner. They talked more than they had in days and covered more subjects than Faye's church friends who stopped by the store.

Only the topic of Law's upcoming departure, three weeks away, was skirted.

"So . . . your sister?" Law broke the silence. "Anything we can do?"

"Nah," Bum said and stared out the side window.

"So you didn't see her?" Wreath asked.

"I saw her."

"She's coming later then?" Wreath asked, but Law gave a quick shake of his head.

"I don't want to talk about it," Bum said.

"What about Jaclyn? Are you bringing her up here?"

"Hey, Wreath," Law said softly. "You should probably let this go for now."

"Thanks, man," Bum mumbled. He leaned his wild shrub of hair back on the headrest, eyes closed.

Wreath looked from him to Law, who searched for a different radio station.

The sound of an "Alabama Shakes" song, raw and mournful, filled the cab. Until she met Law, Mitch and Destiny, Wreath hadn't known anything about popular music, had never been to a concert and had only seen two movies in a theater, both long-ago cartoons with her grandmother.

Bum's breathing evened out, and his mouth dropped open. He looked like she probably had that first day Clarice picked her up on the road. Wreath had been tired and over-wrought. *Was that how he felt?*

Law rested his hand on her leg for a moment and gave her a sweet smile.

"How'd you know his sister wasn't coming back?" she whispered.

"I took your advice and listened instead of judging." His voice was barely discernible over the song.

"But he didn't say anything."

"That's usually how people tell you the most," Law said and put his hand back on the wheel.

41

If Law's theory was right, Bum must be telling them a lot. He spoke exactly zero words until they reached the outskirts of town.

"Can you drop me at the Palomino?" he asked.

"Sure," Law said.

As they pulled through the breezeway, the courtyard looked peaceful, no one out on their steps. The door was closed to the cottage where Linda and Half-Pint lived. The big oaks swayed, and a squirrel scampered up one of the branches.

"Down there." Wreath motioned to the room where Bum and Jaclyn lived.

"Thanks," Law said.

Bum didn't say anything else until he climbed out and closed the truck door. Then he leaned on it, like he'd leaned on the car in that parking lot in Alexandria. "You think Miss Faye'll mind keeping Jaclyn a night or two more?"

"She can stay as long as you need. We like having her," Wreath said.

"She loves you." He looked at the ground as he said the kind words. "Tell her I miss her, and I'll get her as quick as I can." His face had grown almost as red as his hair.

"We'll take good care of her. I promise."

"Another thing." He looked up, past her, still not letting his eyes meet hers.

"Anything."

"I need to talk to you for a second."

Wreath moved across the seat, but he held up his hand. "Not you. Him."

He nodded at Law, who raised his eyebrows.

"Fire away," Law said.

"Privately," Bum said. "It won't take a sec."

"Really?" Wreath asked.

"Really."

Law shrugged, opened the door and stepped out. With his clean-cut good looks and lithe movements, he was startlingly out-of-place against the rundown cottage. Even though his trailer wasn't all that much better.

Looking around, Bum jerked his head toward the end of the row of cottages, and they stepped almost out of sight. Bum alternately scanned the courtyard and looked at Law. The two huddled close, and each spoke in clipped tones, their words too low to distinguish. A short way into their discussion, Law exclaimed and turned toward the truck at almost a run, but Bum grabbed his arm.

Only years of staying out of Frankie's tense situations kept Wreath from flying out of the truck. She held her breath and waited to see who would throw the first punch.

Law finally nodded and looked around the courtyard as Bum had earlier. Their conversation resumed.

Both now faced Wreath.

After a curious ten minutes, they shook hands and approached the truck. Each was tight-jawed, movements controlled. When Law skirted the front of the truck, he was looking around the courtyard like Bum had done earlier. *Was still doing.*

Bum walked up to the passenger door, both hands in his pockets, and looked at Wreath for the first time since they'd picked him up. "Law's a good guy," he said. Then he dropped the pack of cigarettes in her lap. "I try not to smoke."

Without another word, he turned and walked into the room.

Law stood and watched him until the door clicked shut, then climbed into the cab of the truck.

"What was that all about?" Wreath asked.

He started the truck and revved the engine. Then he punched the electric door locks. "I wish you'd never gotten mixed up with Bumgardner," he said.

"That's obvious from the flames shooting out of your eyes. Tell me something I don't know."

"This isn't a joke, Wreath."

"So noted."

His lips pressed together. "Unfortunately you're in too deep to back out now."

"What are you talking about?" She glanced back at the cottages. By nightfall residents would line the steps. "I told you there's nothing between us."

Law put the truck in gear and peeled out. Gravel peppered the empty porches. "He'll either get you killed or be the only thing that can save you from Big Fun. Only time will tell."

42

Faye was reading Jaclyn a story when Wreath and Law got back. J.D. sat at the kitchen table with a piece of paper and a pencil. *Yet another thing he and Wreath had in common.*

"There you are," Faye said. "We were five minutes away from sending out a search party."

"I's learning how to read," Jaclyn said and hardly looked up. "Miss Faye says I can go to school." She turned to Faye. "When? When do I get my school supplies?"

Of course. Jaclyn needed to go to school. Wreath hadn't thought of that. She wondered if Bum had.

"Everything all right?" J.D. walked into the living room as he spoke. His smile faded as he soaked up Wreath's face. He could read her in an instant.

"You'll have to ask Law. He seems to know some kind of secret," she said.

Law looked from J.D. to Faye to Jaclyn, who flipped through a book. She pretended to read, making up words.

"Look how late it is," Faye chirped. Her voice was a blend of cautious cheer. "We'd better get Miss Jaclyn to bed."

"I don't want to go to bed." The bottom lip came out. Then she grew still, and an apprehensive look crossed a face that should have been all innocence. "I want Bum."

"He . . ." Wreath didn't know what he was doing. She glared at Law, who looked the way he had the day she ran away. He had driven home from the motel like a crazy person, weaving through town like he was on the run. Wreath had perfected similar evasive moves on foot the year before.

"He had to work tonight," Law said. With a baffled look on his face, he pulled out his wallet. "But he said he'll buy you a treat when he gets finished." He handed the child a ten-dollar bill, and in that moment Wreath forgot how annoyed she was with him.

Jaclyn grabbed the money and her bottom lip morphed from pout to tremble. "I miss Mommy."

Wreath knelt down. She'd learned to recognize when a meltdown was brewing. "You want me to tuck you in?"

"Can I sleep in your bed?" Jaclyn swabbed at her eyes, and Wreath moved in to hug her.

"You and Samson both." She picked Jaclyn up and carried her toward the bedroom. The dog hobbled behind them.

"I can do that," Faye said.

"I want to."

As she reached the hallway, she turned and pointed a Bum-worthy scowl at Law. "You'd better not tell them anything until I get back."

"Are the doors locked?" she heard him ask as she drew out of sight.

43

Bum punched the pillow instead of punching the wall. Darkness had settled on the Palomino courtyard, and the Saturday-night crowd at the Corral was lively.

He cleaned the bites, changed clothes and tried to take a nap. He even scrawled Jaclyn a note on a fast-food napkin. *Just in case.*

Theriot should be here any minute.

The temptation to destroy the entire room consumed him but he figured he'd break his hand. He wouldn't give Theriot that satisfaction.

Another choice would be to put the pillow over Fred Procell's smirking face. That would be a pleasure.

That maniac shouldn't be out of jail, much less chauffeuring Starla around. Theriot would be furious when he found out. And that seemed inevitable.

When had his sister gotten so messed up?

And poor Wreath. She didn't deserve Big Fun on the loose.

Bum groaned. How humiliating to ask Law to protect her.

Being around Wreath when she was caught up with Law was torture. If she looked at Bum one time like she looked at Law, he was fairly certain he'd drool like Samson with a bone.

When Law sped out from the motel, taking Wreath, Bum wanted to vomit. And yet he'd handed her over to Law like some country-club gentleman. They'd shaken hands on it. On her.

He felt like he'd given away the only chance he had for something decent in his life.

What else could he have done?

With the Theriot explosion ahead, he didn't trust himself to keep Wreath safe.

But, oh, how he wanted to.

Then there was Jaclyn to think about.

Providing for a kid was way harder than he'd realized, harder even than putting up with his sister's BS.

Maybe he couldn't raise Jaclyn . . . but who could?

Wreath was headed to college, and she was younger than he was. Faye and J.D. were old. His parents were worthless. He wouldn't leave one of Theriot's dogs in their care.

What if Jaclyn got put somewhere with people who didn't love her?

He flopped on the sagging mattress, his hands behind his head. He would have to gather up Jaclyn's things. His were crap. Maybe he'd throw everything in the Dumpster behind the Corral. Start over from scratch.

Wreath—*God, she was sweet*—would make sure Jaclyn had what she needed. And Bum would probably be given a new set of clothes in jail, where he was pretty sure he was headed.

He pulled out the package from the pet store and read the enclosure.

Bum had expected to be calmer.

It was after nine p.m., and he knew what he had to do. He had outlined it and planned the timeframe. He wanted to get it over with.

One way or another.

He fingered the package again.

The thought of all that lay ahead—Theriot's orders, the dogs, the violence—kept getting pushed aside by Wreath and Jaclyn. They exhausted his brain. Wreath and Jaclyn. Wreath and Jaclyn. Their names, their faces, whirled through his mind. How was he going to protect them?

It would come down to Jaclyn. That he knew. She needed him more.

He would get away from Theriot somehow and provide for her like a parent should. She needed to go to school, have a room of her own, eat meals that included vegetables other than French fries.

He could get his GED and check out that junior college Wreath and Law visited today. *Was that only this morning?* Wreath would help him with his application. That much he knew.

Knowing her, she would even try to help him with his homework. *And wasn't that a nice thought?* Wreath looking over his shoulder, her long hair brushing against his face, her cit-rus-y scent making math bearable.

The dream world encroached on his common sense—until lights swept the front of the cottage. He glanced through the blinds. Theriot's big truck sat by the porch.

In the next few hours, he would finish things with Theriot. Then he could worry about what would happen if Big Fun found out about Jaclyn.

He hoped he'd be alive for that battle.

44

Wreath didn't cry—not that Law expected her to. She was the bravest girl—person—he'd ever met.

But he thought Faye and J.D. might have a heart attack.

On that winding drive from the Palomino a few hours ago, he considered not telling them. No way would Big Fun be dumb enough to show his face around Landry again.

That hulk was known for meanness, not intelligence.

So now, with Jaclyn asleep and the house bolted shut, Law jumped up from the couch to look out the window. Bum's news about Fred Procell had been revealed. It had gotten dark, and the cicadas were loud. It felt like the middle of the night, but the clock said it wasn't quite nine p.m. Not even a dozen hours had passed since they'd picked Bum up for the drive to Alexandria.

Law should have driven in the other direction. He'd nearly taken Wreath into the arms of the man who could most hurt her.

She hovered in the middle of the room—where she had catapulted as soon as Big Fun's name was uttered. She looked bewildered.

J.D. rushed to her side and stood with his hand on her shoulder. Faye hurried to the phone to try to find Clarice, who should have gotten back earlier in the day.

"What a horrible thing to come home to," Wreath said quietly. "She and Sam spend weeks helping those good people, and she gets hit with this."

"She'll want to help you," Faye said, hitting redial. Her mouth was twisted in frustration.

"She shouldn't have to keep jumping into my drama."

The sharp corner of one of Jaclyn's books poked Law's back and almost felt good. Maybe physical pain trumped psychological torment.

At least the little girl was asleep.

A lump came into Law's throat. *Was this what Wreath's life had been like?* Always in the middle of a crisis? And her mother gone.

He swallowed and willed himself not to let tears form.

When his phone buzzed, he wasn't surprised to see that it was his grandfather. That man had super powers when it came to knowing Law needed him.

Or maybe Faye had slipped in a call. His grandparents loved Wreath for bringing Faye back to them after her husband died. She'd been nearly a recluse until Wreath came along—a grumpy, not very pleasant recluse. Beyond that, Wreath was his grandfather's all-time favorite library patron.

"Hey, Pops," Law said in a low voice. "I thought you'd be calling."

"So you've heard?" His grandfather's voice was hoarse.

"I'm over here now."

"With your mother?" Pops sounded confused.

"With Wreath. At Miss Faye's."

"So Wreath's going with you to the hospital?"

"The hospital?"

As Law said the word *hospital*, Wreath and J.D. looked up, heads cocked.

"To see your mom."

"She's in the hospital?" This day had just gotten worse, a feat he'd not thought possible.

"She's at Waterside in Lafayette. Your grandmother and I are headed there now. I thought you might like to ride with us."

"What happened?"

His grandfather sounded old and tired. Defeated. "She should be fine, but they're not sure about the extent of her injuries."

"Injuries?" The word was high-pitched, like someone else had uttered it.

"I'm sorry, Lawson. I should be telling you this in person. When you said you knew—"

"What kind of injuries?" Law interrupted.

"She was in an . . ." His stalwart grandfather's voice trembled. "She was in an accident. A bad accident."

He could hear his grandmother in the background. She told him they needed to hurry. With his mother, it could be anything. "A car wreck?" Law asked.

"Let us come get you."

"Was she alone?"

"Her boyfriend was there." He cleared his throat. "I don't know . . . he . . . there's no other way to say it—he was killed." When the words finally came out, they were rushed. "Police say he was speeding, lost control."

"Drunk, no doubt," Law said. That monster had lost control years before and been in the process of taking Law's mother with him. He felt a wave of relief, followed by almost physical guilt.

"Lawson? We're headed that way."

"But I have my truck here."

"You can get it later. We need to hurry."

"I'll be waiting," he said woodenly and disconnected the call. Wreath took a step toward him, her expression stricken. J.D. looked pale.

"I struck out," Faye said, walking in from the other room. "Neither Julia nor Shane picked up either. Clarice's flight was held up by that storm in the Gulf, but they're due in New Orleans any minute. Her father's driving them back."

"Wait." Wreath held up her hand. "Law, what happened?"

He felt dazed. "Mom's been in an accident. My grandparents are headed over to pick me up."

"Do you need me to drive you somewhere?" Wreath asked.

He shook his head. Had that overhead light always been this bright? He squinted, then swabbed at his eyes. "Even if I did, you don't drive. Remember?"

She dipped her head. "Do you want my *grandfather* to drive you somewhere?"

"Happy to do so," J.D. said.

"Oh, Law," Faye said, "what can we do for you?"

"Could you keep trying to reach Shane?" he asked. "And Clarice? I'm afraid that Wreath's in danger. Big Fun wasn't happy when she put him in jail."

Wreath caught his gaze. "We should be thinking about your mother, not about me."

He gave a nod and met her in the middle of the den. His feet felt heavy, like his shoes were bricks, and he was relieved when Wreath extended her arms.

With a sigh of defeat, he stepped into her embrace, and they drew each other close.

If only the world would stop now.

"Do you want to sit down?" she asked.

He shook his head. "I need to reach Bumgardner. I'm calling in that favor."

45

Wreath needed answers. And she had to save Bum from whatever scheme he was working. He'd given Law just enough information to petrify her.

The only thing to do was to sneak out of the house.

That idea, which scattered goose bumps down her arm, almost collapsed when her grandfather bedded down on the living room sofa.

He had refused to leave "his girls" until they knew what Big Fun was up to. Clarice had been distressed when she called from the airport to say that he had been released and Wreath needed to be vigilant.

What good was vigilance when he always showed up?

Wreath shuddered.

Jaclyn was, thank goodness, sound asleep in the middle of Wreath's bed, an arm slung over Samson and a smile on her face. At least there was total peace in her sleep.

Law had called at about eleven o'clock. His mother was in surgery, and he would be allowed to see her early Sunday morning.

"What happened?" Wreath asked.

"I'll tell you tomorrow. It's too awful to talk about over the phone." He sounded wrung out.

"Do you want me to come sit with you? J.D. would bring me."

"No! You need to stay put," he said. "Did you hear from Shane or Bumgardner?"

Wreath fiddled with Faye's clunky cordless phone. "Not yet, but Faye talked to Clarice, who got in touch with the district attorney's office. They were supposed to notify us. Big Fun's charges were reduced."

"Reduced? What kind of fool would do that?"

"He made bail and can stay out of jail until his trial, whenever that is."

"He killed someone!"

"Apparently they're having a hard time getting evidence to prove it." She hesitated. "But we can talk about this later—"

"I want to hear now. This matters. You matter." His words were fierce, injected with a spurt of energy.

"He has an alibi. Someone who vouches for him."

"What kind of worm would vouch for him?"

"I don't know," she said. "Some woman says they were together."

"You need a guard," Law said.

At this, Wreath could not hold back a small laugh. "The only guard I want is you," she said. "I've dealt with him before. I can handle it."

The snort wasn't flattering. "He could have killed you," Law said. "Isn't there anything Clarice can do? A restraining order, something like that?"

"Have you been watching police shows with Faye and J.D.?"

His voice was quiet. "Quit, Wreath. This is beyond serious."

"We'll figure something out. Clarice is coming over tomorrow afternoon. You should focus on your mom and grandparents. You sound beat."

"Did you leave a message for Bumgardner? Did you give him my number?"

"You're not listening, Law. This is under control."

"Bumgardner?" he almost growled.

She sighed. "He didn't pick up in his room, and someone at the office said he wouldn't be back until late—right before she hung up on me."

"Try again," he said. "I want him to stay with y'all until I get back."

"Now that's a change."

"Big Fun tried to hurt you. We've got to pull together."

"Please, Law. Get some rest." She wished she could pull him close, the way they had stood right before his grandparents picked him up. "My grandfather's staying tonight, keeping watch from the couch."

"Bumgardner's younger and stronger."

While they talked, Wreath looked from the kitchen into the den, where J.D. and Faye were watching an old movie. "J.D. would jump off a building to save me, and you know it," she said. Her words were muffled when she cupped the receiver with her hand.

"There's safety in numbers. Try Bumgardner again."

Instead she whispered a prayer for healing for Law's mom and calm for his family—and sat on the edge of the bed with her diary. The hall light cast barely enough light to see by.

Dear Brownie, WHAT WOULD FRANKIE DO?

Then with determination Wreath drew a heavy line through the words.

Her hand was steady when she started anew:

> *WHAT SHOULD WW DO? Here's the deal—*
> *Summer is almost over. I will start college headfirst,*
> *no more looking back.*
> *—Tired of giving Big Fun control over my life.*
> *Terrified Bum's in trouble. What will happen to*
> *Jaclyn?*
> *—What's Bum's plan? Faye, J.D., Clarice, even Law*
> *will help him and Jaclyn.*

She chewed on her pen.

> *Everyone looks out for me, and it's time I step up.*
> *—Make sure Jaclyn gets registered in kindergarten.*
> *—Talk to J.D. about my dad.*
> *—Have a romantic date with Law. I want things to*
> *be perfect when he leaves.*

Her pen hovered over the page as she considered the next entry. With a deep breath, she put the point down. The ink blobbed onto the page, soaking through.

Even on paper, Big Fun was a blight.

Enough. Enough. Enough.

She printed in small, tidy letters. *Prepare to testify.* *I'M STRONG! TRUTH! FACE THIS SCUM BAG!*

She put the cap on the pen and quietly closed the journal. Her fingers stroked the familiar cover, and she watched Jaclyn and Samson sleep. Neither stirred.

She slipped her feet into her shoes and stood.

She had to find Bum.

46

The door didn't creak when Wreath slipped into the carport.

She had counted on that.

With J.D. around, hinges, locks, door handles and other contraptions didn't stand a chance of malfunctioning.

What she hadn't predicted were the big fat flat tires on her bicycle.

She hadn't ridden the bike yesterday, but the tires had been fine the day before. Now they were flatter than her hair after she wore a hat.

It was nearly midnight, and J.D. and Faye rose with the songbirds. Wreath had to be back and tucked in with Jaclyn no later than five. If they discovered her missing, they would be crazy worried. And mad, Faye especially.

Reaching for her pump, she grabbed nothing but air. *Where was the thing?* It had sat there every day since she'd moved in.

"Wreath and her air pump are never parted," Law liked to joke.

Her eyes widened.

Law! He knew her better than she thought.

When she eased back into the house, she nearly jumped onto the counter as the icemaker kicked on. She drew in a shaky breath, pushed the back door shut—and spotted Law's truck keys on the hook by the door.

Wreath shook her head. *That would be wrong.*

She padded back toward her bedroom and paused to peek in at her grandfather on the couch. It was the first time Wreath had seen him sleeping, and she had a childish urge to curl up against him.

From fourth grade, she had wondered about her daddy. Looking at her grandfather, her heart righted itself.

J.D. had fixed her unanswered questions, like he fixed everything else.

As she watched, he stirred, his frame too long for the formal sofa. For an instant she thought his Wreath-intuition had roused him. But the whimsical idea evaporated as he settled back, his breathing soft.

Faye would be happy to know he didn't snore.

Wreath blew him a silent kiss and backed out of the room.

Then, ignoring her conscience, she headed back toward the kitchen.

The keys on the hook pulled her gaze. Yes, they were really there.

She knew what she had to do.

One of Frankie's enthusiastic boyfriends had let her drive home from middle school once, eager to win Wreath's approval. She shoved out of her mind the ensuing fracas with Frankie. The boyfriend never came around again.

That, plus Law's quick lessons in the school parking lot, would be good enough. She was seventeen and a quick learner. *Of course she could drive.* All kids her age did.

After tiptoeing to the kitchen counter, she scribbled a nearly illegible note of apology and reached up.

"Where you going?"

The voice was a million times worse than the ice machine, and Wreath gave an Olympics quality jump into the air. She clutched her chest and whirled around.

"Oh, my goodness, Jaclyn," she said in a hushed voice. "You scared me to death."

"Were you leaving me?" Jaclyn asked in a squeaky voice. Her trembling lower lip was visible from the nightlight on the stove.

"No," Wreath whispered and put her finger to her lips. "We have to be quiet. Miss Faye and Mr. J.D. are sleeping."

"Where you going?" Jaclyn had lowered her voice but punctuated the question with a small stamp of her bare foot.

"I was getting a drink of water," Wreath whispered. Frankie had often used that excuse when Wreath caught someone coming or going at odd hours.

"Did you pee on yourself?" Jaclyn's eyes were round.

"Uh, no?"

"Why don't you have your jammies on?"

Looking down at the black T-shirt and blue-jean shorts, Wreath chewed on her lip. "I got hot in my PJs."

"Where's your water glass?"

Has Jaclyn been watching detective TV too?

"I was getting it out of the cabinet." Wreath tried not to look at the clock. She had a lot to do in a short amount of time.

"Then why were you by the back door?"

"It was dark."

"But Miss Faye left the stove light on 'cause she knows I'm scared of the dark."

Wreath loved this child like the little sister she'd never had.

Right now she wanted her back in bed, asleep, fast. If this escapade worked, there'd be plenty of time to answer her questions. "I guess I made a wrong turn," Wreath said. "I'm not even thirsty anymore."

"I am," Jaclyn said.

Wreath squeezed her eyes closed for a split second, then turned toward the cupboard and pulled out one of Faye's old jelly glasses with a cartoon character on it. "Here you go, princess," she whispered.

"Thank you." Jaclyn's voice had gone tiny and sleepy.

"We'd better head back to bed before it's time to get up."

"I wish Uncle Bum would come home."

"He will, sweetie. He will."

By the time Jaclyn fell back asleep, nearly pushing Wreath off the bed with her sprawl, it was closing in on one o'clock.

On the positive side, surely Bum would be back at the Palomino by now. When they had dropped him off earlier, he'd been silent to Wreath and nebulous to Law about where he was headed.

According to Law, it had something to do with Theriot but that wasn't much to go on. And no one did business this late, did they?

Wreath pulled the covers around Jaclyn's shoulders. "Watch over her," she prayed. "Help me too," she added.

Then she glided down the hall.

Step one: She confirmed that J.D. was still asleep.

Next: She lifted Law's keys off the hook.

And she headed out.

Starting the pickup was tricky. The ignition protested when she turned it too far. How could she save Bum if she couldn't get out of the driveway?

When the motor started, it sounded like a jet in the quiet night.

Planting her foot firmly on the brake, she shifted into reverse. A long buried memory surfaced when she reached for the lights. She and her mama were slipping away in the night with her grandmother at the wheel.

"Don't turn on the lights," Frankie had said in an urgent whisper.

"Do you think I'm stupid?" her grandmother barked. "When will you grow out of these messes?"

The memory boosted her resolve, and Wreath eased off the brake.

The truck rolled back slower than her bicycle. Emboldened, she touched the gas pedal and nearly took out Faye's mailbox. At that, she hit the brake so hard she almost decapitated herself with the seatbelt.

Her hands sweated when she gripped the steering wheel and lifted her foot off the brake. Her use of the pedals had finesse this time, and she steered onto the street. Not a car was in sight, so she put the vehicle in drive and touched the accelerator. When the truck didn't roll more than a few inches, she pressed it harder and smiled as she picked up speed.

Mildly confident, she puttered down the street slower than Faye in a school zone.

When she met a car, though, she panicked and swerved to the curb. Could it be the police? Would they arrest her for driving without a license?

A single newspaper sailed from the car, then another. *So that's how the newspaper wound up in Faye's driveway each morning.*

Her resolve soared as she headed toward the Palomino, and she braked smoothly at a red light and a stop sign. Driving wasn't hard at all.

The parking lot at the Corral was still full, something she'd not counted on for a stealth visit. *How late did people in this town drink?* Too timid to navigate through the narrow breezeway, she pulled to the curb and climbed out of the truck.

"Hey, cutie pie, where you heading?" a man called. He held a beer can and staggered toward her.

She jerked back and slammed the door, then wondered if she should have stayed in the truck.

"You looking for some fun?" he called as another guy walked up next to him.

She didn't answer but watched, glad to have the truck between them.

"Snotty, are we?" The drunk headed her way.

Her pulse raced. "I'm meeting someone," she called out. There was not anyone else in sight, and the motel office was dark.

"I bet you are." The guy kept coming in her direction, but his buddy hesitated. Wreath knew a lot about avoiding traps, and she debated whether to go on into the courtyard.

"Come on, Mike, let's get out of here," the other guy said. "You don't want to get pulled over again."

"Ain't gonna happen." The response was slurred, and he swatted at his friend.

"If we leave now, we can still catch some of the action."
The other guy shoved *Mike* as he spoke. "Woof. Woof."

"Hey," Mike's protest lacked heat. He lifted a hand in
Wreath's direction and shot her the bird. "I'll be back tomorrow if you change your mind."

"Ain't gonna happen," she mimicked under her breath
and scurried into the courtyard. She cut a wide berth around
the bar as she headed toward Bum's room.

47

Linda's door stood open, despite the late hour. She sat on the porch, a beer in one hand, glowing cigarette in the other. "You're not very bright, are you?" she asked.

That was rich.

"Have you seen Bum?"

"Girl, you're in way over your head." Linda drew on the cigarette and blew smoke into the hot night air.

Wreath crossed her arms. "I'm seventeen."

Her laugh was sarcastic. "Acting like it too. This isn't any place for kids."

"Your son lives here." Wreath had had enough of people telling her what she should and shouldn't do.

"That's different." Linda studied the end of her cigarette. "There aren't exactly a world of places for him to go." She took a sip of beer. "Get out of here while you can."

Wreath shook her head and walked toward number 22. The cabin, like most of the others, was dark.

"Bum isn't coming back." Linda's voice was low and hoarse. "If you want to keep that sweet body of yours in one piece, you won't either."

Wreath swiveled and planted her feet on the gravel driveway. "Where'd he go?"

After two puffs on the cigarette, Linda spoke. "He's with Theriot."

"Where?"

"You're even stupider than I thought."

"I'm trying to help his . . . nephew." Wreath stared her down.

"Info will cost you."

Wreath fished a few dollars out of her pocket—and couldn't feel the truck keys. Where were they? She tried to act nonchalant but patted and dug in her pocket. Nothing but the money.

Linda grabbed at the bills and shook her head all the while. "I want something else."

"Beer? Cigarettes?" Wreath had never bought either.

"Bum says you might be able to find a place for Half-Pint to go, like a school or something."

"He did?"

"Can you?"

"I know some people," Wreath said after a minute.

"Yes or no?"

"Maybe." She waited a beat. "Probably." She'd yet to meet a person in need that someone in her group wouldn't help. "I'll have to learn more about your son, though." Car doors slammed in the bar parking lot, and the sounds of carousing drifted back to them. "Uh, can we do this later?" Wreath said.

"How do I know you'll come back?"

"Because I don't lie." *Not anymore.*

The bar noises crescendoed. It must be closing in on two o'clock.

Linda looked at her for what seemed like half an hour. Wreath's heart raced. "I haven't trusted anyone since my Mamaw got herself run over."

The need to hurry and a sense of compassion clashed. "My grandmother died too," Wreath said finally. "I'll find a way to help Half-Pint."

The woman lit another cigarette from the glowing end of the one she smoked and blew out a careless cloud of smoke. "Bum's at the big dog fight," she said in a voice hard to hear over the Corral drunks.

Wreath stared at her.

"Hasn't Mr. Cutie told you? He works for Theriot. Tonight's his last big job." She gave a harsh laugh. "Like anyone gets away from Theriot."

Law had been right. Bum wasn't to be trusted. No wonder he was covered with dog bites. The image of the puppies at the State Park and Samson asleep on her bed raced through her mind.

She had to choke out her question. "Where is the fight?"

Linda snorted. "That info would get me and you both hurt." She rose. "Let me hear when you find a place to help my boy. And if you tell anyone I told you that much, sister, I'll bust your face."

With that, she walked in the room and slammed the door so loud the frame shook.

"I hope Half-Pint isn't sleeping," Wreath muttered and headed for the truck, digging in her pockets again for the keys. Still nothing. Had she left them—? *Oh no.*

48

Wreath's wild imagination urged her forward.
Would the truck be stolen? Driven off courtesy of
keys left dangling from the ignition?

She was tempted to cover her eyes as she walked beyond
the office and into the parking lot.

Her legs wobbled.

Law's beloved truck sat where she'd left it.

Whew. That could have been the end of her already precarious relationship with Law.

She eyed it timidly, like it was an animal she couldn't control. Then she looked at the pavement and scoured the parking lot. The glint of metal in the dirt caused her to run.

But it was the cap to a beer bottle, not Law's keys.

She swallowed and peered in the window.

The keys, complete with the monogrammed keychain Law had gotten from an aunt for graduation, dangled from the ignition.

Thank goodness.

With relief, she jerked at the door—and nearly wrenched her arm off. It was locked.

It was that stupid Mike guy's fault. She'd *locked* the keys in the truck in the middle of the night. Even the drunks had disappeared, leaving her alone in front of the crummy motel.

The bar was still open but entering that place at this hour would be her last resort.

Where there's a Willis there's a way. She hadn't pulled out her mother's mantra lately, and it reassured her.

She circled the truck. The passenger door! She hurried to it and tugged.

Locked.

There had to be a way in.

A climb into the truck bed was easy, and she tapped on the back window. How much would it cost to replace this? And would Law forgive her if she busted it? What choice did she have?

She balanced on the tailgate and hopped out of the truck, planting her feet on the ground with the precision of a gymnastics pro. A ten-point-oh. Maybe she should trade her marketing studies for a sport.

Wreath hugged the edge of the buildings as she scampered back into the courtyard. Her head jerked up and down like a yo-yo as she looked from the cottages to the ground. No one was in sight, but she had run long enough to know that people stepped out of shadows.

She was developing a full-blown case of the creeps, so bad that she would have been happy to see Linda emerge from her cottage. It too was dark.

Next to a garbage can filled with what looked like congealed grease, she found a large rock. It was slippery when she picked it up, and she winced. By the time she fell back into the truck bed, she was sweating and wishing for a sink of hot soapy water.

The window propped her up while she caught her breath, and Wreath acknowledged that she had failed. She had gotten swept along, caught up in the frenzy of the summer, and thought she could save Bum. She couldn't even find him.

This wasn't the action of an honors graduate bound for college. You wouldn't find Destiny out like this.

This was the way . . . this was the way Frankie had acted.

DNA followed you no matter where you ran.

But she wasn't that person. She wouldn't smash the window.

Steadying herself with one hand on the roof Wreath prepared to jump down—and noticed the moon roof that Law was so proud of. The *open* moon roof.

She could fit. Sure she could.

Her arms trembled as she hoisted herself onto the roof and slid on her stomach. Should she go in head or feet first?

Feet seemed more dignified.

She snuffled, on the verge of hysteria.

Head first was the only workable option, and she lowered her torso into the opening, legs straight up in the air. In hindsight, jeans would have been a better wardrobe choice than short shorts.

She had hindsight, all right.

Thank goodness good old Mike and buddies weren't still around to see her heinie up in the air.

Her muscles screamed but she was a glorious few inches from being reunited with the keys.

Then she heard a door slam.

Then the voice.

"What in the name of crap are you doing?"

49

W reath, body contorted, peered out the windshield. She was upside-down and could only see a leather belt and khaki shorts.

There was no mistaking that voice, though, no matter how enraged it sounded.

Lawson Rogers stood in front of his truck. Destiny's blue Toyota sat in the shadows.

Wreath shifted to see better, her rump in the air.

Law gawked back.

To say he did not look pleased would be like saying the Palomino was a five-star hotel. His adorable face, an odd shade of yellow under the streetlight, wore an expression that mixed haggard with furious.

Squirming down into the cab, harder than anticipated, Wreath bit her lip until she tasted blood. While she righted herself, Law marched toward the driver's door.

For a half-second she considered not opening it.

But Wreath Willis was better than that.

She looked over at Destiny's car.

Or was she?

Law jerked on the door handle. His face grew, if possible, more outraged.

Wreath turned and met his eyes.

"Open the door," he said. "Wreath—"

The locks made a popping sound as she clicked them, and he yanked the door open but didn't sit down.

"How's your mother?" she asked.

The question seemed to throw him, and the hostile look on his face eased momentarily. "Stable. They took her to ICU after surgery, suggested we come back tomorrow." As he finished the sentence, his mouth tightened. "What—?" He stopped. "What are you—?"

He covered his face with his hands, and the sight made Wreath shrink. "Shouldn't you get some rest?" she said.

"I should." He dropped his arms to his sides and glared at her. "I would if you were safe at home in bed. Where. You. Are. Supposed. To. Be."

"You told me to contact Bum."

"You're not honestly saying this latest insanity is my fault?"

Latest?

He was wound up. "You drove my truck to this dump? After I practically begged you to stay put?" Law ran his hands through his hair, making it stick up Bum-like.

"You shouldn't have let the air out of my bike tires," she said.

It wasn't much, but it was the best she had.

"I drove home from Lafayette to make sure you were safe," Law said.

Wreath felt about as small as one of Jaclyn's new Polly Pocket dolls. "Thank you." Words couldn't convey her level of misery. "I wouldn't have taken your truck if I'd known you'd be home tonight."

"You think this is about my truck? After I find you exposing yourself in front of a bar in the middle of the night?" Law closed his eyes. When he opened them, she braced herself for more. "Could you for one day in your entire life—just one—not take on the whole world by yourself?"

Wreath coughed. There seemed to be something stuck in her throat. "I tried to be that kind of girl."

"What are you talking about?" Law was propped between the open door and the truck frame. His gaze was steady.

"The fun kind."

"Wreath." The word sounded like a moan.

A car door slammed, then another. Wreath jolted. Maybe Bum was back.

But this was Destiny and Mitch, marching toward the truck. Mitch had his hands in his pockets. Destiny, wearing a pink T-shirt with the state of Florida on it, looked anything but calm.

When they got to the hood, Destiny crossed her arms. Her eyes were narrowed and her mouth thin. Mitch looked puzzled.

"She's home from her vacation." One tear tickled its way down Wreath's face as she spoke. "I'm not like them. I'll never be a normal girl." She gave a shaky laugh. "I probably won't be a normal woman either."

"Wreath—" Law said again.

She held up her grimy hand to stop him. "You were right. I got too wrapped up trying to save Jaclyn and fix Bum. I shouldn't have tracked him down when he stole my bike. I never should have come to this disgusting motel." Her voice cracked. "I shouldn't fret about the store, for that matter. It'll be fine." Her tirade trickled to a weak halt.

Law nudged her over as he slid into the seat. "And I used to think you didn't talk much." When he leaned toward her, he smelled faintly of antiseptic, like hand-sanitizer or hospital air.

Wreath leaned in too.

Then Destiny pounded on the hood, making both of them jump. And, if Wreath wasn't mistaken, leaving a couple of dents.

"Dang, Destiny." Mitch grabbed at her hand.

"I'm not staying out here all night." She moved next to the open door. "Have you gone one-hundred-percent insane, Wreath?"

"Des," Mitch said, "that's not helping."

Destiny stepped back as though he had shoved her. "If these two love birds are through making up in the worst part of town, I'm going home." She pointed her finger at them and waggled it. "I suggest you get back to Faye's, Miss Perfect, before they realize you're gone. Your new grandfather might decide to give you your first spanking."

When had Destiny gotten so mad at her?

"They don't know where I am," Wreath said. "How—" She looked at Law and at the keys, dangling from the ignition.

"When Des got in from her trip, she and Mitch drove down to Lafayette to check on me. When the surgeon suggested we leave for the night, she drove me back."

Destiny smirked. "Surprise, surprise when we pull up to Faye's and the truck's gone."

Wreath's face burned with mortification. Those two friends cared enough about Law to check on him. She'd dashed around saving Bum. And taking Law's truck in the process.

Mitch, tall and lean, sauntered up behind Destiny and chimed in. "Looks like you knew how to drive after all." He nodded. "You might consider another lesson or two. Both left tires are on the curb—"

"And your butt was hanging out the moon roof when we got here," Destiny said. "I thought Mitch was going to roll down this lame street laughing."

"Thanks, Mitch," Wreath mumbled.

Mitch cleared his throat.

Law's face was glum.

"I thought I could find Bum, help him." She turned in the seat, her knees bumping Law. "What will become of Jaclyn if something happens to him?"

He shook his head.

She gulped in a breath of air. She couldn't quit. Not with so much at stake. "Bum's acting stupid." *Like I did.* "I wish I could stop whatever he's doing."

"Bad idea," Destiny said.

"And you propose to do that by . . ." Mitch had moved up against Destiny.

"I don't know," Wreath said. "Possibly J.D."

"Right," Destiny said. "Wake up your grandpa in the middle of the night. Risk his life and yours."

"Still not helping, Des," Mitch said.

Law's face was screwed into a confused collection of wrinkles. "Destiny has a point," he said slowly. "But Bumgardner acts like he's trying to do the right thing."

"I keep wondering where I'd be if everyone hadn't helped me," Wreath said.

"Do we have to talk about that here?" Destiny said.

"Des, ease up." Law's voice dripped with fatigue rather than scorn. "Let us think."

Mitch spoke, his tone considering. "Where do you think Bum might be?"

"Probably at a dog fight," Law said.

Wreath threw him a surprised look.

He sat up straighter and exhaled. "Plan C," he said. "I'll take you."

"No!" Destiny yelped. "Look at where we are. Look at what time it is."

Wreath had an urge to hide her face. "Destiny's right," she said. "You shouldn't be out here, none of you."

"It's what friends do," Law said. "We take care of each other."

Destiny banged her hand on the hood again. *Rough night for the truck.* "This has stopped being fun, Lawson Rogers." She turned back to her car, shaking her head.

"Make sure she gets home safe, okay?" Law said to Mitch and closed the truck door as they walked toward the car.

Wreath sighed.

"You know she's not usually like that," Law said.

"I've never seen that side of her, that's for sure."

"She's nervous about going off to school. Leaving home. You know."

"Really?"

Law watched Destiny get into the car. "She's not as good as you at figuring out what she's feeling."

Wreath drew back. *A middle-of-the-night compliment. Wow.*

"Now," Law said, "off to our first dogfight." He paused. "This *is* your first, right?"

Her mouth curled almost into a smile. "Yup."

She felt better.

He put his hand on the key and turned. Nothing happened but a clicking sound.

She shifted closer. "Turn it again, further. That worked for me." He cut his eyes at her before trying again. Another click.

Then he reached toward the blinker and twisted a knob. The look on his face was the same as when he discovered Wreath on top of the truck. "You left the lights on."

Her hand flew to her mouth. "I thought they turned themselves off. That's what Faye's car does."

Law opened the door. "This truck's more basic than that."

Then he flagged down Destiny, doing a U-turn in the parking lot of the Corral.

She lowered her window. "Dare I hope you changed your mind?"

"My battery's dead. Do you have jumper cables?"

"And that's a *no* to the return of reason," she said. "And, no, I don't have jumper cables. I loaned the jumper cables to Mitch the other night when you"—she pointed at Law—"had a dead battery. He never brought them back."

Mitch made a face. "They're in my trunk. My bad."

Wreath was already at Destiny's window. "Will you take us to pick up Bum? Please?"

"My parents would murder me. Dead. Dead. Dead."

"Let's go with them, Des," Mitch said. "Our last summer blowout."

"No way."

"It could be interesting," he said.

"And it would help us out big time. I'd owe you so much, Destiny," Law said.

She looked at Law and not at Wreath. "Get in, but be warned. If we get murdered, I'll kill you."

Mitch chuckled. "Old joke, always funny."

"Speak for yourself," Wreath said.

50

The crowd was rowdier than any Bum had ever seen, and the dogs, somewhere off to the side, were in a frenzy.

Between the booze and the barking, the noise had risen to a brain-rattling point.

His first—and last—visit to a dogfight had the makings of a humdinger. Thank goodness he had avoided the fights until tonight. Maybe the dogs had even grown to trust him a little.

Could he possibly take care of them after this?

Theriot, in charge of it all, told him to quiet people down before someone called the law. Bum had to bite back a smile at that.

With the crush of fools, it was easy to move from scumbag to scumbag. He didn't make eye contact, shuffled his feet, the lackey at Theriot's mercy. "Boss man says you might want to get out of here," he lied quietly to one after the other.

"I paid to see the fight," an oversized thug in overalls said.

Bum made his shrug the picture of nonchalance. "Your choice."

"What about the prizes?" a young guy asked.

"He'll settle up tomorrow."

"After church?" one of the men cackled.

"You'd better pray you do better than last week," his fence mate said.

"You're welcome to stay," Bum muttered to others, "but Theriot says keep an eye open."

"It's a dogfight," one man said. "I got eyes in the back of my head."

You're going to need 'em.

Bum wished he could personally escort every one of them to jail. But the fewer here when all hell broke loose, the more likely Theriot would be caught.

When he was about halfway around the arena—a dirt circle and motley collection of caged dogs—Theriot caught his eye. With the same two-fingered whistle that he used to get the dogs in place, he signaled Bum.

"Boy!" he yelled as Bum balked. "Get over here."

A few spectators poked at him when he passed. "You're in trouble now." "I'm putting my money on him." "I'd like to see you wrestle that Doberman."

Bile rose in Bum's throat, but he arranged a smirk. "Ooh," he said to the cluster of jerks. "I'm scared."

The first true statement he'd made all night.

He was forced to admit he was terrified. Only the thought of Jaclyn's future and Wreath's past kept him moving.

Before he could get to Theriot, Mr. Big Fun himself stepped out from behind a dog-hauling trailer. Bum's stomach flipped, then righted itself. Freed from jail, Procell couldn't stay away from his natural habitat.

Only the hours ahead would tell if it would be a bonus or a disaster.

Whatever happened to Bum, it would be worth it to snag two of the lousiest humans ever to inhabit the earth. If Big Fun went to jail tonight, Wreath and Jaclyn would be safe again.

"Well, if it isn't Starla's runt of a brother." He stepped forward with a sneer.

"I didn't know you'd be here," Bum said.

To Bum's dismay, his sister stepped out from behind a nearby van, a grin on her face. "Bummy! I wanted to come see what all the excitement was," she said.

Theriot stood a few feet away, toothpick in his mouth. He was frowning.

Big Fun pinched Starla's rear. "Your sister's no chump. You had to know she would tell me about the biggest fight of the year."

But Bum hadn't told Starla about the fight. She must have been in touch with Theriot. If only she had been smart enough to stay home, whatever ditch that happened to be.

"Starla." Bum pitched his voice low. *How could he warn her without words?* She seemed stoned or drunk. "I thought you were working in Alexandria."

She swung a playful, unsteady punch at him. "Fred here got me out of my misery."

Big Fun gave a toothy smile. "Turnabout's fair play, doll."

Theriot moved toward them. "Starla!" He went in for a hug and kissed her on the mouth.

A frown moved to Big Fun's face, and he stepped toward them.

"I didn't know you were bringing her," Theriot said. Bum had not known him very long but he could tell Theriot was seething. His face was red, and he looked like he might chomp the toothpick in half.

"You know how it is, man," Big Fun said. "Hard to leave the women folk at home."

"Not exactly a gal's game," Theriot said with a smarmy smile. "But always good to see this one." He kissed her again. "Fred Procell's a fine partner at these shows of ours. Good to have him back in circulation."

Big Fun looked like a dog who had been given a treat—from a handler he didn't trust. "How long we been working together?" he asked. "Seven, eight years?"

Theriot's eyes said *too long,* but he shook his head. "Long time."

"Nearly six," Starla said. "About the time Jac—"

"Hey, sister, you had any supper?" Bum burst in. "There's good barbecue at that pit over there." He grabbed her arm.

Big Fun towered over Starla. "Hold on a minute, boy," he said. "We were talking about old times." He tilted his head, squinted, turned his head the other way. His eyes bored into Bum. "Why do you and that kid keep popping up?"

Slumping his shoulders, Bum shuffled his feet and assumed his best beat-down pose. The old tennis shoes without laces probably helped. "I was looking for Starla," he said. "Hit some hard times, you know?"

Big Fun wasn't drawn in. His eyes narrowed as though Bum had the word *liar* tattooed on his forehead. "That sets me to thinking," he said.

"Theriot, you ready for a hot-link sandwich?" Bum asked. "Or another beer." Everything could be ruined if something didn't happen quick.

"Shut up," Big Fun said. "I'm not through with you."

Theriot bristled. "Don't start that again. This one works for me, not you."

A fight between these two could make everything easier.

But Big Fun backed down and moved aside a step. "My bad," he said. "There's something I been meaning to ask your *helper* about."

"Make it quick," Theriot said. "We got dogs to fight."

"Soooieeee, don't we?" Big Fun said, then rotated toward Bum. "How old's that kid of yours anyhow?"

At the question, Starla edged out of their circle. Wobbling toward the barbecue, she threw Bum a worried look and inched closer to Theriot.

"Um, not quite four," Bum lied. His heart pounded hard enough to hurt.

Big Fun's stance relaxed, not by much but enough to allow Bum to breathe.

Theriot draped his arm around Starla's shoulder. "Didn't listen to your Daddy about how to keep that from happening, did you, Bumgardner?" he said. "That Jack's a cute booger."

"A boy?" Big Fun turned toward Starla who took a half-step behind Theriot. "Didn't you have a kid? A little older than that?"

Starla was staring wide-eyed at Theriot, as though she didn't hear the question. Vans and trucks were placed around the arena to block prying eyes, and Starla and Theriot had leaned up against a beat-up van, almost out of sight.

"Yeah," Bum mumbled. "Starla got pregnant when I was in middle school. Our folks were none too happy."

"Where's that one?" Big Fun's calculating eyes followed Starla.

Bum met his gaze, defiant. "She died."

"That's ugly, man," Theriot said, rejoining them without Starla. "No wonder she's sensitive when it comes to children."

Sensitive about taking care of her own.

"How'd it die?" Big Fun demanded.

This was the conversation Bum had hoped to avoid for the rest of his life. He watched moths fly under the portable lights and debated his concocted answer.

"I asked you how that kid died." Big Fun grabbed his shirt collar.

"It was that thing, where kids die in their cribs, sudden something? I don't remember much about it except Starla was messed up."

Big Fun gave him a shove. "You should have been more respectful," he said. "No wonder your sister doesn't want to have anything to do with you." And he ambled toward Starla.

Bum stood stock still. Theriot watched Big Fun. "Your sister's getting herself deeper in debt," Theriot said. "You better pray the fights go off without a hitch or you'll be working for me a lot longer."

Not on your life.

One way or another, this ended tonight.

51

The first two dirt roads Destiny turned down devolved into creepy, swampy trails. One led to a vacant mobile home, the other to a crawfish pond.

"It's time for all good girls and boys to go home to bed," Mitch said. He ended the sentence with a yawn.

Wreath slumped in the seat. "I was sure it was out here." She hit her forehead on the back of Destiny's seat. "Wasn't this the area Bum mentioned to you, Law?"

He gave a slight nod.

"So much for a big summer blowout," Destiny said.

"We need to save Bum," Wreath said.

Mitch put his hand on Destiny's shoulder. "Okay, one more try," he said. "You know that gravel road where your aunt or somebody used to have that camper?"

"The one by the dump?" Destiny said.

"Sounds like one of my relatives," Law said, and Mitch guffawed.

Destiny put the car in reverse, and they bumped their way to the main road. The car bottomed out more than once, and the floorboard felt like it might break open. "You're paying for any repairs." She looked at Wreath in the rearview mirror.

Wreath was silent, running through every detail Bum had mentioned about Theriot. This was hopeless.

After a half mile or so, Destiny put on her blinker and turned down a gravel road. The rocks sounded like popcorn popping as they hit the bottom of the car.

"Slow it down, Des," Mitch cautioned. "Don't want to ding your windshield."

"Said the guy who didn't bring his car."

"I didn't have any gas." He grinned.

The road, curvier than most in Central Louisiana, ran for a few miles. A dainty crescent moon hung in the distance, lovely but providing scant light. Trees were closer to the road, creating a tunnel effect.

Right about the time Wreath began to feel carsick, Destiny swerved. She narrowly missed a big pine tree and mowed down a stand of weeds.

"Ouch," Mitch groaned as his head flew up toward the ceiling.

Wreath covered her face with her hands. What would it do to J.D. if she died in a car wreck? "We should turn around," she said in a halting voice.

"Don't be a baby," Destiny said. "It's hard to dodge potholes at two in the morning."

"You're doing a good job, Des," Law said, his voice unnaturally calm.

"Suck-up," Mitch said.

"There's not a place to turn around," Law said. "We have to keep going."

The sentence struck Wreath hard. That had been Frankie's philosophy of life. In the past, it had described Wreath's life too.

Not anymore.

She had options that went beyond plunging ahead.

"Let's go back," she declared in a loud voice. "We did all we could."

"No," Law said. "We can't leave Bum on the field."

Guys. She wasn't sure she'd ever understand them.

"I'm willing to keep trying," Destiny said and nodded at Law in the mirror.

Wreath sat back and tried not to think about the contents of her stomach, which plunged up and down with each bump.

After a couple more twists, the road ended—at a sprawling cemetery, surrounded by a chain-link fence. Two huge trees flanked the gate that had an arch that said "Fellowship."

"A dead end," Mitch said.

Law and Destiny groaned in unison. Even Wreath smiled.

"My funny boyfriend." Destiny's voice sounded more normal.

What was going on with those two? They had dated since prom but seemed to drift apart this summer. Wreath and Law's relationship was on about the same trajectory.

"You were right, Des," Wreath said as Destiny maneuvered around the cemetery parking lot. "This was a dumb idea."

"At least you got to see where your dad's buried," Law said quietly.

Wreath's heart leapt into her throat, and she leaned toward the window. "Seriously?"

Law nodded. "My grandparents brought me for dinner on the grounds once. J.D. was putting flowers on a couple of graves. That was the day Pops told me about the wreck."

"We could go look," Mitch said.

"No!" Destiny and Wreath said at the same time.

Wreath reached up and gave Mitch a pat on the shoulder, not quite sure why. "I'll come back in daytime."

"I bet J.D. would bring you." Law's voice was a deep whisper by her ear.

"That's a good idea," Wreath murmured back.

The car had taken on a solemn note, the energy drained as though the engine had run out of gas. Destiny exited the lot more slowly than they had entered.

An armadillo waddled across the road. Two babies followed.

"Those things are hideous," Destiny said.

"Prehistoric steampunk animal design," Mitch said.

"Just a mom and her babies," Law said, his voice almost wistful.

Wreath put her hand on his leg, and he laid his hand on top of hers. Why hadn't she gone to the hospital in Lafayette? Waited overnight. Been there for him the way he was for her.

She touched his leg. "Your mom's going to get well," she whispered.

"You know how scary it is, don't you?" Law said.

She nodded. "I loved Frankie with my whole heart."

The car fell into silence.

Looking out into the darkness, Wreath was swept by a wave of longing. On two or three nights this summer, Wreath had crawled into bed and realized her mother had not come to mind that day. It felt like she'd missed her mom's birthday or forgot to say *good-bye* as she left for school.

During the spring battles with Big Fun, the good Frankie slipped away, replaced by memories of what she had done wrong.

But after her outburst in the bottle cave with Bum, Wreath had felt whole again. Her mother hadn't dumped her, like Starla had Jaclyn. She hadn't drunk herself into a stupor the way Bum's parents did. She'd never been in jail or hospitalized from some freak accident.

Wreath owed it to her mama to make a better life.

The Landry city limits sign came into view, and she exhaled. She'd failed to find Bum and might not be able to save Jaclyn.

This summer she'd moved beyond her past, though. That would have to be enough.

52

C rouched behind a van, Bum dabbed ointment on a
black-and-tan hound, the small act of mercy easing his
heart.

"It's okay, girl." His voice was soft. Theriot didn't want
anyone *babying* the animals. The dog whimpered and calmed
slightly. She had a gash on her right flank.

Bum unbuttoned the cargo pocket on his filthy pants and
pulled out a dog biscuit. The box of treats had cost his supper
money, but his stomach was too upset to eat tonight anyway—
and thankfully Jaclyn would have a good meal at Faye's.

Even if the biscuits didn't work, the small gesture might
make the dogs feel better—and keep them from another night
of horror. "It'll be all right, little Bitty," he murmured, reassuring himself as well as the dog. Naming the dogs was another
mistake but he couldn't stand to treat them like things.

As disasters went, tonight was shaping up to be a doozy.
What was that other word, the one like *disaster*? Wreath would
know. She was smart. Hadn't been stupid like him and quit
school, even when it would have been easy. A horrifying
disaster.

One dog died before he and Theriot arrived that night, a victim of a quick fight that someone put together on the spur of the moment. Theriot had been furious—not that the dog had died but that someone was getting a piece of his business.

Bum had hoped to save all the animals tonight, but his idea was a . . . *debacle.* That was the word. A tenth grade teacher had taught him that, as in, "Your attention to detail, Mr. Bumgardner, is a debacle."

Instructed to toss the body, Bum disobeyed. He buried it in a shallow grave in the edge of the woods. He gagged as he worked and mustered a swift plea that the animal hadn't suffered.

There'd be time enough for those thoughts the next time he laid down to sleep.

Now he had to dispose of this dog and put an end to his work with Theriot.

The hound, smaller and weaker than the others, had been intended for bait. But when Big Fun showed up, Theriot got antsy about the schedule and pulled the dog from the arena—the only good thing Big Fun had ever done.

Unfortunately a pit bull nearby had not gotten the message and ripped into the smaller animal. The crowd of jackals cheered and made side bets.

"Let's get on with the main event," Theriot said. "Get her out of here, Bum, and collect the money. Big Fun, shoot her, how about it? We've got real dogs to fight."

"I got it!" Bum said and yanked her away before Big Fun had pulled his gun. "I'll collect on my way back from the pens." Handling dirty money was easier than keeping dogs out of monsters' clutches.

"Ten-minute break, everyone," Theriot yelled. "Grab a beer and make your bets."

Bum looked around at the camouflage pants and shirts, gimme caps that advertised oil companies and beer, dribbles of snuff in the corners of mouths. The pasture teemed with morons.

They were probably high school dropouts like him. Theriot had turned stupid into a chain of businesses.

Bum's sister, chief stupid among them, sprawled in a lawn chair, and gave Theriot a come-closer smile. Big Fun, his back to them, waltzed across the field and peed in the bushes.

Bum had been forced into meanness this summer, from collecting and paying off bets to checking on ill-treated animals. That was a problem—his efforts to calm them always resulted in bites.

He had done all he could to save the animals, including refusing dogs presented by gamblers in trade for their bills. He had dropped one anonymously at the local animal clinic with a note that promised he'd pay later. Where that money would come from he hadn't a clue.

Samson had been a small victory in a chain of defeats. He had snatched the dog before he could be further mutilated and told Theriot he had run away. The vet bill for that one had drained every dollar he had brought to Landry, but he couldn't let the dog suffer, his back leg dangling.

"I know you took that dog for your kid," Theriot had said a couple of days later. "I've shot people for lying to me."

Bum stared back at him and tensed for the punch. It landed right on his kidneys.

Yet he had not surrendered Samson. One of the few things that he had done right this summer.

He glanced up to see where the moon was. Only a sliver, it told him what he needed to know. It was time for the call. And once more he had to decide whether he could trust Starla in the least.

After tonight, whatever the consequences, he would no longer be an accomplice to evil.

He stood slowly so as not to scare the dog and slipped her one more biscuit. He hoped it wasn't too much.

With a growl, the dog snapped at him.

"Shhh, Bitty." Bum averted his eyes from the area where the blood congealed. No wonder she wanted to take a chunk out of him.

His plan had to work.

The dogs were too aggressive to be set free without expert care. They'd hurt some kid like Jaclyn or get shot by an upset farmer. *Poor things.* Theriot and Big Fun—before he'd gone to jail—had trained them too well.

The dog whined, and Bum looked up. A few yards away Theriot was staring in his direction—until Starla put her hand on his thigh.

Bum's jaw tightened at the sight. Big Fun wasn't the kind of guy to share, and Starla would wind up with another black eye or worse.

She hadn't always been like this. Their upbringing, the belt of their father, dropping out of high school in ninth grade. Those had been to blame, as surely as the revolting toys, chains, and electric prods made the dogs mean.

He risked holding the growling dog and shielded her from Theriot's line of sight. Thankful for the long sleeves—he wore two shirts tonight, despite the summer heat—he heard the fabric tear as the dog latched on.

"You gotta let me help you, girl," he said. "Trust me."

She rewarded his words with a nip at Bum's upper arm, but the action seemed more symbolic than vicious. "That's a good girl," Bum crooned. "Sweet Bitty. Shhh. It's okay." He glanced back again.

He only had a few minutes until he would be summoned to assist with the big fight of the night. Balancing a toolbox full of evidence—including the horrible steel pieces that stretched the dogs' mouths—Bum, dog still in his arms, zipped in and out of the vehicles, mostly beat-up pickups. The animal didn't move, her weight becoming heavier.

Bum put the toolbox on the ground first, letting it slip from his aching fingers. Then he sank to his knees and eased the dog onto a bed of pine straw and leaves. With a quick move, he pushed the box further out of sight and scooped loamy soil onto it.

"Sorry, girl," Bum said again and looped the rope around the dog's neck and tied her to a nearby tree. The dog didn't stir, and Bum ran his finger between the neck and the rope. His own heart pounded so hard that he couldn't tell if she had a pulse or not.

He turned back toward the arena and stopped, twisted, knelt again. He stroked the fur between the animal's eyes, then took off his outer shirt and put it under the dog's head.

A tear slid down his face.

Right before a twig cracked behind him.

He lurched up, whirled, wiped at his face. The zap of nerves, mingled with all he'd seen that night, weakened his knees.

"What are you doing?"

He drew in a swift breath. *Starla.*

"You shouldn't have come out here." He shoved her backwards, away from the dog.

"Neither should you." She sounded perfectly sober as she looked down.

"Rough night to be a dog," he said. "I had to . . . dispose of this one."

She nodded. The silver handle of the toolbox glinted in the dark of the grove, and her eyes lingered there a moment too long.

"Did you get it?" He had once been able to read his sister, following her from one skirmish to another. He had been stupid to ask for her help tonight.

"Let's forget all of that and get out of here before they hunt us down," she said. "You got a car?"

"You know I don't have money for a car."

"We'll hitch. Where's Jaclyn?"

When he didn't answer, she stepped closer. She smelled like weed, mixed with a tinge of B.O. "I don't like you leaving her alone at that rat-hole motel."

"Then maybe you shouldn't have abandoned her." He watched for even a shimmer of shame. None. He shooed her away. "She's with friends, but you need to get out of here." His words were rushed. Time was running out.

She put her hands in the pockets of her pink mini-skirt. "I can't start over. I'm not strong and smart like you."

"Right," he said. "Dumb Bum the dropout."

"Don't call yourself that," she said. He'd never heard her use that maternal voice, not even with Jaclyn. "You're a smart kid. And a good kid."

"I'm burying dogs," he said.

"I see that rope on that one. It ain't dead."

"Starla—" His teeth were jammed together so tight his jaw ached. Truck doors slammed in the background, and a dog barked. "I've got to get back to the dog pens."

She nodded, her posture relaxed. They might have been having a chat on the front porch at home. Bum started walking toward the arena, and she followed.

"You're not half as tough as you make out to be," she said.

He hesitated. "I'm tough enough." Then he strode toward the cages. Theriot was scanning the arena with binoculars, not a good sign.

Starla's footsteps in the damp grass made a soft sound, like that Faye woman's house shoes on carpet. "I got Big Fun out of jail," she said. "I'm the one who gave him the alibi."

"Why would you do something like that?" His voice was too loud. "You put people in danger, even your own daughter. Nice, sis. Real nice."

"Hush." She pulled a handful of money out of her pocket. "They promised me this, said they wanted to take care of me." She shrugged. "He and Theriot both want what the other has."

"They did this together?"

She cracked her knuckles and her feet shifted. "Not exactly."

"Both of those men need to rot in jail."

"Big Fun didn't kill that girl." Starla spoke quickly, her gaze directed behind Bum. "He told me."

"And of course he never lies."

"I needed money," she said. "That job stunk."

"These people are rank—even by your standards."

She drew back. "You didn't have to do all this work for Theriot. You could have stayed in Thibodaux."

Bum was so weary he could have lain on the stubbly grass and slept. "I didn't realize how bad it was until I was in too deep."

She smiled. "You were helping your Sissy," she said, "like you always do." Her voice was sweet and young.

It was hard not to forgive her, but he had given his heart to her daughter. "How could you leave Jaclyn like that?" he said.

"It's rough having a kid."

"I noticed."

She looked down at the ground. "Thanks for not telling Big Fun about her."

"I wouldn't tell him squat."

Starla snickered, the sound as out of place as someone opening a beer in church. "My little girl's done stopped you from cussing, hasn't she?"

For a moment he wanted to smile. Maybe Jaclyn would grow up to be a woman in charge, not a clueless victim like his sister. Maybe she would be like Wreath.

"I've got to wrap this up," he said. "I was stupid to think you would help me." Starla was who she was. If Jaclyn hadn't changed her, nothing would.

"You're not going to get yourself killed, are you?" Starla said. They were a football field away from the crowd, and she had fallen behind again. Her voice was low and tense. "Stand between me and the crowd. Hurry."

When he hesitated, she spoke again. "Block their view."

With a half turn, he had his back to both Big Fun and Theriot—and most of the other losers in Landry, Louisiana.

And he was facing someone who had proven she would do anything for money.

Starla pulled her hands out of her pockets, and he took a step forward. He felt a sliver of hope. Her fisted hands flew toward him, full of crumpled money. "Use this for you and Jaclyn."

"No." He shook his head and gazed over his shoulder. The binoculars were trained on them. "You take it. Leave tonight."

For a split second, she acted like she might force the money on him. He could see a few twenty-dollar bills and a couple of hundreds. His mouth practically watered at the thought of the food it could buy.

It wasn't money he needed from her.

Then she jammed the cash back into her pockets. "I'm going to do better." She walked a yard or more toward Theriot, who had moved the binoculars to a rowdy group in lawn chairs.

"I can help you find help, go to rehab, whatever," he said. "There are people here who will help."

She stopped. "Why would they help me?"

"Because that's what they do. They take care of people."

"I'm going to do better," she repeated. Then she veered a couple of steps the other way. "But I can't do it here."

The sight of her walking away was as painful as Theriot's punch in his stomach. She had failed him. *Again.* "Don't blow that money on drugs," he said in a loud whisper. "Use it for a bus ticket."

Then she stepped back to kiss his cheek. "Tell my baby girl I'll be back. And I love her." And she pressed the cell phone into his hand.

He gazed down at it and forced his mouth not to drop open. It felt warm and slightly greasy and was encased in a camouflage shell. He fidgeted with the ringer button but a small noise nearby startled him, and he shoved it in his pocket.

When he looked up, Starla had headed for the woods.

He pulled out the phone. Dialed. Spoke soft and fast.

Theriot stepped from the shadow of a panel truck. "What you doing, boy?"

53

Wreath slunk through the woods, and mosquitoes buzzed around her head. Law was on her heels. The yellowish lights drew nearer.

When Destiny had swerved off the highway, Wreath tried to talk her into turning around. "We did our best," she said. "Let's go home before anyone starts worrying."

"I've been worrying since we pulled up in front of that motel," Destiny said.

"Let's try this one road," Law said. "Over here."

They skirted the Junque Mart and a narrow road, more like an unused alley, forked. "Which way?" Destiny said.

"This isn't a good idea," Wreath said.

"Listen to her, Des," Mitch said with a big yawn. "This guy probably doesn't want to be rescued. We don't know if something illegal's going on. It may all be legit."

"Bum needs help," Law said.

Mitch looked over the seat, his brow furrowed. "You sure?"

Law nodded.

"I guess we could scope it out from a distance," Mitch said. "Tell Shane what we learn."

And suddenly they were there, no turning back.

"Des, pull over there," Law said. "Kill your lights."

"Back in," Wreath said.

"All right, I get it," Destiny said. "I don't recall asking for a driving instructor."

Law rested his hand on her shoulder. "You and Wreath keep trying to reach Shane," he said, then pointed at the clock on the dash. "If we're not back in an hour, call 911."

"What are you talking about?" Wreath said.

"Stay here with Des. It's safer."

"*You* stay here with Des," Wreath said and half-tumbled out of the car. "I won't be long." She placed her hand on Destiny's shoulder. "You're a good friend."

"Tell me that when you don't need a getaway car."

"You're not going without me, Wreath," Law said. "You stay, Mitch."

But Mitch was already out of the door. "And miss all the fun? I'm going too."

"I'm not staying by myself," Destiny said.

"We can't all go," Wreath said. "It'll be conspicuous."

"Like you're not going to stand out?" Destiny grumbled.

"We need a lookout," Law said. "Wreath and I have got this."

"Come on, dude," Mitch said.

"You watch and see what happens. Call Shane again. Call the cops if it gets bad."

Destiny shuddered and pulled her door open. "When you put it like that . . ."

"Keep the doors locked, and leave us if you have to," Wreath whispered.

"Don't ever doubt it," Destiny said. "We will."

Mitch was fussing as Wreath moved away from the car. Her legs were shakier than expected, but after a quick survey of the area, she nodded at Law. "This way," she said. "Stay low."

That had been ten minutes and ten thousand bugs ago, but the light was getting closer.

"You've done this a lot, haven't you?" Law whispered. He was so close behind her that she could feel his breath on her sweaty neck.

"I've never been to a dogfight in my life."

"Don't be obtuse."

"You saw where I lived. I've done my share of hiking."

"So that's what you call this?" He was agitated. "Did you have to get away from trouble a lot? Before you got to Landry?"

She pivoted and slapped at a swarm of mosquitoes. They looked like an unholy halo around his head. "Could we do this interview later?"

"I *want* to understand you, Wreath." He pulled a twig out of her hair. "I'm looking for clues."

"Don't go getting all sweet on me, or we won't be able to finish this." She walked on.

He stumbled on a root and grunted. "To think that I'm the one who works in the woods," he said. "You're like a panther."

She stopped. "Thanks for rescuing me tonight."

"Will Bumgardner be glad to see us?"

She shrugged and resumed walking. "Who knows?"

"Wreath, stop!" Law said. "You do see all those people across that field, don't you?" He didn't wait for her answer. "Those are bad people, and we weren't invited to their party."

"That's why we're in the woods," she whispered, "so nobody will see us. All we have to do is grab Bum."

And she pushed through a wall of vines—and ran right into the woman she'd seen in McDonald's in Alexandria.

Bum's sister.

Starla flailed her arms and plowed past them.

She never stopped running.

54

Bum almost stroked at Theriot's words.

So this was the way it would end. And Theriot would skate once more. *Did the good guys ever win?*

"Answer me! Where's Starla going? What's the holdup? I've been planning this all summer."

"I, uh, that runt died. I had to . . . you know, dig a hole."

Theriot exhaled. "Don't take so long next time," he said. "You're not burying your grandma."

"I don't want the cops to find him. And Starla had to go to the bathroom."

"Get over to the cages. Now."

Bum scanned the area as he started walking. He should chase Starla and get out of town before Theriot figured out what he'd done. They could grab Jaclyn on their way.

What kind of life was that for a little girl? With Faye and J.D. and Wreath, she was always wearing a new outfit or jabbering about the toy she'd gotten at some restaurant. Her frequent puny spells had lessened.

He had to see this through.

At the very least he'd saved the dogs from further pain.

A blur of movement in the woods caught his eye. He squinted and looked around. Theriot was yelling at Big Fun. Everything else seemed in place. Surely the cops couldn't already be here.

Bum slowed his pace and took a closer look. The movement drew nearer.

His heart felt like the time he tried to do a flip on a friend's trampoline and catapulted onto the ground. He'd spent six months in a neck brace.

Tell me this isn't happening.

Those weren't sheriff's deputies hiding in the woods.

It was Wreath and Law.

Seeing Wreath always brought a spurt of happiness, but tonight it was overridden by paralyzing terror. That Law guy wasn't as smart as he seemed if he let Wreath come here tonight. What if Big Fun saw her? Or if the cops arrested her too?

She was too good to see the likes of a place like this.

Bum watched closer, saw her shake her head. Law put his hands on his hips, and she turned her back on him.

Law wasn't in charge of the deep-woods escapade. Wreath was pulling him along in her wake.

Bum's mouth twitched and he started toward them at a dead run. He tamped down the shout of warning that kept trying to come out.

Before he had gone more than a few feet, they burst out from the tree line and zigzagged toward the row of trucks and trailers.

Wreath had seen him. Her eyes widened, and she started toward him.

Definitely not as smart as he'd thought.

Looking over his shoulder, he saw Theriot raise the binoculars to his eyes. Bum jerked to a halt, then heard Theriot shout into a bullhorn.

Wreath's head swung toward him. Law was a step behind her.

Bum acted like he was swatting at a bug and signaled them to get down.

"I said where's them dogs, boy?" Theriot yelled louder.

Waving the pair back into the shadows with one hand, Bum extended his right arm in a wave as he ran toward Theriot. It was too early to reveal his plan, but he had to save Wreath. "Something's wrong with the dogs," he shouted.

Theriot and Big Fun looked at each other and back at Bum.

"Shut that racket up," Theriot said and hurried toward the dog pens. Big Fun loped along behind him. They looked like villains in a cartoon.

Their path would bring them only a few feet from where Wreath and Law were crouched.

Bum ran toward the two men as fast as he could and stepped from side-to-side to block their path. "Somebody messed with the dogs." Clutching his stomach, he faked a gag. "I think they've been—"

Big Fun shoved him aside. "Move out of our way, you dumb—"

Bum reached out and grabbed his shirttail. "Dogs. Sick." He grabbed his gut again. "Poison."

He could take one of them, but he probably wasn't strong enough to fight both. Together they'd be meaner than the wild hogs his grandfather trapped in the swamp. He had to distract them until Wreath could get away.

"What are you talking about?" Theriot said and looked from Bum to Big Fun.

Bum did a belly flop onto the ground, mimicking a losing character in a video game. It might be over the top but this was the biggest moment of his life.

He pulled a silent plea out of the dusty air. *Watch over Jaclyn.*

His dramatic momentum was stopped by Big Fun's big-booted foot. It settled on his chest and Theriot, toothpick in mouth, pulled a pistol out of the waist of his pants.

No surprise there. Theriot would no more go unarmed than Jaclyn would go to bed without a light on.

The surprise was that Theriot couldn't seem to decide who to point it at.

The brouhaha had drawn a boisterous audience, moving closer and closer.

The scuffed toes of boots drew a circle around Bum, who closed his eyes and ventured a moan. "Poison," he said.

"What the hell?" Theriot said, the gun now pointed at Bum, who was fluttering his eyelids. If he was going to get shot, he wanted to see it coming. "What's he talking about?"

"He's scamming you." Big Fun ground his boot heel deeper into Bum's stomach, like he was putting out a cigarette. "This squirt's trouble. Him and his sister both. Tried to tell you."

Theriot swung the barrel of the gun up from the vicinity of Bum's body toward Big Fun's torso. "Shut up about Starla."

That set off a chain reaction.

The crowd, still close enough for Bum to see grass and mud stains on the hem of their jeans and camouflage pants, jeered. Men shoved and mouthed off like school kids watching a fight between classes.

The boot on Bum's body didn't follow Theriot's orders, bearing down instead.

"I wondered when they'd get tired of sharing the same woman," a gravelly voice muttered.

"She ain't nothing but white trash," another man said.

Big Fun's foot moved into field-goal kicking position, aimed toward the voice. Before he could let it fly, though, Theriot whipped around and slammed the pistol against the unseen guy.

That man fell backwards into Big Fun. When the crowd parted, a sprinkling of stars were noticeable in the sky over Bum's head. A trickle of blood ran down the guy's temple but he was already reaching in his pocket.

Big Fun moved his boot to him. "I wouldn't do that if I were you."

"Anybody else got something to contribute?" Theriot asked and cocked the gun.

The crowd grew quiet so fast that Bum heard a dog give a quick bark, almost like a hushed yelp. *Oh, no!* They shouldn't be conscious.

Theriot looked in the direction of the noise and chewed harder on the toothpick. "Are we fussing like a bunch of girls or are we having us a dogfight?" he asked after a moment.

"Let's win us some money," one man yelled.

"You wish," another said.

"My turn tonight," a third chimed in.

The comments drew a round of laughter, the kind when a kid diffuses a bully on the school bus.

Bum didn't share the relief. He rolled over onto his hands and knees and struggled to rise. Pain lingered from the boot, so pretending to stagger wasn't hard.

"What we going to do with this one?" Big Fun asked and grabbed Bum by the bushy ponytail. If he could ever afford a haircut, he was getting every inch shaved off.

"We'll deal with him later," Theriot said.

55

Big Fun's fingers bit into his sore arm and shoved him toward the dog pens. Bum walked as slowly as he could.

Where were Wreath and Law? Hopefully Law had the sense to get her out of here. He hoped he lived long enough to daydream about why Wreath had come tonight.

But that didn't seem likely at the moment.

"You was lying about Starla's kid, weren't you?" Big Fun said, so low Bum could barely make out the words.

He squirmed as far away as he could, hoping he wasn't giving away Wreath's hiding place. Theriot, gun still drawn, walked a few steps to the side.

"No, I didn't lie!" Bum said, overly loud. *Wreath, get out of here.*

Big Fun gave a satisfied grunt and twisted Bum's wrist until he thought it might snap. "I know that kid's mine," he said. "I always wanted a young'un."

Theriot stepped so close Bum could see a hair growing out of his ear.

"She wants you to leave her alone," Bum said, louder still. "She loves someone else."

Right in Bum's face, Theriot's expression was meaner than a wounded German shepherd. "What you talking about, boy?"

"My sister, she's—"

Before he could conjure up more words to infuriate Theriot, Big Fun backhanded Bum across the mouth. "You slimy troublemaker."

Stumbling backward, Bum barely registered the blood running down his chin—because he could see Wreath hunched over, moving toward the dog pens.

Theriot and Big Fun glared at each other, like a pair of puffed-up roosters about to square off over the same hen. Bum had to keep them focused on each other.

"She's tired of you harassing her," he said. "Ever since you got out of jail, you've hassled her." Sometimes it scared Bum how easily the lies came.

"You —" Big Fun raised his hand.

Theriot, a smug smile on his face, moved between Bum and Big Fun, a circle once more forming. When he spoke his voice was low, his attention on Big Fun. "This Starla business is settled," he said. "She's mine. She told me tonight."

The noise that Big Fun emitted held no humor. "Well, Mr. Big Shot," he said, "I'm the one she lied for."

"I'm the one who paid her to lie," Theriot said.

"What?" For a moment Big Fun looked confused.

Bum felt the same way. *Why would Theriot want Big Fun out of jail?*

The two men were so near that Bum could feel specks of spit as they argued. Ignoring the pain in his gut, he searched for an escape, one that would lead them away from Wreath.

She was no longer in sight, but Law's eyes, topped with a good head of dark hair, peeked from behind a pickup a few yards away.

Big Fun had grown still, his hulking body like the trunk of an oak. "Why would you bail me out?"

"For the fights," Theriot said. "How could you get out of debt from prison?"

"I was working on a plan," Big Fun said.

"I don't care much for your plans."

"You smug SOB," Big Fun said. "Who always found dogs? Who's the best trainer? Who was your banker? I didn't see you out there collecting."

"Who got his mangy self thrown in jail? I wouldn't have used this kid if you'd had good sense."

"That punk's trouble. You should have used a pro. He's probably skimming money for Starla."

The crowd was growing restless. Some shuffled nearby and some yelled from the arena. "Get on with it," some guy with a hacking cough scolded.

"Bring in the dogs," one shouted.

But Theriot was looking at Big Fun, as though they were alone in his living room. "You should have paid what you owed." He pulled something out of his pocket with a swift movement. Bum didn't see the knife until the blade was against Big Fun's neck.

"Whoa," someone said, and the circle dissolved. Men scurried backwards like oversized crawfish.

The two men stared at each other for an endless moment, the gray steel of the blade hovering close.

Sweat trickled down Bum's face. Big Fun looked unperturbed.

The background noise steadily increased, like a half-hearted wave at a football game picking up momentum. The knife blade moved closer to Big Fun's neck.

Bum's heart rate increased, his mouth dry.

"Dogs, dogs dogs," the crowd chanted—from a safe distance. Cowards.

Big Fun threw up his hands and took a step back, the movement causing Bum to flinch. "They're right, man." Big Fun nodded toward the field. "Let's get the dogs. You can slit my throat later."

Theriot cackled. "You can count on it," he said, then shoved Bum. "Get 'em, boy. You're costing me money."

Bum looked around. At least Wreath had escaped. He doubted he'd be as lucky.

The crowd was shouting *dogs* over and over, faster and faster.

Big Fun propelled Bum in the direction of the cages with his boot on Bum's butt.

Theriot was ahead and noticed immediately. "What's wrong with them?" His voice was higher pitched than usual, and he peered back toward Bum and Big Fun. "What'd you do to them?" He pulled his gun as he spoke.

A flash of pink caught Bum's eye. A girl was weaving behind the crowd, a guy following at a less enthusiastic pace. They ducked behind a pickup.

The sight provoked a startled reaction. "What in the name of—?" Theriot said.

"Crazy teenagers," a guy said. "I'd take a belt to a girl of mine for coming out here."

"Well, crap," Theriot mumbled. "I'd better check on them."

Bum gulped in a breath of the hot July air. It had all come down to this, the dust swirling, bugs diving, sweaty, bloated men cheering for blood sport.

Grabbing Theriot's arm, Bum felt the gun brush against his chest. "Poison," he said as Theriot aimed the gun at his face. "Tried. Tell you. Poison."

"You poisoned the dogs?" Big Fun, who had been staring at the girl and the guy, grabbed Bum's throat. "What kind of scum does that?"

"Why you little—" Theriot was cocking the gun as he spoke.

"Him!" Bum nodded at Big Fun. "He wanted to get back at you, about Starla and about calling the cops on him."

"You called the cops on me?" Big Fun moved from Bum toward Theriot.

"Why the hell would I do that?" Theriot said.

If there was one thing Bum had learned this summer it was how animals were baited. The distraction worked; the pair—*friends of Wreath's?*—were no longer visible. With effort, they might escape.

"He poisoned the dogs and plans to run off with Starla." Bum didn't blink when he looked into Theriot's eyes. With a wish for luck, he let the cell phone fall to the ground and nudged it with his shoe. With another step, he was away from it.

"Stop right there," Theriot said.

Bum froze and flung out another of the weapons in his arsenal. "She's gone to town to wait for him."

"He's lying!" Big Fun roared.

Pointing the gun at Big Fun, Theriot looked around. "Where is she?"

Bum leaned in, as though telling a secret. "He was going to steal the take. Starla told me before she left."

Then he went for the kill.

"He has someone calling the cops."

Theriot swore with words Bum hadn't heard even when collecting gambling debts. His eyes were as wild as a dog's before it entered the fighting ring.

His own death might be imminent, but Bum took a split second to enjoy the looks on the faces of both men, circling each other.

The pleasure was brief.

Theriot waved the gun in the air. Big Fun's Toyota-sized fist hit Bum in the middle of his stomach, then square in the face, blood flying out like a wide-open faucet.

His last thought was that the punch sounded as loud as a gunshot.

56

Law threw Wreath to the ground and shielded her body with his. "Get down!"

The chilling chants from the crowd turned into yelling, and Wreath, ear pressed to the ground, could almost feel the stampede.

The men stumbling past paid no attention to them, and she recognized some from town. Others looked vaguely familiar, and she could swear she saw *drunk Mike* and his buddy from the Corral parking lot. No wonder they'd been in a hurry.

She and Law lay in a patch of grass and weeds with cockleburs poking her. She could almost touch the dog pens. She twisted and raised her head like a turtle peeking up from a lake. Had Bum been shot?

"Don't move." Law's voice was quiet. "We're surrounded." He moved, and his cheek touched hers.

"We might make it to the woods, but I can't be sure," she said.

"You're a good person, Wreath. The best. Whatever happens, you know I'm crazy about you, right? Sorry about this summer."

Were they about to die?

She shook her head. The dry grass scraped her skin. Her knees burned, and her head hurt. "You're not giving my eulogy, are you?"

"I was supposed to keep you safe tonight."

"I got you into this," she said. "Let's go."

Trucks were roaring out of the parking lot. Gravel and horns mingled in an unholy chorus. The cloud of dust around the field thickened.

They crawled a few feet, and Wreath halted, twisting her neck. Between the darkness and the dust, visibility was nil.

"Wreath?"

She started at the voice, right at her ear. Destiny moved so close her hair hit Wreath in the face.

"You're supposed to be in the car!" Wreath had to keep herself from screaming.

"I got scared."

"Where's Mitch?'

"Here." Mitch materialized out of the dust. "Where's Law?" His voice sounded like they were at the Landry pizza parlor.

"My father's going to murder me," Destiny said. "As in dead."

"Let's hope he gets the opportunity," Wreath muttered.

"Hey, guys," Law said in a somber whisper. "We'd better shut up and lie low for now." He gripped Wreath's arm, his palm sweaty and gritty.

"Did you see those poor dogs?" Destiny's voice was one octave away from a sob. "They killed them."

"Shhh," Wreath said. "It's okay." She almost reached out to stroke her hair.

"What if they shoot us?"

"They're chicken. Look at the taillights," Wreath said. "They're bailing."

"Someone got shot," Mitch said. "Was it Bum?"

"Mitch!" Law said.

The tumult was quieting, and what had been an indistinguishable roar was the sound of voices. *Close voices.*

Wreath swallowed. She was a pro at running. "We need to break for the woods," she said. "When we get past the trucks, run as hard as you can. Don't stop, no matter what happens."

"Can I hold your hand, Mitch?" Destiny asked.

"I've got your back, Des," Law said.

Wreath led the quartet around the backside of the cages. She looked for Bum as she crawled. What if he *had* been shot? Her hands and knees stung against burrs and gravel.

"Ugh, I'm in dog poop," Mitch said.

"Shut up," Wreath commanded.

"It's gross."

"You'll get us killed," Destiny said. Wreath wasn't sure if she was talking to her or to Mitch.

Truck lights flashed nearby, illuminating the cages. The dogs were motionless, except for one that whimpered and let out a sluggish bark as they passed.

"I want to go home." Destiny was sobbing softly.

"It's okay." Law's voice was low and soothing. "Haven't I always rescued you?"

"Only since she was five," Mitch said with a snort.

Wreath hadn't known anyone that long. "We're almost to the opening," she said. She had gotten her friends into this. They could have watched a movie or hung out at Faye's, played with Destiny's puppy. Normal things.

She stood and lurched a few feet when she saw Bum, lying face down in the dirt.

A sob erupted from her throat, and she looked back at her friends. "Mitch, you lead. Go toward the woods. Law, make sure they get to the car."

Then she changed direction.

She heard a hushed argument behind her, knew the minute they turned toward her.

"We're going with you." Law crawled up next to her.

"Don't risk it," she said.

"Well, isn't that precious?" The question was low and mean.

Wreath froze as a pair of boots stopped in front of her, then one foot almost casually came down on her left hand.

Her eyes watered with pain as she looked up into Theriot's evil smirk.

When J.D. tapped on her bedroom door, Faye was tossing and turning. The re-emergence of Big Fun had saddled her with uneasiness.

J.D. stepped into the room before she could reply to the knock. She'd expected Wreath, and at the sight of this man, she felt almost embarrassed. She patted her hair and hoped she didn't look as old as she felt.

But the agonized look on his face ripped those thoughts away like a Band-Aid from skin. "What?" She jumped up and ran to him. "Who?"

"Wreath's gone."

Faye dashed past J.D. and looked in Wreath's room. Jaclyn was sprawled as always. Samson snuffled, his tail wagging.

She pulled the door shut. No need for the child to be frightened by the conversations that would follow.

They flew to their phones and called maniacally, Shane, Clarice, Law, and the Palomino office. *Nothing.*

Faye paced, while J.D. made one of his lists. For two people who had just gotten acquainted, he and Wreath were as alike as could be. But Wreath had J.D. beat in the mule-headed department.

"Tell me what Shane said again," Faye said.

"That he'd let us know as soon as he heard anything."

"I don't like it. I'm calling Julia to stay with Jaclyn."

J.D. stood and draped his arm around her shoulder. Then he pulled her right up against him. The smell of soap rose from his chest. "Let's go look for Wreath."

She met his eyes, held them. How she loved J.D.

"Shane told us not to," she said.

His eyes were intense. "I can't live with myself if something happens to her."

"Have you tried Law again?"

J.D. nodded. "And you called Destiny?"

"No answer."

"I'm buying Wreath a cell phone," he said.

"And I'm forcing her to use it."

57

Theriot pulled a small pistol out of his pocket and stuck a bigger one in the waistband of his pants.

"You're stupider than that idiot boyfriend of yours," he said to Wreath.

"We need to help him." She began to stand.

Theriot's foot pressed harder on her hand, pinning her to the ground. "You're a little late for that, don't you think?"

Behind her, Law had risen and stepped toward Theriot. "Get away from her," he said.

"My, my, my." Theriot turned the gun toward Law. "What have we here? A high-school love triangle?"

"Law—" Wreath warned. She wondered if her hand was broken, which would hamper her in a fight. And where was Big Fun? She'd seen him earlier from across the field and would rather have Theriot step on her hand than be caught off guard again.

Destiny seemed to be playing dead, and Mitch had scrambled to his feet and was watching.

"Stop right there, boy. I'd hate to shoot you," Theriot said. His gaze went to Destiny. "What's her problem?"

"She passed out," Wreath said.

"She's got asthma," Mitch said.

Destiny did not have asthma. *Did she?*

Theriot made a *tsking* sound. "Kids today," he said, with a shake of his head. "Your parents should keep a closer eye on you." The gun was steady, pointed at Law.

"We just want our friend, sir," Law said. "We don't have any argument with you."

"You trespassed on my property. That's argument a-plenty in my mind."

Destiny sat up so fast that all of them, including Theriot, started. "This isn't your property," she said with a gasping breath. "This is parish land."

"So the Girl Scout awakens?" He moved the gun toward her. "Did you twits poison my dogs?"

"Poison?" Destiny's eyes were wider than a full moon.

"Guess not," Theriot said.

"Des! Are you okay?" Law asked and moved in her direction.

"Stay where you are," Theriot said and hit Law with the butt of the gun. He stumbled and fell to his knees.

"Law!" Destiny screamed

"I'm okay," he said, but he didn't get up.

Destiny looked at Wreath. "Why did I let you talk me into this?" Then she slumped to the ground again.

Was she hurt or acting and what about Law? "She passed out," Wreath said. "They both need a doctor."

"Do I look like the Red Cross?" Theriot asked.

His snide manner snapped Wreath's control, and she lunged at him. "Run!" she screamed. "Run now!"

But before the others moved a blur of noise and movement exploded, and a sprinkling of sticky red drops landed on Wreath. The sound rang in her ears.

Theriot screamed way louder than Destiny had and pitched forward, his heavy weight partially on Wreath and partially on Destiny.

Mitch yelped.

Law didn't hesitate but crawled toward Theriot. Then he grabbed the big pistol from his pants. His eyes were focused behind Wreath. "Good job, man," he said.

Wreath turned to see Bum. He had blood on his face and was walking like a cross between Frankenstein and a zombie. His hair was filled with grass and twigs, and he looked like a scarecrow without enough stuffing.

"You're okay!" Wreath's voice was shrill with relief—and fright.

"I didn't kill him, did I?" Bum's voice came out thin.

Wreath wiggled out from under Theriot, who wasn't moving. She held her hand down to see if he had a pulse but couldn't bring herself to touch him.

"I got it," Law said.

She turned and touched Bum's bloody face. "I thought you were dead."

"So did I," he said. "We've got to get out of here."

"Best idea I've heard all night," Mitch said.

No one seemed to know what direction to move, however, and blood flowed from the top of Bum's head.

Law pulled off his T-shirt and pressed it against the gash.

"You all right?" Bum asked. "He got you good."

"It's just a knot," Law said. "Where's Big Fun?"

Bum touched the blood pouring down his face. It ran onto the tattoo at the base of his neck, a small peace sign. "He's the one who might be dead," he said.

❧

Mitch and Law used a choke chain and leash to secure Theriot.

"I wish we could leave him here to rot," Bum said, holding the shirt against his head.

"Did he poison the dogs?" Wreath asked. She looked calm in the midst of the misery, although her face was pale and her hair was tangled.

A quick shake of his head increased Bum's dizziness. "I need to tell you something," he said, but his knees buckled.

He heard the collection of gasps as he fell to the hard ground, somehow managing to get dirt in his mouth. *Would this night never end?*

He struggled to sit but gave up and lay flat on his back. Strobe lights seemed to flash behind the faces that stared at him. The flow of adrenaline had slowed, and he couldn't get his jaw to work.

Wreath dropped to her knees beside him. "I didn't want to work for him," he tried to say.

She cradled his head in her lap. "It'll get sorted out." Her eyes, full of emotion, roamed across his face.

That look could change a guy.

If only he could keep his eyes open.

58

The handful of remaining camouflaged weasels dispersed when the flashing lights appeared, which could have made Wreath smile. But her entire body shuddered, as though she'd stayed out in the cold too long.

Bum was unconscious and bleeding. Theriot was trussed up at her feet.

Wreath pressed the blood-soaked T-shirt to Bum's head again. "What should we do?" she asked.

"Stay put, I think," Law said. "How's his pulse?" He sounded older, more sure of himself than Wreath felt.

Putting two fingers to Bum's throat, sticky with blood, she shrugged in frustration. "I don't know."

Destiny crawled over and pushed Wreath out of the way. "I've got this." Her voice held such unusual authority that Wreath half expected her to pull out a stethoscope. "His breathing's steady but we probably shouldn't move him." She looked over her shoulder. "Law, what did that first aid teacher say about head wounds?"

Mitch's eyes narrowed. "Are you all right, Des?"

She nodded, two fingers on Bum's neck. "Next time, though, don't let me make a U-turn."

"You're one-of-a-kind," Mitch said.

Then floodlights came on and each of them shielded their eyes with their arms. The field transformed into a cross between a football stadium and a construction site. Behind them were the dog cages, and all of the animals were still. *Dead* still. Beer cans and whiskey bottles were everywhere, and smoke still wafted from the oversized grill.

"Barbecue, anyone?" Mitch said.

"Oh, boy," Law said and his head jerked. "Don't look."

Wreath's gaze had already traveled the few yards. Big Fun, drenched in blood, was splayed out on the ground. A pistol lay a few inches away.

She covered her eyes.

Law, still holding Theriot's gun, approached the body like a veteran law-enforcement officer. When he got close, he nudged Big Fun's stomach with his foot. His sneaker was smeared with blood when it came away.

"Be careful, man," Mitch said.

"Is he alive?" Wreath asked.

"Put your hands in the air," a voice boomed through a megaphone. "We have you surrounded. We are armed and will shoot you if you resist arrest."

"Do you think that's the cops?" Destiny asked.

Wreath shot her a look.

"What?" Destiny said with a sniff. "It could be a rival gang."

"This isn't Miami," she said.

"I repeat. Put your hands in the air."

Theriot emitted a small moan but didn't move.

"Listen to that," Law said. "Even unconscious he recognizes the police."

Then a man's voice called Wreath's name.

Her grandfather and Faye, in jeans and one of Wreath's old T-shirts, ran at her. Tears streamed down Faye's face. "Wreath! Wreath!" J.D. yelled.

"Oh, my Lord, oh, my Lord," Faye was saying over and over.

Shane, not wearing his uniform, was trying to get around them, gun drawn. "Get back," he kept saying, almost in rhythm with Faye's cries.

A trio of officers, also holding weapons, flanked him. "You're not allowed here," one said. Wreath had no idea to whom he spoke.

"Bum needs an ambulance," Wreath said and ran toward Faye and J.D. "And Big Fun might be dead. Theriot got shot." The start of tears burned her eyes as she babbled.

Bum struggled to sit up.

"Do we need the coroner?" Shane asked.

"I don't think so," Law said, again in that strong, mature voice. "It was chaotic. Can't say for sure."

J.D. murmured something indistinguishable.

A deputy with an EMT patch on his sleeve swooped in and took Theriot's pulse, then Big Fun's. "We need stretchers," he yelled.

Then a paramedic moved over to Bum, who unsuccessfully attempted to wave them off.

Two officers, hands on their guns, scurried over and stood over Theriot and Big Fun. Theriot writhed like an earthworm on a hot sidewalk but Big Fun looked dead.

A woman in uniform snapped photographs and uttered the occasional curse word. With gloves, she picked up a cell phone and dropped it into a bag.

"This was some operation," she said to Shane. "I'd begun to think we might never break it up."

"Who called the cops?" Mitch asked.

No one answered, but the photographer frowned. "You civilians need to be removed from the scene."

"Amen," Destiny said.

Bum made a small noise, and Wreath pulled away from Faye and J.D., who had locked her in an embrace. She squatted by Bum, and his eyelids fluttered when she put her hand into his mess of hair.

"You did it," he said and stared into Wreath's eyes.

"Help's here," she said.

"*Youdidit*," he repeated, his words running together.

"J.D.! Shane! He needs help."

Shane, headed toward Big Fun, said something to J.D., who moved their way.

"He's incoherent," she said.

"No." Bum's mouth turned up at the corners. "Want to thank you."

"Don't talk," she said. "J.D. will make sure you're all right."

"You're wonderful."

Wreath's stomach quivered at the intensity in his eyes.

J.D. knelt with the agility of a college guy. "Let's see what we can do for you, Mr. Bumgardner." He pulled a bandanna out of his pocket and gently dabbed at Bum's face.

"I'm sorry I got Wreath mixed up in this." Bum's voice was stronger than Wreath expected.

"Me too," J.D. said. "Although, in case you haven't noticed, she's strong-willed."

Faye barreled past the protesting deputy. "She's never leaving the house again," she said and stepped close enough that a few drops of Bum's blood fell onto her light blue Keds.

Wreath met her eyes. "From now on, I will do whatever you say."

"Where have I heard that before?"

"Where's Jaclyn?" Bum asked.

"With Julia," Faye said.

Wreath felt for a moment like she was in a cocoon, the chitchat erasing the horror around them.

Then an array of law enforcement people swarmed in, yelling orders and trying to corral them. They circled round Bum.

In minutes, a command center of sorts was set up near where Theriot and Big Fun had reigned earlier.

"What is all this?" Faye asked.

"We've called in reinforcements." Shane looked at J.D. "This is going to be a long night."

A Louisiana State Police officer, complete with impressive hat and a patch of stripes on her sleeve, directed an assortment of officers in every direction. Most wore Rapides Parish Sheriff's Department uniforms, while a handful were members of the Landry Police Department.

A swarm of mostly men in Louisiana State Police regalia descended, screeching in at high speeds, lights flashing. Other officers were harder to identify—maybe from another town or parish.

"They're collecting evidence," Faye said.

Wreath managed a smile. *How had she gotten so fortunate?* "Maybe I'll stay home and watch TV with you next time," she said and squeezed Faye's hand.

"What about the dogs?" A deputy asked the woman in charge. "Should we go ahead and—" His voice lowered, and they couldn't hear what he said.

"No!" Bum bolted up and blood gushed from his head. "They'll be fine."

The deputy shook his head, and his voice almost sounded sympathetic. "Afraid not. They're half-dead now. Most are unconscious."

Bum tried to stand but Shane put his hands on his shoulders. "Stay still. J.D., can you give me a hand?"

Bum would not be restrained and fought off Shane. "Don't kill them," he said.

"All right, all right," Shane said but he still had a hand on Bum. "Bumgardner, you need to calm down. Now."

Bum dug in his pockets, and he pulled out a collection of dog biscuits and capsules. His hand shook as he displayed them. "I sedated them so they wouldn't have to fight tonight. They'll wake up in a few hours." Then he made an almost comical face. "You might want to be careful when they do."

One nearby deputy shook his head. "This guy's in shock," the photographer said and snapped photos of Bum.

Shane looked to J.D. "You need to get Wreath and the others out of here."

Bum put a hand up to his head. "I left a dog–Bitty–in the woods."

"It's okay," J.D said. "You did all you could do."

"No, we have to get her. She was the bait dog." Bum covered his face with his hands, his words muffled. "Don't let them hurt her. Please, sir."

Law moved closer. "I'll get her."

"She won't bite if you're gentle." Bum rubbed his arm. "But you might want to wear gloves."

Shane scowled. "I can't approve this," he said. "Law, you need to stay here."

"She's tied up." Bum struggled to stand again. His hair stuck out like the points of a compass, each section going in a different direction. "We can't leave her overnight. She'll be attacked." He closed his eyes. "Again."

"Mr. Bumgardner," Shane said, "you need to stay put."

"I think I know where she is," Law said. "I won't be a minute."

Wreath looked at him.

"I'll go with you." Mitch said.

"Don't leave me!" Destiny hadn't spoken since she'd checked on Theriot.

"We're not sure the area's secure." Shane shook his head. "You three need to stay here."

"I'm a dog lover myself," the kind deputy said. "I'll escort them."

Law nodded, and Destiny said something Wreath couldn't hear and fell back. Mitch meandered like they were changing classes at Landry High.

"Keep a close eye," the woman in charge barked. "Everyone's not accounted for. And none of you can leave the site until you've been questioned."

"Questioned!" Faye put her hands on her hips. "We need to get these kids home. It's clear they're not the perpetrators."

Shane sighed. "They were at the scene of the biggest crime around here in years." He glanced at deputies handcuffing a group of men on the far edge of the parking lot, then to where Big Fun had been put on a stretcher. "They're in serious trouble."

Faye's gaze followed his, lingering on the gray lump that was Big Fun. "They're heroes! You know they weren't involved in a crime."

"Off the record?" Shane said. "I couldn't agree more."

J.D. put his arm around Faye's shoulder again and pulled her close. His lips were in a thin line.

The officer in charge gestured for Shane, who jogged over, nodded a few times and headed back toward Wreath and crew.

"We'll need statements from each of you, plus evidence," Shane said.

"What evidence?" Wreath asked.

"You'll all be searched," Shane said, "and clothing will be collected for blood-spatter evidence." He stopped. "I can't tell you at this moment all we'll be looking for. Some of you may be taken to headquarters."

"Is that necessary?" J.D. asked. His voice was calm as always.

"We'll have to wait and see," Shane replied, but he was summoned again to the officer in charge. She had a cell phone pressed to her ear, and her posture was rigid as a slab of concrete.

"Yes, sir. I understand, sir," she was saying. "Totally unacceptable, sir. I have no idea how they came be at the scene. Understood, sir." Then she looked around the group. "No, sir, I've not spoken with her."

Holding the phone away from her mouth, she spoke to Shane in a voice so low that Wreath couldn't hear, despite inching closer.

Shane drew back.

A man's voice, loud and clearly angry, could be heard on the other end of the phone.

"If you'll give me one mo—" the officer said. Her words were interrupted by another burst of loud words.

"It's Destiny's father," Shane whispered to J.D. "A cop called and told him she was here." He was shaking his head.

"He keeps a close eye on her," Faye said.

"Daddy!" Destiny shrieked and almost tackled the trooper as she grabbed for the phone.

Shane ran his fingers inside the neck of his shirt.

As she hung up, two deputies with a police dog approached. Each had a hand on his gun, which was, thankfully, holstered. They stopped near Bum, who sat on the ground with Faye fussing over his wounds. "Are you Bumgardner?" one demanded.

Bum, propped up with his hands behind him, palms flat on the ground, leaned his head back and jerked his chin. It approximated a nod.

"Thank goodness, you're finally here," Faye said, holding up the red-stained cloth. "He needs treatment."

"Ma'am?" The officer frowned.

"Get moving," Faye said.

The two deputies exchanged a glance.

"Is that him?" one asked.

"His pulse is racing," Faye said. "Help him."

"We're not EMTs, ma'am. Medical treatment is on its way." He nodded toward an ambulance pulling in next to the herd of police cars.

"Step away, ma'am," the deputy said, as he turned to Bum. "You're under arrest for the attempted murder of Fred Procell."

"And that's for starters," the other officer mumbled under his breath.

59

J aclyn cried herself to sleep the next night, scrunched up against Wreath in the middle of the bed.

The mixture of the explosive Saturday night and the frantic day was jumbled in Wreath's brain, which went back and forth, back and forth, like the pendulum on Faye's grandfather clock.

Wreath had spent Sunday going over details with Clarice, while Faye and J.D. tried to distract Jaclyn. Unspoken worry about Bum hung over the house. Law's mother's surgery also added a layer of strain.

Jaclyn had developed the trouble radar that Wreath had picked up as a kid. "I miss my mommy," she said as Wreath tried to lull her to sleep.

"I know you do," Wreath said. *I miss mine too.*

Jaclyn wiped her nose on the hem of her flowered pajama top, a gift from Faye. "When's Uncle Bum coming to get me?"

"We don't know quite yet," Wreath said. And they didn't.

Bum was in jail.

Who knew where Starla was? She hadn't surfaced during the police roundup that had all of Rapides Parish buzzing. Apparently her encounter with Wreath and Law in the woods was the last Starla sighting.

While she had disappeared, the bait dog, Bitty, had been right where Bum left her and emerged from the wood snarling at the end of a rope leash. Law, Mitch, and the deputy kept their distance, the deputy holding onto the rope.

When they approached, Bum was being handcuffed, his eyes steely. Wreath was struck by the similarities between him and the captured dog.

After a quick conference, the deputy removed Bitty from the scene. "Will you take her to the vet?" Bum said.

"You better worry about your own hide, boy," the deputy said.

Then J.D. had stepped forward. "We'll take care of her," he said as the police led Bum toward the ambulance. "And clear all of this up."

"May I go with him to the hospital?" Faye asked and took a step after them.

"You people need to stay put," one of the officers said for what seemed like the dozenth time.

"She wants to help," J.D. said, a rare knot of aggravation in his voice. "Please don't be rude."

"I'll be all right," Bum said, then caught Wreath's eye. "Please take care of Jaclyn."

"We will." Wreath rushed toward Bum.

"Stop right there." The deputy held up his hand.

"Listen to him, Wreath," Bum said with a crooked smile. "He's armed."

"Clarice will know how to handle this." J.D. put his hand on the small of Wreath's back. "She made it home and will meet Bumgardner at the police station."

And Bum had been removed.

The sun had been up by the time they got home-minus Bum-and they were covered in dust and sweat.

Law hurried to Lafayette. Faye and J.D. called their pastor and asked for prayer for Bum and Jaclyn—and all hurt by the Saturday night tragedy.

Would any of them ever forget the sight of Big Fun and Theriot, splattered with blood on the field?

Now, as Jaclyn whimpered next to her, Wreath's body ached with fatigue. She shuddered, and Jaclyn jumped, just short of dozing off. "I hope Uncle Bum's okay," she said in a sleepy voice.

"Me too." Sometimes Wreath thought the child was inside her brain.

"And Miss Clarice . . ." The small voice trailed off into sleep.

Wreath smiled. Clarice had been in and out all day, not complaining that she'd been up most of the night after a long flight.

Her eyes had been troubled when she came from the police station, Bum not with her. But after quietly filling in the adults, she draped a quilt between the couch and coffee table in the den and went into a make-believe world with Jaclyn. *If only they could shield Jaclyn forever.* Wreath hoped the sweet child would never hear the story of last night.

And if she couldn't be spared the hard details of life, Jaclyn now had a circle of adults to protect her. Each took unspoken shifts and read to her or worked a puzzle or played chase in Faye's backyard. They had even bribed her to take a nap with the promise of a snow cone with J.D.

Clarice returned in early evening, fresh from the jail. One look at her somber eyes told Wreath that Bum was not coming home that night. "Nothing moves quickly on weekends," Clarice murmured. "Theriot says Bum pulled the trigger of the gun that they were tussling over with Fred Procell."

"Big Fun attacked him. Bum didn't have a gun." Wreath led her into the living room.

"Theriot didn't get this far without a passel of lies," Clarice said. "A string of people arrested said Bum collected their bets, delivered their payoff, was part of Theriot's inner circle."

"He was protecting his niece!" Wreath's voice rose. "His sister dragged him into this."

"We need to go back over everything you know. This is a complicated case."

Jaclyn rounded the corner from the den.

"Where's Uncle Bum?" She bypassed Wreath and climbed onto Clarice's lap. Her thin, pale arms looked fragile around Clarice's chocolate-colored neck.

"He had a few things to take care of, honey bunny," she said. "He said to tell you he loves you very much and will see you soon."

"When?"

Wreath smiled. A prosecuting attorney couldn't be much worse than Jaclyn.

"Soon, we hope. He said for you to be sweet." She tweaked Jaclyn's nose. "I assured him that you are always sweet."

"You use big words," Jaclyn said, rolling the word *assured* around on her tongue. "Will I learn that at school?"

"You'll learn all sorts of things at school," Wreath said.

"I wants to know how to read, like you and Miss Faye." Jaclyn sounded impressed. "Smart girls read."

"That's right. Smart girls read." Wreath smiled but was grateful when Jaclyn wandered off to find Papa J.D.

"What a resilient soul," Clarice said. "You must have been like that when you were a child."

Now, lying next to Jaclyn, Wreath pondered the decisions ahead—how to run the store and keep Jaclyn and what could be done about Bum. His legal problems, as Clarice had said, were complicated.

Where would he and Jaclyn live once he got out of jail? They couldn't go back to the Palomino, and how could an eighteen-year-old take care of a child?

A tap sounded, and Wreath's bedroom door eased open. The hall light outlined Faye, who looked like a middle-aged angel in her white robe and slippers. She padded across the carpet, and her face relaxed into a smile as she looked down at the bed.

"Hey," Wreath said softly.

"Hey, yourself," Faye said. "You okay?"

"I can't sleep. You either?"

"My head feels like a dozen TV programs are broadcasting at the same time—and, I'll tell you, they aren't comedies."

Wreath patted the bed. "Have a seat."

"I don't want to wake up the little princess," she whispered.

"A tornado couldn't wake her up once she conks out."

Faye eased onto the mattress.

"I feel bad for her, not knowing where her mother is, what's going on with Bum," Wreath said. "A kid shouldn't have to worry about things like that."

"You can't slip much past her," Faye said. "She's an intuitive little thing."

"What will happen to her?" Wreath lowered her voice until it was hardly audible over the hum of the air-conditioning unit. "She can't keep moving around like . . ."

"Like you did?" Faye put her hand on Wreath's arm.

"At least my mom was there for me," she said. "Jaclyn needs a permanent roof over her head. Roots." She yawned. "A roof and roots."

"Why don't we talk about this tomorrow?" Faye started to rise but Wreath grabbed her arm.

"What if Clarice can't get Bum out of jail?"

"Jaclyn can stay with us. I'd love that. Wouldn't you?"

Wreath exhaled. "I don't know about getting her in school, the store, college classes." She shrugged. "It's too much."

"We'll figure it out," Faye said.

Drawing in a breath, Wreath hurled her latest idea out there: "I think I should postpone college for a semester."

"No, ma'am," Faye's voice was low and firm. "That's not an option."

"I'm ahead of where I ever dreamed I'd be," Wreath said, "thanks to you. I could wait until next semester. I won't even be eighteen until December."

"Let's not get ahead of ourselves. Lots of things have to unfold before we make big decisions." Faye stood and pulled the sheet over Wreath and Jaclyn.

"I can't believe y'all went to that field last night. I'm sooooo sorry—."

"Oh, shush," Faye said. "Nothing would have kept J.D. from going." She clasped her hands together. "Like it or not, your grandfather plans to be part of your life."

Wreath looked straight at her. "I like it."

60

The afternoon light was brighter than Bum remembered when he exited the courthouse Monday. He squinted and shielded his eyes.

Even the air smelled better—like hamburgers.

Maybe he'd lost his mind, caged up like one of Theriot's dogs.

People didn't forget what the sun was like in thirty-one hours. *Did they?* That cell was tiny and dingy, its odor a mix of Pine Sol and urine.

Bum walked faster. He jammed his hands in his pockets, a pair of hand-me-down khakis from J.D. They hit him just below his calves but were better than the bloody pants he'd been wearing.

"You hungry?" J.D. asked.

"Jail cuisine leaves something to be desired," the too-nice lawyer said. *Clarice Johnson.* Where had she come from? She walked briskly, all dressed up in a blazer and skirt. She hadn't let Bum get more than six inches away from her.

"It wasn't too bad," he mumbled. At least he hadn't gone to bed hungry.

"Long night?" the attorney asked.

He didn't answer. A few of Theriot's surly customers—yapping like the dogs—were his suitemates, and he'd spent the night keeping watch.

"I could do with a bite of lunch." J.D. said. "What say we grab burgers?" He nodded toward the red-and-white cart parked on the corner. "You have time, Clarice?"

"You buying?" she said with a grin.

J.D., in blue work pants and a plaid shirt, nodded. "You betcha," he said. His voice was calm, his face relaxed.

What is it with these people? They acted like they were on a family outing, not exiting the Landry city jail. "Don't you need to get back to work?" Bum asked.

"I never miss lunch," J.D. said. "You in a hurry?"

To go where? To do what?

Bum gave his head a quick shake. "Not if Jaclyn's okay."

"She was playing at Faye's store when I left," J.D. said. "I think she had sold Wreath a few thousand dollars' worth of furniture."

Clarice—or should he call her Mrs. Johnson—burst out with a laugh. "That child, that child," she said. "If I had half her energy, I'd be on the Supreme Court by now."

"Tell me about it," Bum said, although he wasn't quite sure what the Supreme Court was. He'd put his head down that day and slept through the . . . what was it? Oh, yeah, through the *judicial* branch. He should have paid more attention, but he supposed he'd get firsthand knowledge now.

J.D. steered them toward the grill.

A cluster of cops sat in the shade and shoveled food into their mouths. A handful of other people lined the concrete wall. Some shared chips. All ate burgers.

"What can I do you for, Mr. J.D.?" the vendor asked. "The usual?"

J.D. nodded.

"For Wreath and Miss Faye too?"

"Absolutely," he said, "plus my two guests here."

"And a junior burger," Clarice said. "What does Jaclyn like, Bum?"

"Ketchup, no mustard," Bum said. "Sweet relish. No onions."

"Well done," Clarice murmured.

The cook drew the meat out of a metal vat, and steam floated upward. "You're that lawyer from up near Alexandria, aren't you?" he said.

"Guilty as charged." She smiled.

The vendor nodded toward the police having lunch. "Did you hear what those guys ran into Saturday night? Broke up a big dog-fighting operation south of town."

Bum dropped his head, but his new lawyer stepped closer. "What are they saying?" Her voice was casual.

"Somebody tipped 'em off that there was a big fight, huge purse." He lowered his voice. "They even found the phone the call came from."

Bum stiffened. J.D. drew in a breath. Clarice leaned in. "No onions on mine either," she said, pointing, then kept talking. "They're sure tight-lipped on who their informant was."

"They don't know!" The cook's big white hat flopped as he shook his head, dressing a hamburger as he spoke. "They figure the same person sedated the dogs, saved almost all of them." He put the food into white sacks. "The hero hasn't taken credit."

J.D. drew out his wallet, paid for the food with cash and dropped a five-dollar bill in a plastic cup for tips.

"It's a crazy world," the cook said.

"It sure is," Clarice said and put her hand on Bum's arm. "The world needs more heroes."

61

Wreath was buying a pretend car when Bum, Clarice, and J.D. popped in with burgers.

Even over the scent of onions and meat, a musty smell clung to Bum. His hair was in a knot on top of his head, which should have looked ludicrous but didn't. And he was wearing a pair of pants that fit about like Bermuda shorts.

Jaclyn hurled herself at him and upended the sacks. The food was barely rescued from Samson, whose stubby legs moved faster than one would expect.

"Uncle Bum, I learned to ride a bicycle!" A smile burst across her face.

"That's super, Champ!" Bum knelt, his arms around her, his face in her curly hair.

"Just like Wreath."

He fixed his gaze on Wreath. "Is that so?" he said, his voice quiet.

"J.D. bought it for me. And I'm going to learn to read!" She drew in a breath. "Clarice says we all need to read a lot. Wreath loves to read too. Don't you, Wreath?"

"I certainly do." She forced a smile.

"Did you know she used to live in a van in the woods? Clarice says she's a modern pie-oh . . ." She stopped, her brow furrowed, and scurried over to Clarice, who leaned down. Jaclyn wrapped her arms around her neck. "What was that word you said?"

"Pioneer."

Jaclyn pulled back and looked at Bum. "Wreath's a pioneer." Then she leaned closer, and when she spoke her voice was lower. "That's a good thing."

Bum nodded. "Yes, it is."

Jaclyn's exuberant welcome was the only cheerful thing about the lunch, which was more awkward than Wreath's first day at Landry High. Faye was the only one who pushed Bum for information and spelled out *j-a-i-l*.

"My mommy was in jail once," Jaclyn said, her mouth full of hamburger, ketchup on her chin.

Bum and J.D. both made choking sounds and set their food aside for sips of lemonade. Faye cleared her throat, and butterflies flew around in Wreath's stomach.

Clarice merely smiled, reached over and dabbed at Jaclyn's face with a napkin. "You are a smart girl."

"It sure is hot outside," Bum said.

"I suspect we'll get a shower this afternoon," J.D. said.

Lunch ended abruptly when Clarice said she needed to talk to Bum in private.

"What's *in private* mean?" Jaclyn's eyes were suspicious. Then her face drooped. She threw her arms around Bum's leg. "Don't leave me."

"I'm not going anywhere, silly-willy."

The grownups exchanged glances. Wreath raised her eyebrows.

Jaclyn pulled back to look up into his face. "Did you save them dogs?"

His face flushed the color of an overripe tomato. "He most certainly did," Clarice said. "That's why we need to talk in private."

62

When the bell dinged on the front door a week later—*had it really only been a week since the dogfight?*—Wreath was down on her hands and knees, dusting underneath the Art Deco furniture.

She didn't think she liked the style—too many angles. With all its crevices, it was hard to keep clean She preferred her furniture like life . . . simple. She would reduce the price on this collection. Surely everything would be easier when school started.

As she clambered out from the sofa, she saw the black shoes.

The mail carrier dropped the mail on Faye's desk and waved. "Lots of excitement around here this week," he said. "People still talking about that big arrest. You know anything about that boy? The one everyone's talking about?"

"Not really." Wreath was tired of talking about Bum when he apparently was not speaking to her.

"Sure looks like he helped rid Landry of the worst kind of blight." The mail guy adjusted his bag and headed for the door. "Have a good 'un."

Wreath scrunched back down and focused on a spider web. Store work was easy compared to relationships.

Truth be told, she was tired.

Tired of speculating about what was going to happen—to Bum, to Jaclyn, to Law's mother, even about Destiny, whose father had grounded her for life or until school started.

Tired, if she admitted it, of sharing sleeping space with a five-year-old bed hog. She rubbed her neck. She hadn't slept well in days.

Mostly she was tired of waiting for Bum to talk to her.

He had avoided a real conversation with her all week.

Rumors zoomed around town faster than Faye drove. Wreath had known Bum was a good guy, but he was emerging from this ordeal a hero. Would she ever know the full story?

Since that day when he'd gotten out of jail, Wreath had not had a moment of her own with him.

Faye's house buzzed with activity, a stark contrast from a few months ago when it was tomblike. The crowd for supper had varied from night to night, always with J.D. and sometimes with Bum, who made it a point to take a seat away from Wreath.

He had moved temporarily—and with an argument—into J.D.'s house and passed on supper several nights. "He's overwhelmed," J.D. said and took him a plate.

"I'm glad you're there, Mr. Bumgardner," Faye said when he came to see Jaclyn one evening. "Maybe you can help J.D. with some of those odd jobs he can't keep up with."

Bum gave a slight smile at the suggestion and, according to Wreath's grandfather, had cleaned gutters, weeded a flowerbed, and caulked a shower.

"Want to come see his handiwork?" J.D. asked, his voice steady. But Wreath balked. She wasn't ready to see that house. She had to wonder: *Did Bum have her father's room?*

Clarice and her husband also came nearly every evening. They divided their visits between legal strategy with Bum and playing with Jaclyn and Samson. Twice Jaclyn begged to spend the night with them, and Bum relented.

Law had been by only twice, on the way back from visiting his mom. Those visits were subdued, and he avoided talking by watching a TV show with Bum. Wreath noted that crime dramas were suddenly less popular, though.

Law's mom was weak, and he was taking "some time off" to stay with her. "I'm not sure when I'll be able to go back to work," he said. "I like to be there when she has her physical therapy."

His grandparents, Nadine and Jim, stopped by for coffee one afternoon, and talked softly with Faye and J.D. about their daughter's injuries. Wreath wanted to eavesdrop but Jaclyn was giving her a pretend manicure on the kitchen table, and she couldn't hear over the child's happy chatter.

Both Bum and Jaclyn had gone with Clarice and Sam for a couple of hours Friday afternoon. "I think we's going to talk *private*," Jaclyn had said as Wreath combed her hair.

Bum had run both hands through his hair with such an amusing result that Wreath had escaped to her room after they left and sketched him.

The crazy hair was easy to capture, but the uncertain look in his eyes was impossible to get right.

Finally she gave up and left his face blank.

The household hubbub felt to Wreath like a nonstop stay at a carnival. After a year living alone, she still wasn't used to having so many people around so much. She was happy to tend the store alone today.

Even coming to work had turned into a negotiation. "Let's close tomorrow. Summer's slow, and lots of stores close on Mondays," Faye had said after Sunday lunch. They each still wore their nice church clothes, and Wreath was drying the china plates. Faye never consented to paper and wore an apron over her dress.

"That's not our brand," Wreath said. "What if someone needs a gift?"

"Or an emergency end table?" Faye raised a brow. "Thanks to you, our brand is good. Take a day and go have fun."

"Running the store is fun."

Law and Bum were watching television with J.D. in the den, and Wreath didn't miss Law's quick glance back her way.

"Well, it is," she said.

"You mean that, don't you?" Faye said quietly.

Wreath nodded.

"Have at it. I'm picking my battles, and this one goes to you." Then she popped Wreath playfully with a dish towel. "I'm dragging Mr. Bumgardner to Lafayette tomorrow for some decent clothes."

A weird choking sound came from the den, and Law gave a rare laugh. "Good luck, buddy," he said to Bum.

Jaclyn, smiling more each day, had gone along that morning "to help Uncle Bum choose the right colors."

Wreath, with an unexpected lonely hole in her heart, went back to her dusting. "Take that," she said to a cobweb.

This she could control.

63

Clarice's voice called out as the bell jingled again. "Hello? Anyone here?"

A pair of black pumps moved her way.

"Over here," Wreath called and crawled out from behind the grouping.

"Taking a nap?"

"I wish." She hopped up. "I didn't expect you today. I missed you while you were in Haiti."

"Likewise. We don't find enough time to chat."

Wreath gave a little shrug. "Life's been weird this summer, hasn't it?"

"Indeed."

A yearning ran through Wreath. "Want to have a seat?" She pointed at a green vinyl couch. "Mid-century? Or Craftsman? Or"—she wrinkled her face—"Art Deco?"

"Art Deco, of course," Clarice said and eased onto the settee, her back straight. She was a stately, attractive woman.

There was a moment of silence, the big clock in the back ticking.

"How are you doing, Wreath?"

"I shouldn't have gone to the dogfight," she blurted. She had needed to get that off her chest. Clarice had done so much for her and been dragged back into the Big Fun mess.

"None of you should have gone." Clarice raised her brows. "But I admire your spirit."

Wreath hesitated. "I vowed to quit lying, so I have to tell you I'd probably do it again. It was reckless and dangerous, but a lot of wrongs were righted that night."

"Please don't do it—or anything like that—again. You all could have been killed." Her face was, for Clarice, stern. "Law enforcement should be allowed to do their jobs."

"I was worried about Bum."

"You have to learn to trust the system."

"It's hard," Wreath admitted. "At least I learned to trust you. How'd you put up with me all those months?" She tilted her head. "When I almost gave up on Bum, I thought of how you never quit on me."

Tears welled in Clarice's eyes. "Oh, Wreath, how I adore you. You're smart, astute, and loyal . . ."

A flush crept up Wreath's face. "Am I applying for a job?"

Clarice chuckled. "Almost," she said. "I need to talk about your college plans. I've got a proposal for you."

64

Wreath zoomed to the junkyard Tuesday afternoon. A crow cawed in the distance, and another answered. A woodpecker's *rat-a-tat* echoed through the trees.

She propped her bike against a tree and stood for a moment. Peace, elusive for the past few weeks, washed over her. She inhaled the woodsy smell. A hint of honeysuckle lingered, about the only flowering plant left in the July oven.

A tiny chickadee chattered from a nearby branch. A pair of cardinals flew deeper into the brush, one of them singing a happy sound.

A mockingbird seemed to lecture. "Do it. Do it."

"Oh, shut up." Her voice caused the bird to fly from a nearby oak. It landed atop a hickory a few yards away. "Do it. Do it," the bird chirped.

What about her plan? Rapides Parish Community College, not some New Orleans university. Working at the store. Helping with Jaclyn. Getting to know her grandfather.

She glanced up where the leaves draped overhead. It looked almost like the bottle cave.

Then she saw them.

A string of orange *No Trespassing* signs had been posted on a row of trees, with a boundary of orange ribbon, stretched out like the police-scene at the dog-fighting arena.

Someone had laid claim to her junkyard.

Wreath yanked at the sign. It would not give way, the plastic strong, the nail deep into the tree. Putting one foot on the tree, she pulled again. Sweat poured down her neck.

"Want me to do that for you?"

She whirled so fast she bumped right up against . . . Bum. He put his hands on her shoulders. The dappled light gleamed on his— Her eyes grew wide. "What happened?"

His hands dropped. "It looks dorky, doesn't it?"

She studied what was left of his hair. "I think I like it."

"Then why are you frowning?"

"You've barely talked to me in more than a week," she said, "then you show up here? What's that about?"

His eyes did not meet hers. "I didn't know what to say. I made a mess of things."

"You took on a ring of criminals."

"And almost got you killed. I'm sorry, Wreath."

"What are you doing here?"

He kicked at the grass. Were those *Vans* on his feet? "I wanted to see what this place was like. Clear my head."

Wreath's eyebrows shot up.

"Guess it wasn't a great idea." He tapped the *No Trespassing* sign. "I'm not exactly in good with the cops."

"J.D. says you're a hero."

"Your granddad's too nice for his own good."

"Did you really call the cops from Theriot's personal cell phone?"

He brushed off a mosquito and did not answer.

Her eyes widened. "You're wearing short sleeves."

"Faye's idea." He rubbed his arm, his fingers lingering on the scars from the dog bites. "I see where you get your stubborn streak. She is kind of sweet, though."

"I probably wouldn't use the word *sweet*." Wreath couldn't keep her eyes off his hair. It looked tame. Normal.

Not like Bum at all.

He looked around. "You lived here alone for a whole year?"

"The critters and me. They weren't as bad as the men you worked for." Wreath stared at him for a second and ducked through the dense brush. She held a branch back to make a passageway.

He followed without a question.

"Careful. Fire ant bed," she said.

He leapt over the rotten log. "You did this every day?"

She nodded and forged ahead. Nature had reclaimed the land over the summer. The vines and undergrowth were as thick as if she'd never existed.

Will that be what happens if I go away to college?

Weaving in and out of the rusted buses, trucks, and cars, she leaned back and let the sun beat down on her face, then pushed on toward the old van. "This was my camp." She pointed. "I ate by that bus. My bedroom was in here."

She put her hand on the VW door where she'd slept but stopped. Instead she led Bum to a gold Dodge Coronet and hopped up on the hood. She patted the warm metal. "Care to join me in my home theater?" She lay back. "This was a great place to look at the stars."

Bum hoisted himself on the hood and lay down next to her.

"The night noises get super loud out here. All those stars made me realize I was part of something bigger."

"I couldn't have done that," he said.

"But you took care of Jaclyn." She sat up. "And tried to get your sister out of trouble. That's braver than running away and living out here. Harder too."

"I was so afraid, Wreath." His voice sounded raw. "You shouldn't have come out there that night."

She snorted but didn't comment.

"Did you hear that Clarice is working on a deal for me? First offender, helped the cops, stupid kid, that sort of thing."

"Does that mean you won't have to do time?"

"Not sure. We have evidence that I didn't pull that trigger, but this is still serious." He shuddered. "That jail makes this place look like a resort."

"Is that where Theriot is?" She resisted looking over her shoulder as she said his name.

He gave a quick nod. "They're holding him without bail. His lawyer's fighting it, and Clarice says he may get out."

"And Big Fun's still in the hospital?"

Again, a nod. "Critical condition."

She shivered. "I'll be glad when he's back in prison." She paused. "You're not going to do any more stupid things, are you?"

He tapped his fingers on the hood. "I'm only eighteen. I doubt I've done my last stupid thing."

"That's not reassuring." Wreath shifted. "Please don't break Faye and J.D.'s hearts."

He frowned. "I don't plan on it."

"It'll crush them if you run off or something."

"Like Starla, you mean?"

"Like me." The words felt like a confession.

He shook his head. "I'm staying in Landry for now, getting Jaclyn settled down."

"J.D. mentioned he's helping you find a job."

"*Helping* doesn't cover it." Bum sat up straight, his feet on the silver bumper. "He put in a good word to the owner of the animal clinic. She remembered Samson, but . . ." He hesitated. "I had to confess I dropped a dog there once. That dog Bitty's there, too, for the time being." He looked down. "The others are at the parish shelter. . . except one had to be put to sleep."

Wreath put her face in her hands.

"He never stood a chance," he said. "The cops said he was too mean. Only because people made him that way."

"At least you stopped the ring. No telling how many other dogs you saved."

His face flushed. "The clinic really takes good care of animals. I want to work there so bad. Maybe it'll make up for all the dumb stuff I did for Theriot."

Wreath studied him. "Do you think you'll get the job?"

"The manager asked if I'm willing to work Saturdays." The corner of his mouth lifted. "I hope it works out because you've seen how much Jaclyn eats. And she'll need school supplies and"—his words were getting faster—"the job's only twenty-five hours. I have a panic attack thinking about it."

"I've had a few of those myself, most of them right around here." She clasped her fingers. "You can't take the future all at once. It's overwhelming. All we have is right now."

"I wish I had half your brains."

"Said the guy who pulled off his own sting operation," she said. "You're plenty smart."

"We'll see soon enough." He hopped down and paced around the car. "Clarice lined up a GED class as part of the plea bargain. I might be able to start at RPCC in January." He stopped and peered at her. "How about you?"

Wreath shook her head. "I'm thoroughly confused. She's come up with a major scholarship to Evangeline College in New Orleans, but I already have everything in order here."

"What would change your mind?"

"I want to do the right thing, but how do I know what that is?" Education had been her mother's constant dream for Wreath. "Frankie made me promise to finish high school and go to a good—" She stopped.

"Are you all right?" he asked.

"You helped me figure something out."

He threw her a confused look. "Are you shi—kidding me?"

She smiled. "Close one, buddy. Jaclyn would be all over that."

Bum pulled at the neck of his preppie shirt. "She's a challenge."

"At least she's not in the Palomino." She hesitated. "I went by with information for Half-Pint. There aren't any programs around here, but Law's grandfather is checking into something through the library."

"I heard," he said. "Linda tracked me down through Clarice's office. Wanted me to tell you thanks." He looked up at the trees overhead. "I'm lucky. Clarice and Sam suggested they keep Jaclyn during the week. Or whenever I have to work."

"Wow."

"They've asked me to stay there too." He shook his head. "I've been on my own a long time. Even with my folks, I pretty much took care of myself." He sighed. "I've made so many lousy choices."

She stared at him. "Now's your chance to make better ones."

❧

A squirrel scurried up a pine tree as they wound their way silently back toward the road. A rabbit hopped across the path. The birds jabbered.

"How'd you get out here anyway?" she asked.

He pulled a key ring out of his pocket. "J.D. loaned me his truck. Want a ride to town?"

"Sure."

As Bum loaded her bike into the back of the truck, Wreath looked back at the junkyard. The posted signs shone in the late-afternoon sunlight, and in the distance, she could hear the hum of machinery.

She had a new opportunity for college.

"Do it. Do it." The mockingbird flew out of the tree as Bum negotiated the turn toward downtown. "Do it. Do it."

The trees nearby swayed with a strong breeze. Wreath swallowed. *I miss you, Mama.*

65

Faye walked to the front of the store when the truck pulled up, relieved that Wreath had ridden back with Bum. Perhaps they could help each other heal.

Throwing her a wave, Wreath didn't come toward the boutique but dashed to the hardware store. J.D. would be thrilled.

She was tempted to join them but these solo encounters mattered. Wreath inched closer to J.D. like a feral cat afraid of being trapped.

As Wreath disappeared from sight, Bum lay his head back on the seat. The haircut and new clothes looked good on him, and he had smiled—honest-to-goodness smiled—when he looked in the mirror at the store.

"Wowser, Uncle Bum," Jaclyn had said. "You look pretty."

They'd all laughed. Jaclyn was right. He cleaned up nice.

If only the inside were as easy.

What a summer.

Faye sighed and straightened a few throw pillows in an antique cotton-picking basket by the window display.

A playful tapping at the back door pulled her eyes off Bum, still in the truck, and Faye scurried toward the rear, looking through the peephole. *Julia.*

"Hello, soon-to-be gone neighbor," Faye said.

"Hello, soon-to-be-someone-else's landlady." Julia was loaded down with colorful canvases of all sizes and placed them on the workroom counter. "I'm clearing out the last of my things and wanted to see if Wreath thinks these will sell."

Faye cocked her head. "She's next door."

"Excellent!" Julia's beautiful smile grew. "She's giving J.D. a chance?"

"More and more every day."

"Is he over the moon?"

"That's an understatement." Faye cleared her throat. "It's almost too tender to watch."

Julia laughed. "You're becoming a softie."

Faye groaned. "My cantankerous image has taken a beating, that's for sure." She steered Julia toward the showroom. "Look out there. Something's going on, but I don't know what."

Bum no longer had his head down but still sat in the truck.

"What's he doing?" Julia said.

"I suspect it has something to do with our girl."

"Are they . . . I thought Wreath and Law . . ."

Faye made a face. "If there's anything I know less about than teen love, I don't care to hear what it is."

"Is Bum good for Wreath?" Julia asked.

"Other than nearly getting her killed the other night?"

Julia's face paled.

"Bum's got depth. It's just not been mined yet," Faye said. "Law is a good young man, although Nadine says he's struggling too."

"Watching these kids this summer . . . I had almost forgotten what a time of change it was," Julia said. "A season of firsts. Everything's new, nothing feels certain."

The two watched as Bum got out of the truck and lifted Wreath's bike from the back. He parked it and fastened the lock that was draped around the seat.

"Is it true that Clarice has offered to let him and Jaclyn live with her?" Julia asked.

Faye nodded. "J.D. thinks Bum's a little proud—and a little old—for that."

"Perhaps." Julia glanced at the big clock. "I'd better get back to packing."

"Wreath did mention she wants to throw you a party, right?"

"I tried to talk her out of it, but—"

"Save your breath. When she sets her mind on something . . . Besides we've got quite the list." Faye counted on her fingers. "You leaving for art school, Destiny and Law off to Tech, Mitch to LSU, Jaclyn in kindergarten. I'm sure I'm forgetting something."

Pushing on the heavy door, Julia paused. "Have you rented the apartment?"

"Too much going on." Faye rolled her eyes. "I may let it sit. I can barely keep the store open."

"Tell Wreath to take a look," Julia said. "I have a lot that I hate to throw out. I hoped the new tenant might want it. Wreath can probably sell it."

Faye's eyes went back to Bum, who was straightening plant displays in front of J.D.'s store. "Leave it," she said. "We'll find some use for it."

66

The winding road wasn't as spooky in the afternoon light, and J.D. navigated the potholes as though he'd been out here many times.

The thought of him here alone hurt Wreath.

They pulled into the cemetery parking lot, two weeks after the midnight ride out here with her friends.

Wreath rolled down her window. Wildflowers grew on the edge of the gravel parking lot.

"It's peaceful," she said.

"Some days."

Side by side, but not touching, they walked from the truck to a chain-link fence and J.D. pushed the gate open.

"Will you go first?" she whispered.

He nodded, not speaking, and headed toward the middle of the cemetery, carefully walking around the graves. He occasionally picked up a faded flower arrangement that had blown over or brushed dust off the top of a tombstone with his hand.

"Lots of friends out here," he said. "We probably should do a better job of keeping this place up."

Wreath barely acknowledged him, scanning the granite monuments for her father's name.

"It's right over here." J.D. cleared his throat.

She was tempted to turn back toward the truck. If she had her bike, she might pedal right back to town.

But she was the one who had asked to come.

"They're buried under that tree," he said.

They approached the graves, now clearly visible. The stark names engraved on the marble made Wreath's heart stammer.

The first stone said Lynn Morris Everest, *Loving mother and wife* under an engraved dove. New silk flowers in bright summer colors sat in small urns attached to the sides. Someone had placed a small bouquet of red roses, like you'd cut from a yard, on the grave.

The clouds above were white and fluffy, the sky summer blue. A bird or two flew around the trees at the edge. They chirped as though part of a holy choir.

"That's your grandmother," he said. "How I wish she could have known you."

Next to it was a matching stone with an anchor engraved by the name: John David Everest. *Beloved son, friend to all.* Those words were worn slightly by weather. Underneath, the words were newly etched: *Father to Wreath.*

Wreath reached for J.D.'s hand and clung. Tears sprang into her eyes. "When did you do that?" she whispered.

"At the beginning of June."

"But you hardly knew me."

"I knew you were my granddaughter."

Neither spoke for a few moments. J.D. took off his glasses and wiped them on his shirt. "I wanted to bring you here then, but I wasn't sure you were ready."

She turned toward him, a sob breaking from her throat, and he engulfed her in a hug, the same kind of hug her daddy might have given had he been alive. A hug Frankie would have given. Tight, reassuring, steadying.

"Does it ever get easier?" she asked. "Losing the people you love?" Her tears soaked through the dress shirt he'd worn.

"You never stop missing them," he said, "but you have to keep going. So I guess that part gets easier."

She pulled back, and he handed her his ever-present bandanna. She blew her nose. "So you bring flowers out here a lot?" She walked toward the graves and picked up one of the red roses. She held it against her cheek and inhaled its scent.

He smiled. "Faye brought the roses. She said she needed to talk to Lynn, make sure it was okay that we are getting married."

"That's kind of sweet. Kind of weird too," Wreath said. "I hope she got the all-clear since you bought that expensive ring."

J.D. laughed, the sound not as out-of-place as Wreath would have thought. "I'm still looking for the right moment to give it to her."

"I wondered."

He laughed again.

"Thanks for bringing me here," she said.

When they climbed into the cab of the truck, they were both quiet and J.D. turned the key only far enough to lower their windows.

The breeze, hot but not too humid, blew through the truck.

A mockingbird landed on the gate into the cemetery. "Do it," it sang. "Do it."

"Uh, J.D.—I mean Granddad." She covered her face with her hands for a second. *What should she call him?*

"Either's fine." He touched her shoulder lightly. "I am grateful that you're letting me into your life. Most people would have cut me out for what I did to you."

"You didn't know."

"Do it. Do it." The mockingbird had moved to a nearby tree branch.

"About the future," Wreath said. "I need advice."

J.D. had a strained look on his face as he turned toward her. "If this is about Bum and Law, Faye might be a better person to ask."

Wreath couldn't hold back a chuckle. "It's not boy advice."

Now he looked serious.

"It's about college."

"Faye and I plan to pay for that," he said. "No arguing."

"Clarice wants me to go to Evangeline. She's arranged for a scholarship. She knows someone."

"She knows everyone," he said. "So are we talking about when you finish at RPCC?"

"When I finish this summer. Like in two weeks."

He swallowed hard. "This must be the hard part of having a granddaughter. That's a fine school," he said, "and New Orleans is a fascinating place and not too far—although maybe not a grandfather's first choice."

"I'm not sure I want to leave Landry. Do you think I should stay here?"

"I can't say that." He put his hand in his pocket. "If you decide to go, we'll always be here for you."

She touched his hand. "Thank you."

He pulled out a small package. She recognized the jewelry store's cream paper and gold bow. "For you." His hand trembled as he handed it to her.

"I hope you got Tomas to give you a discount." She grinned.

"Twenty percent off," he said with a wink.

"Not bad." And then she grew still as she opened it. A pewter anchor on a thin silver chain lay nestled in the box. It was the same design as the one on her dad's tombstone.

"It's gorgeous," she said and ran her fingers around the edge.

"John David wore one, a gift from Frankie when he turned sixteen. I've not seen one like it since, but this one is awfully similar. Our friend Tomas swapped out the chain."

Her fingers rubbed the medallion, but she couldn't speak.

"The anchor had a lot of meaning to John David—hope, faith. Your father, despite his mistakes, was a steady young man."

"Was I a mistake?" The anchor suddenly burned her hand. "Teen parents. Messed up lives."

"Not at all," he said. "You're like that anchor to all of us, a reminder of hope and faith." He curled his lips into a rueful smile. "I doubt John David and Frankie were doing much long-term planning at that moment, but you are most certainly not a mistake."

"Would you fasten it?" Wreath lifted her hair off her neck.

As the necklace settled against her skin, she looked up and smiled at her grandfather. "I can see where my dad got his steadiness," she said and kissed him on the cheek.

67

L aw stood outside the door.

He wore a button-up shirt Wreath didn't recognize and a new pair of khaki shorts.

"I went by your house," he said as she unlocked the door. "Working Sundays now?"

"I'm showing a guy from Lafayette the Art Deco set," she said. "New back-to-school clothes?"

"My grandmother got tired of seeing that same T-shirt and sent me to Target." He bowed. "You like?"

"Very much." She looked down at her toes, then lifted her head. "I've missed you."

"Ditto."

Wreath gave him a quick kiss. She wanted to lock her arms around him and never let go.

"Whoa! Nice!" Law put his hand behind her head and pulled her closer. "I'd better buy more new clothes."

"It's not the clothes, goofball. I've missed you, and—" She felt timid. "There's a lot to talk about." He was going to be proud of her.

"What a crazy summer," he said.

"How much longer will your mom be in the hospital?"

"She's coming home in a few days, then starts physical therapy." He rolled his head from side to side, the way he did when he was nervous. "That guy almost killed her, Wreath." He looked down at his feet, then back at her. "How do you do it?"

"I'm not sure I'm following."

"I almost lost her. It's freaking me out."

"It's impossible to explain." Wreath touched his hand. "Something shifts inside you."

"Did your mother change when she found out she was sick?"

"Probably." Frankie had been agitated that Wreath would be alone. She spent a lot of time apologizing for not being a better mama. Those memories hurt more than the others.

Law ran a hand through his hair. "My mom's acting . . . different."

"Different *good* or different *weird?*"

"Good, I think. She wants to quit partying, be a grownup. She even told me and my grandparents how much she loves us." His voice sounded shaky.

"Are you okay?"

"Wiped out," he said. "The chair in her room makes into a bed, but the hospital staff is in and out all night." He rolled his head around again. "I'll be glad when she's out."

"Will she stay with your grandparents?"

His mouth twisted. "I don't think she's quite there yet. She doesn't like depending on them."

"Will she have a sitter?"

He shrugged. "We'll know in a few days."

Law looked like he was about to collapse.

"Come, sit." Wreath steered him to an overstuffed sofa, shabby chic, with red checks that looked like a picnic table-cloth. She pushed him gently onto it. "Faye sent chocolate cake with me. How's that sound for a pick-me-up?"

"You know me well." He put his head back, and his eyes fluttered shut.

She stared at him. He was so cute. Maybe this summer hadn't been the dreamy time she'd longed for, but Law had been by her side when trouble broke out.

He was her best friend.

Since both of them were going off to school, they'd have a special bond—and a shot at fun. They could share campus visits and meet in Landry for the weekend. They'd joke about dorms and cafeteria food and term papers.

She'd let Faye and J.D. buy her a phone, so they could text and talk.

Law, as usual, had been right all along. Going away to school was the right thing to do.

"I want to hear everything that's going on with you," Law murmured in a sleepy voice not unlike Jaclyn's. "Mitch has been up to the hospital a few times. Destiny too. She would have called you, but her parents are big-time upset." He shifted his lanky body. "Did you say cake?"

By the time Wreath returned from the workroom kitchen, Law had assumed the Faye-napping position, eyes closed, mouth open. After setting the dessert on a magazine, she stood and watched him.

Then she bumped the end of the couch, eager to tell him about her big decision.

Law slept on.

She swept and emptied the trash into the bin in the alley, not looking at the garage apartment. At least by going away to school, she might not miss Julia as much. *How far was Savannah from New Orleans?*

The bell on the front door tinkled as she walked back in from the alley. Tomas stood inside, ready to pick up his furniture. He spoke Spanish on his cell phone and looked as hip as he had at the jewelry store. He wore a bright green pair of pants and a tight white knit shirt. Today he wore a hat.

"Hey," Wreath said in a quiet voice and pointed toward Law, who had closed his mouth.

"Hangover?" Tomas asked. But before she could explain, he dashed toward the Art Deco pieces. "They're fantastic," he said and plopped onto the settee. Good thing that Law chose the overstuffed sofa for his nap. "This place is cool. Have you thought of opening a Lafayette location?"

"No, but you inspired us to consider hiring a driver."

Before he paid, she gave him a tour of the store and sold him another lamp and a pair of orange and green throw pillows. "Now if I can wake my friend up, we'll load it." She raised her voice but Law burrowed down further.

"I got it," Tomas said and grabbed the end tables. Wreath followed with the lamp, and together they manhandled the chair. But they couldn't finagle the couch out the door.

Wreath stood flustered by the window when J.D.'s truck pulled up in front of the hardware store. She should have known he wouldn't leave her on her own. "Just in time—"

Bum jumped out of the cab and scrutinized Tomas. "J.D. thought you might need a hand." In slacks and a knit shirt, he looked like he'd come from work at an office.

"Dude, can you help me get that Art Deco settee? Ms. Wreath here sure is pretty, but we can't quite manage it."

Was Tomas flirting with her?

"She's stronger than you are," Bum said and marched into the showroom, then stopped. "Uh, Wreath? What's Art Deco?"

"There." Tomas trailed Bum in and pointed. "Isn't the color great?"

Bum didn't answer but picked up the settee like it was one of Jaclyn's toys. His eyes watered. *Was he laughing?* "Lead on, sir."

Wreath grinned. "You have furniture-store potential."

While Bum and Tomas arranged the furniture and lashed it down, Wreath walked over to the couch. "Law?" She shook his arm. "You awake?"

He rolled over and rubbed his eyes. "Man. I must have dozed off." He reached for the cake. "Thanks." He rubbed his hand along her cheek. "Everything's going to work out, isn't it?"

"What do you mean?"

"I'm glad you're staying here. Things always fall into place."

She grew still. "I thought you wanted me to go away."

"That was before." He took a bite of cake. "After this summer—"

"I'm going to Evangeline," she blurted. "In New Orleans."

Law set the cake plate back on the coffee table. "You're messing with me, right?" He rubbed his eyes again and left a smear of chocolate on his cheek.

Wreath tilted her head. "Why do you make it sound like a mistake?"

"You're seriously going?"

She nodded and caught a glimpse of Bum rearranging the furniture in the bed of Tomas's borrowed truck.

"What happened to helping with the store, getting to know your grandfather, all that?"

The simmer in her gut roiled to a boil. "Isn't this what we wanted?" she asked. "To get out of Landry, learn new things, prepare for the future?"

"You did this because of me?" He looked paler than when he arrived.

"No," she admitted after a long silence. "You made me see things from a different angle, and that was huge. But I did it for me." *And Frankie.*

"Great." He rolled his head around and popped his neck. "Glad I didn't mention going to Mars."

"Why would you say something like that?" she asked. "Clarice got me the offer. How can I pass it up?"

He took a gulp of the water she'd brought with the cake. "You're probably making the right decision." He stared right into her eyes. "You always do."

"You don't think I'm a good enough student for a better college, do you?" Her doubts burst out like Old Faithful. "What was I thinking? I only got this because Clarice pulled strings with a friend on the board."

"Clarice didn't get that scholarship. Wreath Wisteria Willis did. The girl who beat me out for the top spot in our class."

Law was saying the right words but his delivery seemed off. "Thanks for pushing me," she said. "I wouldn't have the guts to go if it weren't for you."

"Wreath," Law groaned, then buried his face in her shoulder.

Over his head, she could see Bum and Tomas close the gate of the truck and shake hands. And to add to her anxiety, Mitch and Destiny pulled up in Mitch's car and almost sprinted in.

"Anyone home?" Mitch called out.

Law straightened and ran his hands through his hair. His messy hair.

"So, I guess you told her," Destiny said. "I hope you're happy, Wreath."

"We hadn't gotten there yet." Law's voice was low.

"Gotten where?" Wreath looked from Destiny to Law.

"Like you haven't been working on this all summer," Destiny said.

Law wouldn't meet Wreath's eyes. "I'm going to RPCC so I can help with my mom."

"What?" Wreath couldn't have heard what she thought she heard.

"I came over to tell you, but you started talking about New Orleans."

"But you wanted to build a new life," she said.

"I can still do that."

"You told me to think bigger." She looked around the room wildly.

"I meant that."

"Amen to that, Sleeping Beauty." Bum walked in as Tomas pulled away from the curb. "Can you believe she's getting everything paid for? Is she smart or what?"

Law frowned.

"You got your hair cut," Destiny said.

Mitch cracked his knuckles. "Guess you and Law can hang out, now that he's staying in town."

"Cool," Bum said but he stared at Wreath.

She was sure the color drained from her face proportionate to the flush climbing up Law's. Destiny's expression was impassive. Mitch looked bored.

"What are you doing here?" Law's gaze on Bum was steely.

Wreath drew in a breath and pointed to the spot where the furniture had been. "He loaded that furniture for the customer from Lafayette."

"Why didn't you wake me up?" Law said. "You living here these days, Bumgardner?"

Bum looked cheerful, an odd look for him. "I guess I do," he said. "Faye's renting me her garage apartment."

68

Wreath fluffed up the final flower and tossed it onto the red-and-yellow tissue-paper garden at her feet.

Now for the string.

Then she'd start on the arbor. Since the Sunday mess, her friends hadn't been by with offers to help.

"Ooh, my favorite colors." Faye came through the front door with an armful of vintage tablecloths. "I ironed these."

"I was going to do that."

"You need to get ready for school."

"I have two more weeks," Wreath said.

"I'm clearly better with an iron." Faye glanced at the wrinkled bowling shirt Wreath wore.

Wreath studied the happy face in front of her. Faye's hair was held back with a headband, and she wore a bandanna-patterned shirt and a pair of close-fitting jeans. Bright red toenails peeked out from beaded flip-flops.

Faye glanced down. "Did I spill tea on me or something?"

"I was thinking about how happy you look."

"You were thinking how sour I was when you came in a year ago."

"That too."

"I was pretty awful, wasn't I?"

"Define *awful.*"

"Smarty pants. Now that you're going off to Evangeline, you'll be impossible to live with."

"And you won't have to! I'll be in the dorm, remember?"

The smile on Faye's face faded. "Don't ruin my mood. I'll count the days until you come back." She fidgeted with the hem of the tablecloth. "You will come back, won't you?"

"This is my home," Wreath said. "I'll always come back."

"I can't handle this sentimental jabber. We've got a party to plan." Faye lifted her hands, neither of which sported the engagement ring. *When was J.D. giving it to her?*

"Let's go over the guest list and pad it with a few of your friends from church." Wreath flung a tablecloth over an old card table, rescued from Faye's attic. "As you see, my friends are avoiding me." She wasn't sure Law would ever speak to her again.

"It's only been three days. They'll come to their senses."

Wreath debated how far to push it. "I want a big crowd, like we had last Christmas. Clarice and Sam and Mr. Estes. Those women you used to play bridge with."

"Need a hand?" J.D. strolled through the front door. In his work pants and chambray shirt, he radiated a kind of working-man's charm. He never hurried. Wreath fingered her anchor necklace.

"Always!" Faye moved toward him for a quick peck on the lips.

"You look pretty," he said in a soft voice, and Wreath noticed the quick pat he gave her rear end. "Thought you might want help with the party."

Wreath bit her lip. "Umm, the back door's sticking again. Would you mind taking a look, J.D.?"

Faye frowned. "I put some things in the alley yesterday, and it was fine."

Wreath shrugged. "Probably swelled up with the humidity." She pointed to the paper flowers. "Do you have time to tie the twine on these, Faye?"

J.D. had already made it to the door and opened and closed it a couple of times. "Seems all right now."

Wreath hurried toward him. "Let me show you." She made a production of pushing it open and led him into the alley.

Then she whispered her plan to him.

During the middle of Wednesday afternoon, J.D. popped back into the store.

"I need to run a few errands." His cheeks were flushed. "Thought I'd see if I could talk my fiancée into coming along."

"But we've got so much to do for the party," Faye said.

J.D.'s forehead wrinkled. "Surely you can pull the chip-and-dip together by Saturday?" He winked at Wreath.

"I can't go off and leave things."

"I'm over here," Wreath waved. "Look at me." She waved again. "I've got it covered." She picked up Faye's purse and shooed her toward the door.

"Are you sure?"

"She's sure," J.D. said. "Thanks, Wreath."

Whew! She hoped she had talked her grandfather into giving Faye the ring before the party. They were such a great couple.

As J.D.'s truck pulled away, she fished around in her backpack for her journal.

LOVE, she wrote in big block letters using different-colored markers and pulled out her favorite green pen. July 29. Hard to believe. Party day was August 1. Then she'd pack and leave for college.

She chewed on the pen, then jotted the questions the summer had brought. She hadn't exactly had the romantic summer of her dreams.

What's up with Law? How do I feel about him? What's the deal with Bum? She chewed on the pen. *Do I want to date at college? How do you know when you're in love?*

She pulled out the colored markers again.

LOVE. LOVE. LOVE. It sure is complicated.

But Julia had waited for Shane. J.D. had healed Faye's broken heart.

In some ways this summer turned out even better than I dreamed. She pondered.

LOVE makes you feel alive.

69

Bum walked down the stairs at his new apartment. Julia had left him all sorts of stuff. To think that he'd be living here next week.

When he got to the bottom, he started across the alley and gave the door to the furniture store a tug. But it was locked.

He raised his hand to knock, then let it drop. He didn't want Wreath to think he'd be popping in all the time because he lived nearby. And she hadn't exactly celebrated when he told her about the apartment.

Her stunned silence had made him feel like running back to Thibodaux. Why wasn't she pleased? He was doing what she'd suggested.

At least Law would be here. He might be bored enough to hang out some. With Jaclyn at Clarice's and no enemies on his trail, Bum was crazy restless. He'd been by the animal clinic a couple of times to check on Bitty, who rewarded his kindness with a growl. The manager had said be patient.

Patience wasn't a talent of his.

Rounding the corner, he deliberated. Maybe he'd stop and see J.D. But a note was taped to the door. *Gone for the day. Back Thursday.* Wreath's bike was chained to its post.

A clatter drew his notice to the furniture store.

Wreath wrestled a ladder into the display window on the other side of the front door. In the process, she knocked over a large container of something. Her face was flushed, and her hair was a mess.

What an awesome girl.

And why wasn't he inside helping?

He burst through the doorway and was almost to the step up to the window when she turned.

"My gosh!" she yelped. "You scared me to death."

They both grew still. *Was she remembering that first day he'd come looking for her?*

"It's been a wild summer, hasn't it?" she said after a moment.

He nodded and moved up into the window. "Need a hand?"

The sun beamed. "Desperately," she said.

"Is this some sale or something?"

"It's the big party Saturday." She rearranged her hair into a topknot on her head and fanned herself. Then her brow furrowed. "Faye did tell you that you and Jaclyn are invited, didn't she?"

"Yep. Thanks." He reached for the twine and tacked it to the wood on the edge of the display space.

She reached for the other end, and her hand brushed against his. Bum didn't plan to grab it and hold on, but he couldn't seem to help himself. *He had it bad.*

Wreath quirked her head and glanced down at their joined hands.

He let go and dropped his eyes. "I'm sorry I sprang that apartment news on you like that."

"It stung that Faye hadn't mentioned it. Stupid, huh?"

"She planned to tell you." He cleared his throat. "All you guys were sitting around, like you were having a party or something, and I—I was a jerk."

"So was I." She nodded toward the twine. "Let's pull it tighter, and we'll attach these letters later. I mean if you'll help me."

"This is more fun than wandering the aisles of the Dollar Barn," he said.

A little burst of laughter came from Wreath.

This girl could break his heart if he was stupid enough to let her.

Wreath was asleep when Faye got in Wednesday night. The past few weeks had been exhausting—and J.D. had been unusually wound up about taking care of personal business that afternoon.

Usually he was low-key but maybe the horror of the dog-fight and Wreath's college decision had gotten to him.

A sample of lemon bars for the party sat on the table with a note. *Don't eat all of them.*

She nibbled one and smiled. Wreath was so good at everything—but at least Faye was the better cook.

Tonight Wreath didn't rouse when she checked on her, wasn't awake for the smile at the way Wreath clung to the edge of the bed, even though Jaclyn was at Clarice's. The ever-present journal was face down on the nightstand.

The house would be lonelier when Wreath moved to the dorm.

She had changed life in ways Faye couldn't have imagined. And she was so happy that Wreath would soon be her granddaughter.

70

L aw and Bum arrived downtown together late Friday afternoon, causing a mild ruckus.

"I told you your friends would be back." Faye pointed.

Wreath watched them approach. "But you didn't predict
they'd be together."

"Never dull around here," Faye said.

"You're a prophet." *But still not wearing the engagement ring.*

Faye smiled when Law and Bum entered. "If you're in the
market for furniture or vintage clothes, boys, you've come to
the right place."

They threw a confused look.

"She hasn't been drinking, if that's what you're thinking,"
Wreath said.

The guys hooted, a tad louder than the joke warranted.
They seemed as nervous as she was.

"My assistant here seems surprised to see you together,"
Faye said.

"Faye!" Then Wreath looked at them. "Stunned is more
like it."

Everyone laughed again. So they wanted to pretend everything was normal . . .

"Bum called me from J.D.'s this morning," Law said. "Told me there's work to be done before the party."

"I thought you were mad at each other," Wreath said.

"I owe Law a big one. He told the vet I had a way with animals, dogs especially."

Wreath's brows rose. "I hope they didn't notice the gnaw marks."

Law guffawed, again over-loud. "Let us help."

"Aren't you upset with me?" She couldn't meet his eyes.

Law looked at Bum. "Like you said, she doesn't mince words."

"You've been talking about me?" Wreath crossed her arms. "How weird is that?"

"It does seem odd," Faye said.

"You haven't finished that front window," Bum said, "and you said you had a ton of other things to do."

"Did you make something for that window?" Faye asked. "It looks bare."

"I'll get it done," Wreath said.

"If we all jump in, we can take it easy tomorrow," Faye persisted.

"I want to do it. I mean, I have an idea." Wreath put her hands on her hips. "Why don't you and J.D. go out for dinner or something? The three of us can finish up."

"Now this is different," Faye said under her breath.

Law moseyed over to where Wreath was, and Bum cleared his throat. "Miss Faye, didn't you have some plants for me to move?"

"Plants, right." Faye watched Wreath. "They're at the hardware store."

Law glanced toward Bum, his head cocked.

Bum returned a swift nod and headed toward the front.

"This won't take long," Faye was saying as the door swung shut.

"I probably should have called first," Law said, "but I had to see you. Try to patch things up." He ran a hand through his hair. "Things are kind of mixed up, aren't they?"

"You think?" She gave a choked laugh. "Insert life. Turn on blender."

Law rewarded her with his cute, crooked smile. "We can't let this summer end like this."

"You're the one who nearly punched Bum for loading furniture Sunday."

"I had just woke up," he said. "That's a lousy excuse, but I was out of it." He sighed. "And jealous."

"Bum and I are friends," she said. "Like you and Destiny."

"It's not just Bumgardner." The color drained from his tanned face. "This sounds horrible, but I was jealous that you were getting to go to school in New Orleans."

She drew in her breath. "Law, I—"

He held up his hand. "I'll get my chance to go away, Wreath."

He circled the chair to where she stood. "Look at how you've changed the people here. My mom needs that from me."

"I couldn't save my mother." The words were almost a whisper.

"But you tried. That's what I want to do."

"I get it."

He put his hands on her shoulders, his eyes locked on her. "This past year, you not only moved to Landry." He tapped his chest. "This sounds unbelievably corny but you moved in here too."

"That *is* corny." She inched toward him. "But sweet."

"Can't change maybe be for the good?" Law's voice wasn't as steady as usual.

"I'm counting on it." Wreath was hypnotized by the look in his eyes. She gulped in a breath of air.

"I'm not sure what you and I have, but I don't want to lose it." He brushed her hair back from her face.

She blinked. "Do you think we can see how school unfolds? Take things as they come?"

"Will you go out with me if I come visit?" he asked.

"That can be arranged," she said with a smile.

Voices grew louder on the sidewalk, and Law pulled back. "Can we end the summer on a happy note?"

"I'd like that," she said as he leaned down to kiss her, the clock ticking in the background.

Wrapping his arms around her, Law put his chin on her head. "Wreath, in summer, Wreath, off to college," he murmured. "You're awesome."

71

Jaclyn was the first to arrive at the party, riding on the shoulders of Clarice's father.

"There's our guest of honor," Wreath said, a catch in her throat at the sight of her big smile and frilly red party dress.

Wreath leaned closer and put a plastic crown with large pink stones on her head. "You get a tiara, and I crown you my helper."

"Yippee!" Jaclyn slid to the floor. "Did you know me and Samson's living with Miss Clarice and Mr. Sam? And I've got another new grandpa, Papa Estes."

"That's wonderful." Wreath felt an urge to cry. "Want to put the party favors on the table?"

Jaclyn cocked her head. "What's a party favor?"

Wreath's eyes stung. "We're giving everyone a little present."

Jaclyn's eyes roamed up and down her. "I like your dress."

She glanced down at the red-and-yellow miniskirt and bright yellow top. "These are Faye's favorite colors."

"My dress too." Jaclyn fingered the skirt, her hair shiny, her face scrubbed. Her smile was the only outward sign of the pale, dirty child who had panhandled at the flea market.

Julia and Shane arrived next and came through the front door holding hands. Julia, radiant as the art-student-to-be, wore a bohemian dress, also red and yellow, well above her knees. Geometric leggings finished off the look. She'd bought the outfit from Wreath's Junkyard Couture line and modeled it for the website.

"Our next guest of honor." Wreath bowed before Julia with a flourish.

Jaclyn ran from the table where she'd placed bottles of bubbles. "You get a tea-arrow," she said. "Can I put it on her, Wreath? Can I?"

"So much for that cute up-do," Wreath murmured, but Julia knelt, smiling. Shane watched the process and swallowed.

"Is Faye on to you yet?" Julia asked when Jaclyn scampered off.

"If she is, she's hiding it well," Wreath said.

"Your sign may tip her off." Julia grinned as she looked at the red letters strung together in the window. *Congratulations, Faye and J.D.*

"I just hope J.D. gave her the ring," Wreath said. "And that Bum manages to trick them into parking down the street."

"I don't think he's had much experience with surprise parties."

"He's a fast learner," Wreath said.

"Uncle Bum's staying at Papa J.D.'s," Jaclyn said from the other side of the room.

"Bat ears," Clarice whispered. Moving toward the window, she motioned to Wreath. Julia and Shane followed. "Has Starla contacted Bum?"

"Not that I know."

"I don't think Starla's in the area," Shane said. "We've run every lead." He hesitated. "What if she never comes back?"

"Bum has a crude, handwritten guardianship," Clarice said. "We're working on making something legal, with Sam and me sharing responsibilities with him."

Julia looked at Jaclyn, who was blowing bubbles with Clarice's father. "How could someone do that to a child?"

"Scared," Shane said. "Selfish."

"Too young to have a child," Clarice added.

Wreath felt another shift.

In ways, Frankie was like Starla. Young, for sure. Scared at times. Maybe immature.

But she'd seldom been selfish.

And she never once—until she died—gave Wreath reason to doubt she'd be there.

Thank you, Mama.

One of the paper flowers blew in the breeze from the air-conditioner.

A steady flow of friends from church arrived, the women all wearing red.

Even the pastor was early, overdressed in a three-piece suit and carrying a small Bible. *Were preachers ever off-duty?*

Law, handsome in a sport coat and tie, arrived with his grandparents. His eyes grew wide when he saw Wreath. "You look gorgeous."

"As do you."

He winked, and her heart gave a little flop.

Destiny, wearing yellow, came with Mitch. Wreath had not been sure she'd show and met her near the door.

"Are we good?" Wreath asked.

She shrugged. *A start at least.* "Please, Des. How can I make it at college without you to lean on?"

Destiny studied her, then gave a slight nod. "It's been a hard summer."

"Fall will be better," Wreath said. "I'm sorry I wasn't more fun."

"I wasn't that great myself." She looked around the room, anywhere but at Wreath. "Can we drop it?"

It might take a while, but they'd be all right.

Mitch shuffled his loafers and looked from one to the other.

"You ready for LSU?" Wreath asked.

"Pretty much, other than renting the tractor-trailer rig to haul all the stuff my mom has bought for the dorm."

Wreath frowned. "What kind of stuff?"

"Sheets, towels, blankets, a bedspread that matches my roommate's, but don't tell anyone." He moaned. "A refrigerator big enough for one bottle of water. You name it."

"I don't have any of that," Wreath said, "and I'm leaving in two weeks."

"You've got this." Destiny waved a gift bag in front of her. "It's a hostess gift from my mother. I think she felt bad about blaming you for my behavior."

Wreath shuffled her red heels.

"I hope it's not one of those little refrigerators," Mitch said.

Law ambled up and gave Destiny a hug. "Could be a microwave," he said.

"Why don't you just open it?" Destiny said.

Wreath pulled out what looked like a terry cloth cape, monogrammed with a giant green *W* with smaller *W*s on each side. *Was this something for the dorm?* She was in so over her head.

"It's a shower wrap," Destiny said.

"I knew that," Law said.

"Don't let my mother see it," Mitch said.

Destiny swiped at him. "You two have no couth."

"Guilty," Law winked.

"Now that your college hygiene is taken care of, where's the happy couple?" Mitch asked.

Wreath looked back at the big clock. "They should be here any minute." She scoured the room and yelled. "Is everyone ready?"

The guests grew quiet.

"Don't just stand there," she said. "Talk."

"Wreath." Law laid his hand on her arm. "Relax."

"I want it to be perfect."

"It already is." He touched her crooked tiara stuck on by Jaclyn.

"Here they come," Jaclyn squealed.

"That's just Bumgardner." Law said and took a step closer to Wreath.

"Are you sure?" Wreath murmured. The guy in the sport coat with an open-collared dress shirt looked more like a candidate for office. His hair was unnaturally tame.

"Uncle Bum!" Jaclyn flew across the room.

"Told you so." Law draped his arm around Wreath's shoulders.

Bum enveloped Jaclyn in his arms. "You look be-yoo-ti-ful!" he said with a huge smile.

Wreath slipped a step away from Law.

"They're parking the car," Bum said to the room at large. "I told them I needed to help arrange something. I don't even know what."

The crowd laughed and lined up around the showroom.

Her grandfather opened the door for Faye, his hand resting on her shoulder as she entered. "Happy engagement!" everyone yelled.

"Surprise, Miss Faye! J.D.!" Jaclyn ran forward.

Faye's face drained of color, a contrast to the gorgeous red silk wrap dress she wore. Her legs were shapely, a pair of espadrilles on her feet.

Wreath's eyes traveled to her hand. *Darn it!* She still didn't have her engagement ring. What was up with that?

J.D. wore a suit with a yellow-and-red striped tie, and he, too, looked around for Wreath and gave her a thumbs up.

"You are so sneaky." Faye rushed over. "I knew you were up to something."

"Surprised?" J.D. asked, his hand now around Faye's waist.

"*Et tu*, J.D.?" she said before raising her face to kiss him.

The confusion in the room was loud and fun.

Jaclyn got lots of whistles and cheers at the announcement of her impending entry into kindergarten, and Julia presented her with a ginormous basket of crayons and blunt scissors and every kind of school supply.

"And, now," Wreath said, "how about a speech from the happy couple?"

J.D. took Faye's hand and led her to the arbor covered in the red-and-yellow tissue flowers. He cleared his throat and motioned for Wreath to join them.

"My granddaughter's anxious," he said, looking around the crowd, "that I haven't given my fiancée her engagement ring."

Faye stilled.

"I thought it might be fun to do so tonight, Wreath."

"Nice move, Grandpa," she said, and the crowd roared. Everyone moved closer.

"Faye," he said and reached into his pocket. He pulled out the cream-and-gold box. "You and I were blessed with long, happy marriages—but have somehow been given a second chance at love."

"Aww." Everyone swooned in unison.

"You *are* still willing to marry an old hardware store owner like me, aren't you?"

Faye put her hands together. "If you're willing to marry an old furniture store owner like me."

Applause flew through the room.

"Ahem," Wreath said. "Are you forgetting something?"

People laughed, and J.D. handed Faye the little package.

Tears trickled down Faye's cheeks as she tore into the box, and she gasped when she saw the ring. "Did Wreath pick this out?" she asked as J.D. slipped it onto her finger.

"I wish," Wreath said. "Turns out my grandfather has good taste in jewelry."

"But she helped me find the store and bargained for the best deal."

"That's our girl."

"Show us the ring," someone said, and the crowd began to chant. "Show us the ring."

Faye waved her hand like the Queen of England.

J.D. smiled, and Wreath thought she saw his eyes glisten as he walked toward her. "Want to help me with another surprise?" he asked and leaned in to whisper into her ear.

Wreath's eyes widened, and she blinked back tears of her own.

"Look at them," Faye said. "They're ganging up on me already."

The jubilant crowd laughed again.

J.D. stepped closer to Faye. "Wreath and I have noticed a problem," he said in that calm voice of his.

Faye's face grew serious, and she looked around. "What is it?"

His voice grew louder. "The ring doesn't look as good as it should."

Faye's brow furrowed. "It's exquisite."

The crowd murmured, and J.D. held up his hands for silence. "Don't you think it looks lonely?"

"I do," Wreath said.

J.D. scanned the room. "Is there a preacher in the house by any chance?"

Faye's eyes flew open as their pastor wove his way through the crowd. *That's why he had his Bible!*

"I might not have been clear earlier," J.D. said. "To clarify, Faye, will you marry me tonight?"

"The license," she said in a hoarse whisper. "You made up that whole story about getting it early for insurance purposes."

"I did," he said, and his first show of nerves appeared. "How about it?"

"Yes!" Faye said and looked toward Wreath. "Is there a maid of honor in the house?" She turned again. "And I need a bridesmaid." Her gaze settled on Julia. "You there, wearing the tiara."

Then Faye put her finger up to her cheek. "One more thing, J.D. Don't you think we need a flower girl?"

"Absolutely," he said solemnly.

"Jaclyn, can you march down a pretend aisle?" Faye asked. Half of their friends were weeping by now, but Jaclyn sashayed to where they stood like she'd been in a dozen weddings.

Faye whispered to J.D.

"Ahh, yes," he said. "I need some men to stand up with me. Jim?" He gestured toward Law's grandfather. "Shane?" The deputy stepped forward. Then J.D. looked to the side. "Silas?"

Wreath watched for one of the Sunday school crowd to step out.

But instead Bum came forward, a self-conscious look on his face. "Are you sure?" he asked.

"Never been surer," J.D. said with a smile, then turned toward Faye.

"That's my cue," the preacher said and faced the crowd. "Dearly beloved . . ."

"You know how to throw a party," Law said.

"Where'd you find that ring?" Destiny asked.

But Wreath was staring at Bum. "Is your name really Silas?"

"J.D. forced it out of me. Told me I didn't want a nametag at the animal clinic with *Bum* on it."

"Silas is kind of cute," Destiny said. "Old-fashioned."

"Nerdy," Mitch said.

"I think I like it," Wreath murmured.

"Did you see me, Uncle Bum?" Jaclyn ran up to the circle. "I threw flowers!"

Wreath reached down to pick up Jaclyn. "Group hug," she said and moved toward her friends. They had made it to August. College was ahead.

"You were right," she whispered to Law, who wedged himself next to her.

"Good," he said with his heart-stopping grin. "But what are you talking about?"

"We pulled it off," she said. "Summer of fun."

She dove into the hug.

WITH GRATITUDE

Thank you from the bottom of my heart to the readers of *Wreath, A Girl,* who asked for more of Wreath's story, and especially to readers who e-mailed me about the ways Wreath affected their lives. (I'd love to hear how Wreath has touched your life. E-mail me: judy@judychristie.com.)

Many people nudged me forward in special ways, including: friend and eagle-eye copy editor Kathie Rowell, Claire Griggs, Ethel Haughton, teachers Brad Campbell and Ashley Shinpoch, Kathy Murphy and her international Pulpwood Queens Book Club, author Lisa Wingate and granddaughter Gracie. Never doubt the power of a word of encouragement.

Then there was the writing space so generously offered by Christie Greene. Thank you!

My deep appreciation goes to Jamie Chavez, the kind of editor every writer needs. She has helped make Wreath's story shine from the early days in the junkyard.

And thank you to the many creative souls who brainstormed covers and art ideas: Tasha Brown, who designed this cover; Melanie Pace, editorial assistant (and high-school student!); coach Jeni Chappelle; creative director Amber M. Dent; designer Marcus Mebes; high-school artist Abby Nickels; and all-around expert Jim Wilson. Stay tuned for more about Abby's art and special covers for future *Wreath* releases.

Love and thanks to my husband, Paul, and to the memory of our mothers, Betty Brosette Pace and Eva Barnhill Christie, who inspired Brosette & Barnhill, our fledgling publishing company.

If you'd like to be part of Team Wreath, e-mail me: judy@judychristie. com.
There's lots of Wreath fun ahead!

BOOK CLUB & CLASSROOM DISCUSSION QUESTIONS

1. Why is the summer after high school graduation intense for Wreath and her friends?
2. How does Wreath change the lives of those around her? Why did she get involved with Jaclyn? What does Wreath fear? What makes her happy?
3. The summer reveals a lot about Frankie. What are some of the things Wreath learns about her mother?
4. Why is Bum drawn to Wreath? How does she feel about him? What words describe him?
5. How would you describe Wreath and Law's relationship? Is it moving forward?
6. Did you find similarities in the junkyard, the bottle cave, and the cemetery? What do different settings reveal about Wreath?
7. What role do dogs play in this story? What do the animals reveal about other characters?
8. In what ways do Wreath and her grandfather change in the weeks after they connect?
9. What are Destiny's feelings toward Wreath? How did they develop?
10. Julia recalls her summer after high school and all the firsts of life. In what ways are Wreath, Law, Destiny and Mitch experiencing this coming-of-age?

Dear Reader:

Thank you so much for reading *Wreath, In Summer,* the second part of Wreath Willis's story. *Wreath* readers are special people, and I'd love to hear from you. E-mail me, judy@judychristie.com, or write Judy Christie, Box 6103, Shreveport LA 71136.

Lots is going on in the world of Wreath, from writing contests to book clubs and class discussions—and you can be part of the fun. To stay in touch, please sign up for my e-newsletter and follow Wreath on Instagram, **www.instagram.com/wreathwillis.**

A high-school reader told me recently she wants to start a **Wreath Book Club**, and I'm thrilled. I have free discussion questions and journaling activities to share, and I'll send them your way if you'd like. I have a story guide to help you write your own story, too—a novel or your memoir.

There's more: I love working with teachers to put Wreath in the classroom. Or perhaps you'd like to discuss Wreath at your library or organization. Just let me know how I can help!

If you'd like to be part of **Team Wreath,** with inside info about Wreath and a chance to win signed books and offer feedback and more, e-mail me: judy@judychristie.com.

Stay tuned for *Wreath, To College,* book 3, coming in 2016.
Happy Reading!
Judy Christie
For more information on Wreath, see www.JudyChristie.com.

ABOUT THE AUTHOR

Just like Wreath, **Judy Christie** has kept a diary since she was eleven years old and still has all of them. A former journalist, Christie's first newspaper job was editor of The Barret Banner in elementary school. She loves to read, write and talk about books, and "Wreath, In Summer" is the second Wreath Willis novel. Visit Christie at www.judychristie.com and sign up for her e-newsletter to stay up on news about Wreath. And follow @WreathWillis on Instagram.

27228795R00245

Made in the USA
Middletown, DE
14 December 2015